ABOUT THE AUTHOR

Charles Courtley, now living on the Essex coast, did a great deal of amateur acting earlier in his life. In more recent years, he has written short stories (two of which were produced for radio) and two currently unpublished children's books. From 1972–1990, he practised as a barrister, mainly in London and the South Eastern Circuit – both prosecuting and defending in criminal cases. He is now a military judge, presiding over court-martial cases, which have included a number of serious criminal allegations over the years. Charles Courtley is a pseudonym.

WIG BEGONE

CHARLES COURTLEY

Matador
5 Weir Road
Kibworth Beauchamp
Leicester LE8 0LQ, UK
Tel: (+44) 116 279 2299
Fax: (+44) 116 279 2277
Email: books@troubador.co.uk
Web: www.troubador.co.uk/matador

ISBN 978 1848761 735

British Library Cataloguing in Publication Data.
A catalogue record for this book is available from the British Library.

Typeset in 11pt Bembo by Troubador Publishing Ltd, Leicester, UK

Matador is an imprint of Troubador Publishing Ltd

Printed in Great Britain by the MPG Books Group, Bodmin and King's Lynn

This book is dedicated to my wife, Jane, for without her love and support it could never have been written.

My heartfelt thanks also to Vanessa Lamb, whose inspirational sketches grace the back of this book and to Terence Compton whose work, on behalf of Matador, has been invaluable in preparing it for publication.

PROLOGUE

The Lord Chief Justice's good eye gave me a stony stare through the one clear lens of his spectacles as I re-entered the room. I searched desperately round for a sympathetic face – surely, there must be one? Not the other judges, who sat by his side, that was for sure.

I felt myself breaking into a cold sweat.

Only an hour beforehand, the disciplinary hearing at Galahad's Inn having at long last finished, I'd slunk into the anteroom; such a friendless place, adorned with paintings of long-dead judges. A marble bust of yet another ancient judicial luminary from the distant past wearing a full-bottomed wig was my only companion.

Outside a gentle rain fell on the Inn's venerable buildings which surrounded its fine square with an elegant fountain spouting in the middle. Soon the environs of the Inns of Court with their air of calm authority would be lost to me forever. Charles Courtley, the poor boy from the sticks, who had no previous connections with the law and was so determined to succeed in the competitive world of the Bar, was about to receive his comeuppance.

Of course, there were always other jobs I could do, I reflected gloomily; working in an office as a law clerk (a fate worse than death) was one unappealing option – or becoming a mini-cab driver which, at least, would mean that I remained self-employed.

But no 'Tunes of Glory' at the Old Bailey, as a leading advocate in all the big criminal cases earning large sums of money and living in style in a house in Montague Square near Regent's Park. Something very dear to Andrea's heart – she had spent her childhood there in a grand house before her father lost all his money on the Stock Exchange.

Darling Andrea who had supported me faithfully whilst I sweated through the Bar exams, what kind of life would I be able to offer her now?

After my mother died, I'd left Cornwall with a small grant to study law in London and took up residence in a one-roomed bed-sit in Earl's Court At the same time, I was expected to work for a solicitor as his articled clerk. A visit to the Old Bailey changed all that – what I really wanted to do was to become a great advocate – swaying juries with the power of words!

Andrea, a hard-up trainee nurse herself, lived in the same building as myself. After she invited me to her place for a supper of baked beans and pork pie (washed down with a bottle of Algerian wine) we fell in love and married soon after. She encouraged me to take the plunge – and take the Bar exams instead.

Glancing through the window, I noticed a fully-robed barrister rushing back to his chambers from the nearby Law Courts – his gown billowing behind him – followed by a gaggle of solicitors' and barristers' clerks; one carrying his law books. His crisp, curled wig accentuated his air of importance.

Miserably, I turned away from the window pondering – would I ever wear my wig again? – so recently bought from Ede and Ravenscroft for the princely sum of £500.

Woebegone was the way I felt although 'wig begone' might be a more apt way of putting it.

How had it all come to this? Well, here's the tale.

ONE

'Charles Courtley,' declared the Treasurer of Galahad's Inn, eighteen months before. 'You are hereby called to the Bar of England and Wales.'

That was it. Finally, I had achieved my dream and become a barrister. True, it had taken me some years to pass the exams but I had made it at last! Now for the formal dinner in the grand surroundings of Hall and then the last bus home – I reckoned I had just about enough money on me for that.

Frankly, Andrea and I were still very hard up. Married for three years, we were living in a dingy basement flat in Peckham; all we could afford. Not only was it damp all the year round and freezing cold in winter but constant electrical shorts often announced themselves with a loud bang. It was also miles away from the nearest tube.

The call ceremony took place in 1972 and I was about to eat the last dinner in Hall required of me. These twelve compulsory events were regarded as being equally important to passing the exams. Nonetheless, it felt good to sit down at the high table in Hall that night as a barrister and not a student. For the first time, I wore my brand new bar robe over the pin-striped trousers and black jacket which would be my uniform from now in. The fact that these items were bought second-hand from Moss Bros. worried me not at all.

Full of good food and faintly sozzled, I caught the last bus to Peckham. The three-quarter hour journey gave me time to reflect.

Barrister at last! It felt good but there was a problem. I had no income or indeed any expected in the foreseeable future. In fact, I was totally dependent on my darling Andrea to keep us from starving.

The following week, I was due to start a year's pupillage – a period spent with an experienced barrister during which I could expect to earn little or nothing. Indeed, during the first six months, I had no 'right of audience' before any court anyway so Andrea, who now worked as a hospice nurse (and that not a well-paid job) was required to keep me. Her wages covered the rent of our flat and basic necessities but there wasn't enough to finance anything else. My barrister's robe had been a present from my parents but how was I going to afford the wig or any of the other expenses?

By now somewhat subdued, I got off the bus and a minute later let myself into our flat. After routinely kissing both Andrea and our two cats, Katie and Winston, who were wedged either side of the bed, I crawled next to them and instantly fell asleep.

I woke up to a flash of inspiration. Despite, or perhaps because of, my hangover from the night before, I decided the answer was not, as I had been contemplating as a last resort, working as a petrol pump attendant in the evenings but to visit the bank manager without delay. At that time, loans were not so easily available but wasn't I now a professional man?

As it turned out, this middle-aged and respectable chap was prepared to give me a working overdraft in the princely sum of £300 and to celebrate, Andrea and I treated ourselves to a slap-up lunch in a fine restaurant in Dulwich. This was a classic mistake – the £50 bill punched a considerable dent in the overdraft facility at far too early a stage of my career but it was worth it.

So I didn't have to exchange a pair of jeans for my pinstripes each night and troop off to the local garage to work the petrol pumps. I could concentrate on pupillage and what a great experience that would prove to be!

Such affairs were arranged pretty informally in those days. A barrister acquaintance of mine told me that Rex Huggins in his chambers might be prepared to take me on as his pupil.

'He's got a mixed common law practice so you should see a bit of everything with him. I'll bring him up to the pub one night for a drink.'

Rex turned out to be an affable chap in his early forties who looked every inch the successful barrister – exquisitely dressed in a dark, three-piece suit with a melodious voice to match. After we had imbibed a considerable amount of alcohol, I simply asked him if he could take me on.

'Can't see why not,' replied Rex eyeing me up and down. 'You seem the right sort of chap!'

This simple assessment would not meet approval now but what mattered most then was to be able to absorb the ethos (as well as the alcohol) of the ancient profession. That was far more important than any amount of legal training. Despite all the criticism levelled at the snobbery and elitism of the Bar at that time, it didn't really matter about your class, school or university as long as you fitted the mould – and your pupilmaster was responsible for ensuring you did.

So the first six months of my pupillage was truly traditional. I followed Rex round the various courts, read his briefs and most importantly (or so it appeared at the time) enjoyed and shared his lifestyle. That included regular visits to Tom Tug's wine bar in the evenings, as well as indulging in 'reasonable lunches', as Rex somewhat euphemistically called them. When we weren't actually in court, he believed wholeheartedly in these, and I remember spending many enjoyable times in such establishments as Simpson's in the Strand, Sheekey's in Soho, and last but not least, the Cock Tavern in Fleet Street.

Then the inevitable day came when I actually met the head of chambers – a figure seen as remote as Zeus on Mount Olympus.

Rex and I had returned to his room in chambers one day in May after a leisurely 'reasonable' lunch. He said he intended to settle down to some paperwork, a euphemism for indulging in a pleasant snooze prior to being brought tea and biscuits by the junior clerk. Unfortunately, a slim brief now lay upon his desk which apparently caused him a moment's apprehension. Work suddenly became a distinct and unattractive possibility. Leafing through the papers however, he laughed as he spoke.

'Ah, a little gaming matter in which Lionel is going to lead me. Apparently this firm wants to open another casino in Piccadilly and their solicitors have instructed Lionel to make an application for a gaming licence to the Bow Street Justices next week. Con's set down for four-thirty this afternoon.'

He tossed the brief aside and settled down in his chair for a snooze anyway. No further work was required. After all, Lionel Coggiter QC, the head of chambers was an expert in gambling law, and only needed a junior because all Queen's Counsel were required to have one in those days. So Rex was brought in to play a pretty nominal part in the case.

In due course, Perch, the hawk-faced clerk summoned us to Lionel's room at the front of the building looking out on the Temple lawns which on a sunny day looked very attractive. Sunshine dappled the grassy borders which neatly squared the rows of red and white roses. According to legend, it was in this very place that the Yorkists and Lancastrians had picked their respective emblems and sworn allegiance to rival Kings in the fifteenth century.

Lionel Coggiter sat in state behind his vast desk for all the world like a mediaeval potentate about to receive homage. A true Edwardian, born in 1909, he was at the height of his powers. Tall and thin, he had the ascetic look of an early Roman emperor. Every inch a patrician, he sat calmly puffing his magnificent pipe with its distinctive silver shank. Clouds of fragrant smoke filled the somewhat stuffy room as we all trooped in.

I tensed with anticipation. Now I was about to see one of the finest legal minds in action.

The con (conference in legal parlance) began. Lionel sat peering at the plans of the interior of the proposed new casino with a large magnifying glass.

'The bar area,' he stated in his clipped upper-class drawl, 'is far too near the gambling tables. The Justices won't allow that to be sure! As you are well aware, gentlemen, they do not approve of the admixture of the social vices, as they are sometimes called – namely, the consumption of alcohol and participation in games of chance. According to my analysis of your plans, it will be just too easy for a customer to purchase a cocktail or a glass of champagne and proceed to the gaming room nearby.'

'But surely, that's the point, Mr Coggiter,' the instructing solicitor, Mr. Snood replied. 'Gambling takes place in another room altogether. You can't even order a drink in the same area; surely that will satisfy the Justices' objections?'

Lionel removed his rimless half-moon specs and silver-stemmed pipe at the same time. A slight arching of the eyebrows and a pursing of lips indicated that a pronouncement was imminent. This was the moment when he really earned his vast consultation fee – which I duly noted was marked on his brief at 400 guineas.

'It will be for me to undertake that task, Mr.Snood and it is my firm opinion that this is an impropriety which could well cause the application to fail…'

Rex Huggins now spoke. I couldn't blame him for wanting to contribute to the debate but I'm sure that later he regretted that he ever opened his mouth.

'One suggestion might be to construct a small lobby off the bar through which you actually have to go before going into the gaming area.'

We all waited with bated breath for the great man to deliver his judgement. Personally, I thought it was an entirely sensible idea.

'Wholly inadequate in the circumstances. A punter suitably fortified by the stimulus of alcohol would venture naturally out of the room, pausing only momentarily in the lobby on his way to gamble. As Milton puts it so well...

Who shall tempt with wand'ring feet
the dark unbottom'd infinite abyss.

I conclude therefore that the bar must be built much further away.'

There was simply no answer to that, and Rex did not even attempt it simply salvaging his dignity with a resigned grunt of respectful agreement. I was much impressed. The oracle had spoken (using such splendid language) and Lionel had earned every penny as the great Edwardian performer he undoubtedly was. He exhibited that sort of condescending grandness which you see so clearly when you leaf through the period's photography, or watch the early jerky newsreels. You can picture the men dressed in frock-coats, spats and carrying canes; the women wearing elaborate gowns or dresses with their fantastic hats strolling together along the golden avenues of nostalgia. Lionel was a traditional head of chambers in that he was a complete despot. They were his chambers; he held the tenancy from the Temple and the senior clerk, Perch was more akin to a personal manservant than a booking agent for the barristers. The latter, always immaculately dressed in black jacket and striped trousers, always referred to 'Mr. Lionel' in a hushed tone of respect. It harked back to those days in previous centuries when barristers actually lived communally in the Inn, eating their dinners in Hall in the evening and the clerk was employed to wait on his 'gentleman'.

Chambers life, in fact, seemed very leisurely. The rough and tumble of criminal work was regarded as being rather down-market and common and only my pupilmaster and the junior tenants indulged in it at all. Most of the work undertaken was the drafting of civil pleadings and opinions, written by hand, between the civilised working hours of ten in the morning and five in the evening. There were applications before Masters in the High Court, of course, made conveniently 'over the road' in the Strand. That entailed a visit to the 'Bear-Pit' where the Masters' rooms were clustered but this was regarded as being the high point of advocacy by many barristers because full hearings in front of civil judges were so rare.

A glass or two of sherry often accompanied lunch in one of the Inn's halls and tea, if not taken in chambers, would be sipped at Twining's in Fleet Street, or the common room at Galahad's Inn (where the muffins were exceedingly good). Then at five, most of the barristers packed up for the day. Lionel, for example, would don his homburg whilst Perch held out his midnight-blue overcoat with its satin lapels, before the Great Man embarked on the ten minute walk to his flat in Gray's Inn.

TWO

The weeks flew by amiably enough but I began to long for the first six months to be over, after which I would gain rights of audience at last. My retired father, living in Penzance on a small pension couldn't be expected to help with our finances, so as court work for pupils was scarce in Rex's chambers, I devised a way of getting to my feet as soon as possible by obtaining a dock brief.

Quite often defendants weren't represented when they appeared in the crown court on a committal for sentence and barristers were assigned to them on the hoof. Dock briefs were normally taken by the old hacks, who were otherwise out of work and hung round the court precincts waiting for a court official to dole them out. So it was that I travelled down to the Inner London Crown Court and duly picked one up almost straightaway.

The defendant assigned to me that day was an ex-publican called Dearwood. In his mid-forties, he began to gamble heavily – and always lost! He took to stealing from any available source and had built up a considerable number of previous convictions. Whatever the sentence, custodial or otherwise, Mr. Dearwood went straight back to the bookies.

Now he was up before His Honour Judge Oliver Brumble (known as Olly), in breach of two suspended sentences, no less, by virtue of committing even more offences. It looked really pretty hopeless with only one glimmer of hope. Probation was an outside possibility but unlikely due to Dearwood's age. Nonetheless, I prepared a peroration which I hoped would tug at Olly's heartstrings. I spent hours on its preparation, scrawling it all down so I could repeat it virtually verbatim. It was all about the undoubted evils of gambling and how, once it becomes an addiction, it could drag any one of us down into the pit of hell etc, etc... The trouble was that I doubted very much whether Olly had any heartstrings to pull, as that certainly wasn't his reputation.

He was a pudding of a man with appropriately raisin-like eyes studded in a blancmange face. To make matters worse, he sported a large black mole; next to a small down-turned mouth. In regency times, I suppose, a dandy might have regarded it as an adornment but Olly was no dandy. His circuit judge's robe always looked as if half his lunch had been spilled down the front. Thick black hairs also sprouted from the mole giving him altogether a terrifying appearance; quite acceptable in those halcyon days before political correctness when judges were expected to look the part.

Olly's approach to sentencing was also pretty basic; one which would not be appropriate today. He listened to both sides of the case in dead silence and then, more often than not, pronounced one of three sentences.

You'll go to prison for nine months!
or,
You'll go to prison for eighteen months!
or,
You'll go to prison for three years!

No reasons were ever given. It never crossed the judges' minds of yesteryear to give any. After all, the man was only in court because he deserved punishment and he must know that meant prison; that's what happened!

Of course, with the enthusiasm and naivety of youth I was going to change all that.

Probation had never been tried on Dearwood before. Surely now was the time to give him one last chance. Such a sentence was not entirely unfeasible, as there was a suggestion in the pre-sentence report that it might be appropriate as positive help could be given to aid the defendant with his gambling problem. Olly however, was known to be none too keen on probation regarding it, as did so many judges of his generation, as a let-off.

After discussing the pre-sentence report with the client, I made my way from the cells up the stairs into Number Three Court. I arrived at the very moment that Olly marched in and was greeted by a sonorous caterwaul from the usher.

'O..O..Yea! Oyez!.... Oyez....... Let all those who attend before this court today draw near and give their attention! God save the Queen!'

Seamus, Olly's usher was doing his bit using his best parade ground voice as only an ex-regimental sergeant-major in the Irish Guards could. No touchy-feely nonsense in those days in order to help everybody to relax in a caring atmosphere; so essential in our own age where discipline is a dirty word.

Throughout my career, I've always regarded the court usher as being a very important person and made it my business to cosy up to them, dripping with politeness if not actual smarminess. What better way after all, of discovering the foibles of the judge and the particular mood he might be in?

So when Olly retired to consider one of his cases, I ventured out into the vestibule and offered Seamus a cigarette noting that he was in the act of rolling his own minuscule roll-up.

'Don't mind if I do, sir – ah, you're the young fella we've not seen before. Now, here's a piece of advice. When you're addressin' Olly be as brief as you can, he's heard it all before. Oh, an' watch Courtley!'

I was fazed for a moment. I could hardly watch myself, now could I?

Seamus noticed my consternation and grinned twisting the corner of his mouth giving him a lopsided look.

'He's the magistrate who's sitting on Olly's right side. Small and shrivelled man as he is, you probably haven't noticed him.'

Judges always sat with magistrates on committals for sentence but I'd been too nervous to register this old cove who bore my own name.

'Used to be the Chairman of the Bench at Aldgate Magistrates Court until last year when he had to retire. Now, he comes up to Sessions instead nearly every day. He's a hard old bugger, so he is an' always encourages Olly to put the sentences up.'

I gulped. My hands holding my precious notes of mitigation began to sweat.

'So probation hasn't got much of a chance then?'

Seamus gave me a sly look tapping his nose all the while.

'Let me have another of them, ciggies young fella an' I'll tell you what we'll do. Your case could be the last one in the list, see. Olly always likes to get away at three o' clock sharp so he can catch the three-twenty to Sevenoaks. Now what if I call you on at five minutes to the hour?'

'Olly will be watching the clock!'

'So make it really short and sweet which he'll thank you for. There's a fair chance he'll go along with you too an' slap down Courtley who gets on his nerves anyway.'

All thought of my eloquent peroration had now fled.

'What shall I say then, Seamus?'

'Just say something pretty simple which'll go down well with him when he's in a hurry! Like – *Your honour sees what that fine man, the probation officer recommends. Do I need to trouble you further now so late in the day?* '

Seamus' prediction about what would happen turned out to be absolutely correct; in fact, even more so.

At the end of the prosecution's case against Dearwood, Olly glanced at the clock, (it was precisely five to three), and turned to Courtley. This particular individual (no relation, thank God), who wore huge glasses with bottle lenses which made him look like a demented toad, shook his head vigorously but eventually subsided after heated whispering.

Olly turned once more to the front of the court.

'We needn't call upon you, Mr. Courtley – stand up, Dearwood. We're putting you on probation. Don't offend again or you'll be in for the high jump!'

With that, he rose and strode out; the magistrate following in his wake, glaring at me all the while.

I managed to gasp out that I was much obliged but I doubt that he heard. I felt cheated. How could I possibly justify the £10 marked on my brief, (the going rate for a dock brief in those days) when I had submitted nothing?

However, there were compensations. Principally, I had made a firm friend in Seamus who spoke to me again when I left court and was only too eager to accept another cigarette.

'Well done now, young sir! You'll be in Olly's good books an' mine too for that matter. Useful to know that when you come down here regular like.'

He winked and suddenly I was engulfed in a feeling of euphoria. It might have been a modest start but I had appeared in court in my own right for the first time and earned some money!

Seamus must have read my mind. 'Pop along to the taxing office now, lad, and they'll pay out today. That's what the hacks all do. A dollop of cash will come in handy, I'll be bound.'

'I'll do that, thank you...' Then I had an idea.

'Perhaps if you've got a moment, I could buy you a cup of tea, Seamus. You could tell me all about your judges?'

I might still have been wet behind the ears at the age of twenty-three but I had learned one thing. Everybody likes to talk about their work and what better topic was there for ushers to discuss than the judges they serve every day!

'That's a fine idea indeed it is, but you run along an' cash up that brief. The taxing office will be closin' sharp at three-thirty. I'll be getting the teas in the canteen in the meantime.'

The clerk in the taxing office dished out the money and boy, did it feel good – £17 (£10 on the brief and £7 for a conference with the client) – in crisp new notes from the bank. Andrea and I would treat ourselves royally that weekend, I thought. We would pop down to our local Steak House and indulge ourselves with a couple of bottles of claret and a few ports to follow.

Over steaming mugs of tea in the public canteen down in the basement, Seamus described the judges he had worked with over the years. He was the longest serving usher there having done the job since the late 1950s when he left the army. He was able to give me very useful information which I duly stored for the future.

One last word about Olly. As it turned out, I did many cases in front of him in London before he retired. That's because as a junior barrister you tend to do the less well-paid work and defending and prosecuting committals are remunerated at a pretty low rate. Olly hated sitting after three o' clock so this sort of work was ideal for him – as Seamus knew so well.

I became used to his total lack of charm and in all the years I appeared before him, I never recall him once smiling. Coupled with his sour demeanour, he had an unattractive habit of moving his arm in an upwards chopping motion when he wanted the defendant to stand up for the sentence. Grimness was the order of the day. Thank goodness the death penalty had been abolished because he would have looked the part with a black cap on his wig, about to pass the ultimate sentence.

Seamus was quite sorrowful when I told him that most of the barristers thought Olly a hard and unsympathetic bastard.

'Oh, sir. They've got him all wrong, you know. Olly's got a heart of gold beneath that crusty manner... why, one day, he came in late weepin', weepin' buckets, he was. His faithful old bulldog had died that very morning. His wife had to take the hound to the vet to be put to sleep. He loved that dog like a child.'

Well Hitler apparently loved dogs too, but that hadn't stopped *him* from becoming a nasty piece of work, I couldn't help thinking.

THREE

Unfortunately, Perch didn't approve of one of chambers pupils joining the hacks down at Inner London.

'The chambers of Mr. Lionel, sir,' he sniffed, 'being a well-established and respectable set, I'll have you know, do not approve of the pupils 'anging round London Sessions for a dock brief.'

Perch always called that court by its old name – a throwback to the time when the grim old Edwardian building – situated across the river in Newington Causeway – housed the old County of London Quarter Sessions, precursor of the Crown Court.

I frowned. The last person I wanted to offend was the senior clerk.

'I'm very sorry, Perch, but frankly, I rather needed the money.'

'*Money!*' Perch stared at me as if I had uttered an obscenity, 'pupils are not expected to make any of that. Don't you have any private funds then, sir?'

'No,' I answered lamely, 'unless you class an overdraft facility as *private funds* that is – but anyway, it's reaching its limit.'

I pictured Andrea, myself and our two cats, Katie and Winston all huddled round our one-bar elecric fire on a recent, particularly cold night with the meter money running out and decided to be bold. 'So I simply must *try* and earn something, now that I can, in theory.'

Perch didn't reply to that; clerks never discussed financial affairs with their guv'nors in those days but, in fact, he did do his best to help me out. He had contacts with a firm called Overlayes who regularly prosecuted shoplifters on behalf of the big stores in London. The pay was meagre – £8 on the first brief and £5 for any other case in the list on the same day. However, it was paid work and I made the most of it.

So now I found myself in the *real* world of a young barrister dealing with petty crime. The reasonable lunches, afternoon tea in the Temple and watching Rex pontificating at the Old Bailey or, on occasion, the Court of Appeal, became a thing of the past. Now, I was frequenting much seedier places.

Aldgate Magistrates' Court, indeed the majority of these places in the inner London area, were all courts with a faded, daguerreotype feeling about them. Built in the late Victorian age, they contained the narrowest of docks, with just a ledge for the prisoners to sit. The Stipendiary Magistrate presided opposite on a dais, sitting in a high-backed leather chair, pushed back into the shadows. The only light came from a domed skylight in the roof and dull sidelights set in dark oak panelling on every side.

A pervasive odour of tobacco, urine and dirt, faintly alleviated by the whiff of furniture polish tended to linger, but most of all, you smelt the despair in the air – the tang of pathetic, criminal misery.

The two resident magistrates at Aldgate were Laurence – 'Lorry' – Longden and Geldard – 'Geldy' – Lurcher.

Longden terrified everyone; criminals, young lawyers and rookie policemen alike. A glass eye set in a gaunt, etched face glinted alarmingly as he glanced up from his register and surveyed the criminal content of his court each morning.

'Take that chewing gum out of your mouth,' he would bellow to a sour faced youth. Or –

'Take that ridiculous hat off!' – to a Rastafarian, still spaced out after last night's *ganja*. 'Your lawyer tells me that your religion forbids you ever to remove it. Well, it's not a faith I recognise.' Political correctness had not yet arrived in the courts in those days.

Of course as a prosecutor, I was spared all this but then the day came when Overlayes instructed me to defend for the first time. I was in for a baptism by fire but as I was conversant with Lorry's peculiarities, at least I knew what to expect.

Except, of course, sod's law prevailed. I found myself appearing in front of his colleague Geldy instead. The latter was an unknown quantity as far as I was concerned.

The way the brief actually came to me couldn't have been worse either. Originally, my client – an Italian motorist visiting London – had been represented by another firm of solicitors. Half-way through the trial he had sacked them, not being happy with his barrister, and instructed Overlaye's instead. The allegation was that he had assaulted a lollipop man at a zebra crossing.

I met Mr. Jacometti for the first time at court on the adjourned day of the trial – the complainant having given evidence on the previous occasion. I was left in little doubt as to my client's expectations of me.

'Hey, you do better than the other guy, ok? He let that old bastard lie – the man say I get out of the car and *breaka* the stick over his head! *He* hit *me* – *poka* the stick through the window into my face!'

I squirmed – I could see that my first defence trial was destined to be a loser.

Later, after the hyperactive Italian in the dock had spewed forth the last of a cascade of meandering and irrelevant lies, I made my closing address.

Geldy Lurcher stared at me for a moment. The half-light of the late December afternoon accentuated his likeness to Boris Karloff, with the shadows etching the hollows in his broad, saturnine face.

'You don't remember the lollilop-man, do you, Mr. Courtley?' the Magistrate dripped sarcasm. 'The rather *infirm* complainant of this assault, who gave evidence on the last occasion. Of course you don't, you weren't here. Now, I shall retire for a while to assess the evidence. I don't suppose it will take me more than ten minutes…'

Time for you to sup an afternoon cup of tea, I thought gloomily, *as I'm sure you've made up your mind already!*

I escaped thankfully to the improvised police canteen where somebody who was now a good friend of mine habitually dispensed very welcome refreshment.

The tea was made in Sarge's little cell. Not in modern, polystyrene containers either, but good, solid enamel mugs with the Metropolitan Police badge on the side. Sarge – the Court Sergeant – had commandeered the smallest cell in the custody block some years before, installed a wheezy electrical heater and dispensed sympathy liberally with the tea, (but only to the favoured few). I was one of them, having cultivated his friendship early on. After all, wasn't the Court Sergeant the power behind the list in every busy Magistrate's court? In that context, good relations counted for much. A tactful and polite approach made all the difference between getting your case on at a reasonable time, or right at the end of the court day- when justice tended to be tempered not with mercy, but judicial irritability instead.

'Old boy playin' you up then sir?' Sarge removed the roll-up from the side of his mouth and gave me his lop-sided grin.

I don't think I ever knew his name; everyone just called him Sarge. Spectacles with thick black frames covered twinkling eyes and enhanced his look of amiable authority.

'Mind you, Geldy's got a point. Old Mr. Gringe, the lollilop-man *is* pushing seventy after all and he suffers from a bad leg as well. Wounded in the Korean War, he tells everyone.'

Pity I hadn't known, I thought but had no time to reply as the Magistrate was coming back into court sooner than expected.

Geldy was forbidding to look at; nightmarish actually, his

sleek black hair and pale face redolent of Count Dracula. Even the voluble Mr. Jacometti was suitably cowed.

'The case against you is proved. As a punishment, I have in mind a short custodial sentence, Mr. Courtley, and a recommendation that your client be deported immediately.'

'You *cannota* be doing this, please *-ees* not fair! ' yelled my client as Geldy duly sentenced him to seven days inprisonment and ordered that he remain in custody pending deportation. It wasn't until I later saw him in the cells that his real anger was vented.

'*You!* You allow this thing to 'appen. Call yourself my lawyer – English justice *steenks!*'

Sarge patted me sympathetically on the back as I left the custody block later having told my unhappy client that he could always appeal although I didn't hold up much hope of success.

'Never mind, sir. You know what they say, can't win 'em all.'

I nodded glumly. Still, it certainly would have done my morale a power of good if I'd won not necessarily all of them but at least this one – my first!

FOUR

Rumours were rife in the Devereux pub where as a pupil, I inevitably picked up most of my information about chambers splitting-up and assuming new forms. As Lionel Coggiter's set was already full up, I had to look elsewhere for a tenancy. Then it was that I learnt that Tufton Crump was extending his chambers at Number Three Tabernacle Buildings and one afternoon, I just happened to casually mention this to Rex.

'I know dear old Tufton, I'll give him a ring.' Rex reached for his phone as we sat in his room in chambers. 'Of course, he's a Labour M.P, (Rex was known to be a diehard Tory) – but, thank God, not one of those loony lefties!'

This I had already found out for although Tufton represented a mining constituency in Wales with a large majority, it didn't prevent him living stylishly in a Holland Park detached house stuffed full of valuable works of art. Indeed, as I was to discover, Tufton was a quintessential Welshman, armed with a lilting baritone voice, and thus able to play dual roles—*the boyo from the valleys who'd done well in the big ceety, see,* and a suave member of the ruling classes. It only required a slight alteration in his accent.

Whilst I was thus musing, Rex was speaking on the telephone and suddenly the dice of life fell in my favour; double sixes both sides. My luck and both Tufton were in. Moreover, the latter was prepared to interview me straightaway!

'I'll send him up then,' Rex was saying. 'I can vouch for him being a sensible sort of chap, always buys his round – and that kind of thing.'

I left chambers in a daze to make my way to Tabernacle Buildings. All Tufton knew about me was that I was Rex's pupil and as this was long before the days of CVs, assessments, character references and appraisals, everything depended on what personal impression I made on the man.

Pump Court, where Tabernacle Buildings are situated, has hardly changed in centuries. Sets of barristers' chambers still huddle round a small square with a row of cloisters like a monastery on one side. Any pumping activity has long since vanished and the origin of the name is obscure. Broad white boards with barristers' names painted on them in black adorn the various doorways instead.

My eye travelled down the one situated outside number three; Tufton Crump's chambers. The hand-painted black letters danced before my eyes—Would I see my own name painted on such a board soon? That was the ultimate accolade of the young, aspiring barrister to be made a tenant in a set of chambers.

I felt a commotion behind me which jolted me out of my reverie.

''scuse me, guv,' a gangling youth with an alert face badly marred by acne, hefting a huge suitcase, brushed past me.

Later I was to become quite friendly with Spotty Nick as he was, rather unkindly, known. He was the outdoor clerk of a firm of solicitors who sent Tabernacle Buildings a great deal of work. He proved to be a useful buffer between ourselves and the more unsavoury of the clients – but more of that later.

I followed Nick up the stairs as he pulled the unwieldy suitcase behind him. He struggled into the clerk's room where Leslie Divott, the senior clerk stood, stock still; his head cocked to one side like an inquisitive bird. He was striking a pose which I would come to know well.

'Got all the briefs for tomorrow then, Nick?' he barked.

'My principal will be down with the last minute ones, but here's the most of them…'

Nick opened up the suitcase on the floor revealing piles of briefs with the names of clients printed on thick cream paper, neatly tied up with red ribbon. I stared round-eyed at the sight.

These were just the briefs for the next day's court appearances at the Magistrates' and Crown Courts. This was a wealth of work indeed! None were allocated to any particular barrister at that stage; this was the responsibility of the clerk, giving him enormous power. Open-mouthed, I just gawped. Then the bird-like figure turned to me.

'What do you want, *Sah?*'

'I've come to see Mr. Crump, I believe he's expecting me…'

'What chambers are you from, *Sah?*'

'I'm only a pupil – oh, you mean the head of my pupil-master's chambers, that's Lionel Coggiter Q.C.'

Leslie had blue-grey eyes like a cat, and I began to feel like a mouse about to be pounced upon. He was not a physically impressive man, but he could reduce most pupils to quivering wrecks. It was only later that I learnt that underneath a hard exterior, he was essentially a kind man.

'I said what chambers – not the head! Are you ignorant, *Sah?* Name of the clerk, *Sah?* That's what I want to know!'

'Oh, sorry. Of course – it's Perch of …'

'Thank *yoooou*, *Sah!*' Leslie gave me a mocking little bow. 'Him and me will be 'aving a talk about you but in the meantime…'

He strode across the room to a closed door; rapped on it twice and opened it with a flourish.

Tufton sat behind a massive desk; an un-tipped cigarette poised at an angle in one hand, conservatively dressed in a blue, pin-striped suit, which blended well with a pale pink shirt. This was further smartened by a starched white collar, detached from the shirt as was still the custom. He was a small man with curly black hair, sparse on top with large bagged eyes; the lids with a tendency to droop as he spoke. A snub nose ending in a point like a parsnip gave his face a slightly wistful look.

'Come in! Come in, dear boy.' His voice was deep and rich. 'You've come about a tenancy have you? Now, let me tell you we intend to specialise in crime even more than we do at the moment. Defence work, I should add.'

'Oh, yes just what I want to do.' I cringed inwardly remembering that my defence experience amounted to representing a compulsive gambler when I had said nothing and the unfortunate Italian who had just been thrown out of the country.

'Rex prosecutes mainly, of course. You don't want to prosecute, do you? Leslie's not much in favour of it for beginners.'

'Well…I…' *Please God don't let him ask how much defence work I've actually done.*

But Tufton didn't seem to require any information from me.

'Civil work is out too. We intend to eliminate it altogether. You don't want to do that, do you?'

'Oh, no.' I felt much more confident now. Civil work in any form filled me with dread.

'Good, good. I'm glad Rex sent you over, he's a fine chap whose views I respect. We'll let you know…'

The phone rang. Tufton picked it up in one hand, the cigarette in the other vaguely gesturing in my direction. I took this as a sign of dismissal and left, breathing a sigh of relief that no-one had asked what I might be able to contribute to chambers.

A week passed and as was my wont, I was propping up the bar in the Devereux, sipping my first pint when Tufton walked in unexpectedly – he was more likely to visit Tom Tug's (the only wine-bar in that area at the time) than a mere pub.

Fate intervened again. I happened to catch his eye as he pushed his way towards the packed bar. He beckoned vigorously; I joined him.

'By the way it's *yes*. Leslie will be dropping you a line in a few days. Let's have a drink to celebrate.'

* * *

'You mean it was as easy as that?' Andrea enquired.

'All done and dusted,' I said airily. 'Tufton has said that I can start at the end of September when my pupillage with Rex actually finishes.'

I picked up the cheap bottle of sherry, shared the remaining contents between us and returned to our one ramshackle armchair. Contentedly, I glanced at our two cats who were, as usual, happily hogging the one-bar fire. I felt in an expansive mood. 'To be offered a tenancy at this early stage is quite a thing, darling; I've made it actually.'

'Made what exactly?' Andrea didn't sound very convinced.

'The grade... Well, a foot at least on the legal ladder.'

'Yes, but no money. Anyway, if you're now a tenant, you'll have to pay rent, won't you?'

'Ah...' I had been pushing this worrying thought to the back of my mind but now I was obliged to tell her of a piece of conversation I had had with Tufton the other night after the few celebratory drinks.

As a new tenant, I expect a slightly lesser advance of monthly rent from you, Charles dear boy – fifty pounds to be exact but rising to seventy-five thereafter...

'Fifty pounds now!' Andrea banged her glass down in shock. 'Where the blazes are you going to get that from?'

'Crown Court work, of course. Now that I have a place in chambers, it will be coming fast and furious. Admittedly, the Magistrates' Court cases which I've been doing recently don't pay much but -'

'Much!' Andrea was really cross now and rose to go to bed. 'Nothing you mean! That firm which you've been working for haven't actually paid a penny, have they?'

24

'No...' I pondered for a moment. 'That's true to form though. Solicitors never pay counsel's fees until the last possible moment. Barristers can't sue them, you see, that's the legal position.'

'Oh really!' Andrea was very angry now. 'Well, perhaps in that case, you'll find yourself a job which does pay because we haven't got any money. At the moment, I possess just over two pounds which will have to feed us for the rest of the week! Now, I'm going to sleep.'

Having clambered into our rickety old bed which doubled as a sofa, she switched off the sidelight plunging our one room in darkness.

I had some thinking to do.

The next day, I came up with a possible solution at least in the short term. Another visit to the bank manager was required. I made an appointment for the following day but in the meantime Lesley made contact. He had a trial lined up for me – at the Old Bailey – which meant that I had to cancel the appointment. The vexed question of finance would just have to wait.

'New firm of solicitors too, *Sah*! So best foot forward please.'

I was soon to learn that this was one of Leslie's favourite expressions and called for only one reaction. Refusing the case was quite out of the question and the fullest possible commitment was expected. Therein lay the secret of success as one old QC had told me at a Bar dinner.

Work on each case as if it's your first one, my boy. A barrister, however successful he might appear in the eyes of the world, is only ever as good as his next case...

As I took the brief home to study that evening, I told Andrea our discussions about finance would just have to be postponed. My devoted wife, giving me that special smile which has always been one of her most lovable characteristics, gave a resigned reply.

'Then tomatoes on toast for supper until I get paid at the end of the month!'

FIVE

The Old Bailey occupies a special place in British criminal history. It is a redoubtable and doleful place despite the accretion of modern courts, added to the original main building in 1973. Thickly carpeted in an aquamarine colour with light wooden panelling on the walls and green leather in abundance on walls, benches and chairs, the decor was an attempt to lighten the atmosphere but nothing could reduce the sense of intrinsic anguish.

That anguish always floats over you as you walk through the present entrance, turn left and make your way to the original gateway to the building, now only ever used on ceremonial occasions. From there, a sweeping staircase leads to the first floor (which houses the original four courts), and vast murals hover in the heights above your head. There's a biblical resonance, (about it all) emphasized not only by the pictures straight out of the Old Testament, but by the motto – *God will punish the wrong-doer and protect the innocent* – written in stark black letters below the ledges of the cupola.

I suppose the venerable Edwardian architect who designed the place wanted it to resemble a cathedral so those who venture inside feel uplifted but it never had that effect on me. The necessity for such a place is a reminder of human failure and not its success. After all, apart from those who actually work there in one capacity or another, for the rest it is a place of misery, hate, misguided passion and death. Most people who attend have left in various degrees of despair. Lives which have been taken away or ruined may be reconstructed for an hour or so but only in theory; the damage can never really be put right.

A pretty grim scenario, you might think, therefore it's not surprising I entered the building that day with a dry mouth and a prickle of sweat on my forehead. One clammy hand held my barristers' blue robe-bag and the other, the brief – the covering page of which I can still recall having so avidly studied the contents the night before…

IN THE CENTRAL CRIMINAL COURT

Regina versus Leroy Bunker.

BRIEF FOR THE DEFENDANT.

Floater

SHERABLE AND SALOCK SOLICITORS,
2 LUDGATE CIRCUS,
LONDON EC4.

Next I ventured up to the reception desk in the main hall behind which a huge City of London policeman stood. Beside him was a flunkey dressed in a smart dark-blue uniform with red epaulettes on his jacket.

'Excuse me,' I croaked. 'I'm the defence counsel in the case of… er… Leroy Bunker. I'm floating apparently…'

Of course, that certainly wasn't meant literally. On the contrary, I felt that the marble floor was remarkably close and I might just collapse on it in a heap. The word 'floater', (written on the brief by my clerk), simply meant that, as yet, my case had not been allocated a specific court.

The policeman extended a ham-like hand for my brief and

examined it with care, no doubt he had to check my authenticity.

'Ah, yes… it's Wintry.'

My mouth fell open. I knew I was dazed with anxiety but surely I hadn't got the seasons all mixed up? Was it not a muggy and sweaty London afternoon in mid summer?

My confusion must have registered because the policeman chuckled.

'Judge Cedric Wintringham – Wintry's his nick name. His Lordship will be dealing with the floaters today. In Court One.'

I dragged myself up to the robing room; my heart in my boots feeling that I was about to face trial. What a debut here – appearing in the most notorious courtroom in the land!

But all that had to be briefly put aside. First and foremost, I needed to introduce myself to the client and take his instructions. Personal qualms had to be ignored. One thing I had learnt from pupillage was that the client must always think you are totally confident and in charge – otherwise, why should he want to be represented by you?

I was lucky in one respect: Leroy was no hardened villain but a seventeen year old youth with no previous convictions. He was charged with dishonestly receiving a cassette-tape player, (although portable, these precursors of Walkmans and the tiny technical gadgetry of today were still quite large) from a mate called Dwayne. Dwayne had noticed this desirable object sticking out of a woman's shopping bag as she walked along Balham High Street. He 'lifted' it and later sold it to Leroy for a couple of quid. My client always maintained that he didn't know the item to be stolen – Dwayne was a friend and had assured him it was totally 'legit' in effect giving it to him as a present. However, the prosecution's case was that Dwayne had handed it to Leroy quite deliberately so that the latter could 'hide' it for a while, (unlike Dwayne, Leroy was not known to the police). Later, it would be sold on and the two of them would split the profits. Anyway, the fact that he paid so little for it meant that he must have realised it to be stolen from the outset.

Dwayne had pleaded guilty to the theft in the Magistrates' court and was duly punished. Leroy had also attempted to plead guilty to receiving on the basis that he had physically been in possession of the machine but denied any dishonest knowledge. The Magistrate indicated that Leroy should accordingly plead not guilty and so the latter elected trial by jury, as was his right. The Old Bailey wasn't busy as it was August so the case had been duly transferred from Inner London where there was a considerable back-log.

'Court One, innit guv?' Leroy's eyes were like saucers in a pleasant brown face, now putty-coloured with anxiety. 'Wha' ah gonna get if ah go down?'

Surely not long, I thought, bearing in mind that he was a young lad with no previous convictions. But as this was the Old Bailey, how did I know? Yet I needed to sound positive.

'Now Mr. Bunker, you mustn't think like that. My job is to get you off,' – and had no chance to say anymore as a burly prison office entered the interview room and announced. 'Bunker's up in court one now! You'd better get upstairs yourself, sir… a.s.a.p!'

I had already learnt some salient facts about Cedric Wintringham in pupillage. He was now one of the oldest judges at the Old Bailey, having at one time been a senior prosecutor there. He was reputed to be rigidly religious but had never shown any scruple about prosecuting cases which involved the death penalty.

Court Number One at the Old Bailey is absolutely unique. No court I have appeared in over the years possesses its cavernous dimension for a start. It was built in the days when there was nothing touchy-feely about justice and the full rigour of the law was best displayed in an atmosphere of ponderous pomp. The judge's bench seems to go on for ever down the width of the room. Behind it are a number of stately chairs reserved for the Lord Mayor of London and the aldermen who sit with the judge. These dignitaries attend on occasion and indeed the judge sits at the side of the Lord Mayor with the sword of Justice hanging appropriately above the former's head.

Tentatively, I made my way to the back of counsel's row on the side, well away from the eminent QCs (known as silks) who normally sit at the front. Moments later, the court usher entered the court-room and bellowed – *All Rise!*

In came a procession splendid to behold – initially. First of all there was an alderman wearing a fur-trimmed gown tied with velvet ribbon, followed by the Under Sheriff attired in a frock-coat with a magnificent ruffled cream stock round his neck. Finally the judge made his entrance, and what a disappointment that turned out to be!

Judge Cedric Wintringham was not a High Court Judge so did not wear the red robes trimmed with white fur of that office. Instead, he wore the plain black gown habitually worn by Old Bailey Judges. He was a small, rather bent man with round spectacles perched on a beaky little nose. Could this chap really have been a leading prosecutor who so regularly dispatched villains to the gallows? Insignificant in appearance, his voice did nothing to dispel that impression.

'Ye..e..e..s, Mr. Cutherbertson?'

This was said in a thin, reedy voice ending in a whistle.

A sturdy man with greying swept-back hair clearly visible under his wig stood up. He proceeded to make a flowery speech; the content specifically concerning the exceptional quality of justice meted out in this building, as constructed by the City Fathers for just that purpose etc, etc… Only later was I to discover that this eulogy was regularly delivered at the Old Bailey, whenever any City dignitary graced the place with their presence. 'Cuffs' was a senior Treasury Counsel; one of the favoured few who prosecuted full-time for the Director of Public Prosecutions at the Central Criminal Court. They were a very close-knit band indeed, as exclusive as the Freemasons with equivalent privileges to boot. So grand were they that they did not need to take silk; their mere existence vouchsafed their special status. I couldn't help feeling that to my client all this would appear rather frightening but thankfully, he was not yet sitting in the dock.

Dermot Cuthbertson finally completed his peroration and the Alderman and Under-Sheriff looked suitably gratified by the shower of compliments. Then another splendid figure made his appearance known, this time from just underneath the bench.

This was Valentine Voyce, the Court Administrator and the Senior Clerk of Arraigns. Seemingly, all he ever did was to attend court at the beginning of each trial and put the indictment to the accused. This he did in a graveside voice striking fear in the heart of the most brazen of defendants who was left in no doubt of the solemnity of the law.

Rumour had it that he was at his best in the morning before midday when he consumed his first, (and by no means last) schooner of sherry causing him to be rather slurred and unsteady in the afternoon.

'My lord has a floating case today,' he said disdainfully as if forced to utter a profanity, 'the case of Leroy Bunker in which Mr. Everard Rockby prosecutes...'

He said it in such a way which made it clear that this name was a very familiar one at the Central Criminal Court.

A large florid man stood up in front of me. 'Indeed, I appear for the Crown in this matter, M'lud. Unhappily, I do not know who defends if anyone. No counsel has yet introduced himself him to me...'

Oh Gawd that's my fault, I thought. I should have gone up to the Bar Mess and made myself known to him.

'I appear to represent Bunker, My Lord...'

A curious sound like a squawk came from the back of my throat.

Voyce turned portentously towards me. I felt far more nervous of him than I ever would have been of the judge.

'You are?' he growled.

'Courtley, sir. Sorry... Nobody ever asked for my name.'

Voyce sniffed audibly but did not deign to reply.

'Bring Bunker up!' he commanded.

Poor Bunker stood in the same place as Doctor Crippen, Lord Haw-Haw, the Yorkshire Ripper and other celebrated malefactors, quaking as Voyce read the indictment to him.

'Prisoner at the bar, you are charged with dishonestly receiving stolen goods against the Queen's peace. How say you, guilty or not?'

'Not guilty!' To his credit, Bunker spoke much more emphatically than I had moments before.

Voyce faced the judge and stated in a tone of amazement. 'He denies the charge, M'lud!'

'Can we try it now, Mr Voyce?' Another whistling sound emanated from the bench.

I froze. Oh, please God no. I'd heard all about Wintringham's way of trying cases. Appeal-proof on the face of the transcript if the matter ever reached the appeal court, his method remained hideously unfair to the defendant. The defence case was always put to the jury accompanied by a leer of disbelief and delivered in a sing-song voice straight out of a Gilbert and Sullivan operetta.

'M'lud, no. Your lordship has far more grievous matters in your lordship's list. I have consulted the list officer who informs me that Mr. Recorder Cameron will be able to take the case at twelve o' clock in West Court Four.'

'So be it,' grunted Wintringham and that was that. Bunker was whisked away to be replaced by another wretched defendant.

I thanked my lucky stars I had escaped, but what about this recorder of whom I had never heard? – and where the hell was West Court Four?

SIX

Just across the road, that's where. In fact, next to the Magpie and Stump pub facing the main building. This pub had acquired a notorious reputation in the early years of Queen Victoria's reign when convicted murderers swung on the gallows outside the old Newgate Prison on the same site. Before then, the criminals had been conveyed from that grim old place down Snow Hill, across the Fleet ditch, leaving the City of London at Temple Bar, to make their way to Tyburn Tree where Marble Arch now stands. The general populace could accordingly goggle at any point en route, if unfortunate enough to miss the public hanging itself.

Later executions were relocated, taking place just outside the prison itself and the Magpie and Stump became popular with the gentry. The mob had no alternative but to crowd into the street whereas a gentleman for a few shillings (often accompanied by his wife or mistress) could partake of a mutton chop and a pint of claret and repair to an upstairs room to watch the entertainment.

Just after the Second World War, the warehouse next door had been hastily converted into four shoddily built courts and that's where I now went. Shabby (and long since demolished) this whole building might have been, but it was still the Old Bailey and this was my very first trial. I can still visualize the plywood benches for judges and counsel finished in a cheap walnut veneer and smell the aroma of disinfectant mixed with furniture polish. The docks at the back were made of the same cheap material as the other fittings with the exit from them simply leading to a fire-escape (where defendants were promptly handcuffed) at the rear of the building.

Mr. Recorder Cameron turned out to be an amiable enough tribunal. Seeing how nervous I was, he allowed me to get on with the trial without interrupting. The same could not be said for Everard Rockby however, who constantly chipped in as I struggled to take my client through his evidence in a coherent manner.

'Don't lead! Please don't lead! My Lord, I must protest – my learned friend is leading this witness quite disgracefully – virtually telling him what to say!'

Matters were only to get worse when he cross examined. 'Now then, Bunker, you have said that this...ah...tape recording device was given to you by Dwayne for a very small consideration. Is that not so?'

'Yeah. 'e wanted two pahnd for it. I fought that cheap, right if that's what ah fink you're gettin' at.'

'That's precisely what I am getting at. Two pounds was a very cheap price indeed for an item which sells on the high street for at least fifteen pounds. Wasn't it?'

'I dunno – 'e could have bought it off a market stall – anywhere really.'

'Exactly. You had no idea where it had come from originally so believed it to be stolen, didn't you? You knew it couldn't be legit as you choose to put it.'

''e said it was legit, dinnee? No need to ask anyfink more abaht it, was there?'

'You closed your eyes to the obvious, didn't you Bunker? If you'd pressed him on the point he'd have told you soon enough. Furthermore, you knew him to be a convicted thief, didn't you?'

'Ye..ah?...Might 'ave done, ah s'pose.'

'So!' Rockby said triumphantly. 'You drew the only

reasonable inference that was possible in the circumstances – That it must have been stolen!'

'Wha' – don't unnerstand what you mean by innerference, like but it could have been nicked, yeah.'

Rockby sighed with satisfaction and sat down; his cross-examination complete.

I stood up to re-examine.

'So you might have suspected it to be stolen but didn't really know or believe it to be, did you?'

'Not when you put it like that, nah.'

'Now, my learned friend is not just *leading* but actually putting words in his client's mouth! Mere suspicion is no longer enough to establish the requisite dishonest state of mind and that's exactly what Mr. Courtley has got the witness to say,' protested the furious Rockby.

'You're probably right, Mr. Rockby, but what has now been said can't be unsaid, can it?' the judge observed.

This exchange was significant because a leading case on the law of receiving stolen property had only recently been decided by the Court of Appeal. For there to be a conviction, it was laid down that any person found in possession of stolen property had to actually know or believe it to be stolen. Mere suspicion simply wasn't enough.

So Bunker had a defence alright; one that Rockby, as the prosecutor, was required to disprove. My leading question had helped to bolster it but that didn't mean that he was going to get off.

'Quite simply, members of the jury, Bunker's state of mind at the time is clear. He didn't ask any question about this device because he must have known what the answer would be! He is guilty of the charge.' Rockby laid it on the line in his closing speech.

When I rose to address the jury, I was nervous; my hands shook and my eyes were glued to the notes in front of me. I felt I also sounded thoroughly unconvincing. Brought up as a law-abiding citizen, a dire thought for a defending barrister kept invading my mind; the very fact that Bunker was there at all pointed to his guilt. However, poor young Bunker wasn't me but a somewhat underprivileged and inarticulate youth and I was determined to do my best. Sweating profusely, I sat down after twenty minutes.

When the jury were sent out on the conclusion of the judge's summing-up, I had but one thought: *Be quick, for God's sake, and put Bunker and me out of our misery!*

A half hour passed. The jury trooped back in.

When I heard the magic words – *not guilty* – ring out, I was to experience that feeling of pure joy which can come only once to an advocate in his first trial. What made it even more special was that the foreman of the jury gave me a sly wink as he pronounced the verdict.

I stood up and requested my client's release which was granted. I felt as if a huge weight had left my shoulders. On leaving court, my gown billowed with the draft from the door. Now, I really did feel I was floating!

Rockby and I travelled down together in the lift. Although inclined to be pompous as I knew, he had the grace to congratulate me on a 'good result'.

I couldn't help telling him. 'That was actually my first trial, you know. I never expected an acquittal. Whilst I was speaking to the jury, the vibes weren't at all good!'

Rockby looked at me in horror.

'Dear boy, you don't speak to a jury, you make submissions to it – and what an extraordinary expression to use, vibes! I suppose you mean vibrations, although that is hardly an aesthetic expression…'

Perhaps it wasn't but I was only using a word common amongst us twenty-somethings at the time. It originated, of course, from one of the Beach Boys greatest hits, 'Good Vibrations' – but I don't suppose an old fogy like Rockby had ever heard of them.

Back in the robing room of the main building, I rang my clerk.

'I heard already on the grape-vine. You've become a real defender, Sah! Sherable's want you again on Monday, back at the Old Bailey. The brief's coming down this afternoon.'

* * *

So I was back at the Old Bailey on the following Monday and coincidentally once again in West Court 4. This time, however, I drew the short straw because Wintry was sitting there that week – Court 1 being closed for the duration due to routine maintenance work.

I was defending in a wife beating case; a burly Jamaican who had married an Irish nurse. He was charged with beating her so badly that he broke her rib-cage piercing the heart-sack which almost caused her to die. He admitted assaulting her with an open hand, but denied that he had ever intended to do her really serious harm.

The defining moment came when I made the fatal mistake of asking my client this question.

'Now, you admit you hit your wife in anger, don't you? – and you accept that you injured her quite significantly?'

'Yes, sir.'

'But you emphatically deny, don't you, that you intended to cause her the serious bodily injury which, in fact, occurred?'

'Yes, sir.'

There was a pause.

'As that is your claim...' The judge's reedy voice cut in. 'Perhaps you might demonstrate to the jury how you actually struck her?'

'I hit her like this.'   BANG!... CRACK!

As the panel of the witness box which he struck was made of the same cheap material as all the other fixtures of the court, it didn't take much for the defendant's open hand to cleave through the walnut veneer and leave a split in the plywood. The point was only too well made as I realised when the judge gave the jury a meaningful look. My honeymoon in the law had ended almost as soon as it began!

There were no acquittals this time. Instead, Wintry doled out a heavy eight year sentence instead – delivered in his usual thin and whistling tone.

SEVEN

I stared at the brief, bound up in pink tape as normal, with the name of the client and instructing solicitor endorsed on it. Enclosed was a police charge sheet alleging that the client had committed an assault occasioning actual bodily harm on an employee at the formers builder's yard in the Old Kent Road. The instructions revealed that he wished to plead not guilty and elect for trial at the Crown Court. Perhaps not surprisingly, Legal Aid had been refused as he was the sole proprietor of a prosperous building company but no private fee was marked either.

The firm of solicitors, J. Le Malle, Brasper and Co. was one I knew briefed chambers a great deal – I had seen spotty Nick delivering the briefs – although I had not actually worked for them myself thus far.

It was another hot summer's day and I was formally dressed in the conventional barrister's uniform of pin-striped trousers and black jacket worn, in those days, whatever the weather. Not the most comfortable garb to be wearing at that time of the year but what was making me hotter still was a feeling of indignation. Was I expected to work for nothing? Particularly, as attempting to earn a living was very much on my mind that day.

Earlier, I had finally managed to visit the bank manager and our meeting hadn't gone quite as I had hoped. In his office at the rear of the bank, Mr. Tinby examined the state of my account with an air of disapproval.

'£300 seemed to us to be a reasonable overdraft facility at this stage of your career, Mr Courtley yet now you ask it to be extended to £1000.'

'Quite so,' I decided a confident tone was required. 'Because Mr. Tinby, circumstances have changed significantly since we last met. I've been taken on as a tenant in chambers and am now conducting cases at the Central Criminal Court on a regular basis.' (This was a slight exaggeration but I wanted to convey the right impression) – 'therefore substantial fees are accruing to me all the time.'

Mr. Tinby was a fussy type with a toothbrush moustache which accentuated a rather prissy mouth.

'That may well be so, Mr. Courtley. But we at the bank are concerned about your cash flow. Money coming in as well as going out, you know. Your bank statement indicates that that you are now in debt to the bank to the tune of.. ' He peered at the document in front of him. '- £290.50, and your receipts have been nil.'

'Indeed, indeed.' I waved a hand expansively. 'All barristers suffer from a continual liquidity problem as I explained before but I shall tell my clerk to attend to the matter immediately.'

'I suggest you do that straightaway, Mr. Courtley. The bank is willing, on this last occasion, to assist temporarily but only by increasing the limit to £500.'

So, back in the clerk's room, I wasn't in the best frame of mind as I contemplated what to do next.

It was now one-thirty and I was due to appear at Aldgate Magistrates' Court at two o' clock. It would take at least twenty minutes to get near it on the underground and it was a five minute walk from there. I might just make it on time if I left chambers straightaway. Then I thought; to hell with it – I wasn't going to court for nothing! It was time to take a stand and confront the clerk.

'Leslie!' I said in a commanding voice, striding into the clerks' room. 'I possess a private brief here from Le Malle, Brasper and no fee has been marked on it. I can't go to court without this being done. It's quite impossible.'

Leslie swivelled round in his chair and stared at me. His blue-grey eyes remained totally expressionless.

'Yes Sah! Of course, Sah! Very remiss of me, Sah! Please hand back the brief if you'd be so *kaind!*'

I handed over the papers puffing my chest out proudly. This was the way to deal with the clerk. I wasn't just a pupil any more, I was a fully-fledged member of chambers now and absolutely determined to be treated as such.

Leslie scribbled on the brief and handed it back to me promptly. I had won! Of course, I wasn't expecting a substantial fee only a reasonable figure to reflect the fact that it was privately paid...

Written in Leslie's neat hand and underlined, appeared the words.

NO FEE

I gaped for a moment and wondered about the etiquette of the situation. Surely somewhere there was a query about barristers not being allowed to work for nothing! There had to be impropriety about being expected to work for zilch!

I was about to protest but it was too late. Leslie was back on the telephone; two actually as he was jabbering into individual handsets glued to each ear.

Meanwhile Dennis, the junior clerk, cast me a sly glance. Much less volatile than Leslie, he was nonetheless able in his own inimitable way, to put young barristers down just as effectively.

'Leslie's a bit annoyed with you, sir. Mr. Brasper sends a lot of work to these chambers and this case is a bit special-like comin' in at the last minute. The client's doin' a bit of work on

Mr. Brasper's house at a reduced price and he thought we wouldn't mind sending someone to court for nothin'. 'Course, I could always return the brief out of chambers but it seems a pity. There's four trials from that firm tomorrow at London Sessions and I'd have to return those as well.'

'I understand, but...'

Dennis tapped his watch.

'Ten to two, sir. Don't want to keep the client waiting, now do we? I'll ring the warrant office and tell 'em you're on your way but I'd get goin' if I was you.'

And, of course, that's exactly what I did.

You could say that this was the beginning of a significant learning curve. Life as a young barrister might involve visits to the Crown Court – including the Old Bailey – but these tended to be rare events in practice. This was a shame because for such work we were remunerated directly by the court and not by the solicitors. As it turned out, much of my time would be spent working for solicitors who often didn't pay at all – either because, as in the above case, we were expected to work for nothing – or that they simply 'forgot' to reimburse us from the legal aid fees paid to them.

J Le Malle, Brasper were one of the worst offenders and indeed, there were good and bad elements about Ferdy Brasper's close relationship with chambers. A good thing was that he commandeered a great deal of work obtained through his extensive contacts with the warrant officers and gaolers of the central London magistrates' courts. Quite how that operated, I never made it my business to find out but this was long before the days of 'Duty Solicitors'. So when a villain asked for a brief, it was generally FB who got the call. Moreover, he sent virtually all his work to chambers and it was invariably well-prepared. The bad thing was though, as I indicated before, that he never paid up! This seemed particularly unfair as he looked remarkably prosperous in himself, flashing abundant gold accoutrements about his thick -

set body, often clad in a suit of pale mauve cloth which I thought rather garish.

By contrast, Ferdy's partner Le Malle, never came to chambers. We were told he was a 'property lawyer' and a 'company consultant' who would never allow his reputation to be stained by dealing with crime; at least other people's malfeasance that is. Then one day, he visited South America on 'holiday' and somehow failed to return. Rumour had it that arrival back in England would have meant him being instantly arrested for a substantial fraud involving millions of pounds. Accordingly, Ferdy discreetly dropped his partner's name and henceforth the firm became known as 'Braspers'.

The firm was popular enough with clients but not so much with police officers who frequently 'verballed' Ferdy up. This popular police practice was usually employed to conveniently place words of admission of guilt in the mouths of criminals at the time of arrest, but did not normally extend to their legal representatives. However, Ferdy seemed an exception perhaps due to the fact that he enjoyed a devoted following of villains.

One of the milder sort of verbal was – *Braspy says never to tell the Old Bill nothing*. Another, one not so mild perhaps, was – *Braspy's my brief and bent an' all. He'll fix an alibi for this blag!*

Whether Ferdy was actually bent, as a barrister I never needed to know. I was aware though that he worked very hard making himself available to clients night and day.

The other firm that sent a lot of work (and didn't pay either!) was the outfit which employed Gus Garden as its managing clerk.

You could best describe them as 'phantom' solicitors. When I started, they were known under the moniker of Ball and Floris Flood which later changed to Eric E. Evidge. Indeed, the whole thing seemed to be run on a shoestring by Gus and of the actual partners there were no signs whatsoever.

Gus was a laid-back lanky chap with black shoulder-length hair which flopped about an affable face and matched a drooping Mexican moustache. On one occasion I was actually obliged to travel down the Commercial Road in search of his offices. He hadn't been able to visit the Temple the night before to offload his briefs and I was asked to pop into his premises first thing in the morning instead. It all seemed pretty academic anyway as Gus' briefs were notable for their lack of content. Usually, you got no more than a back-sheet with the name of the defendant inscribed upon it and nothing else. Written instructions were never included or a proof of evidence from the client.

So the following day found me trudging wearily along a lorry-bound London thoroughfare; the nearest tube station being miles away.

The change of name had only just taken place, as I discovered on approaching the front door of a rather dingy building. This housed, as well as Gus' firm, a collection of dubious – sounding companies; import and export agents, it would appear, in unspecified commodities.

The bottom nameplate, identifying the occupants of the ground floor, bore the legend-

BALL AND FLORIS FLOOD, SOLICITORS

Underneath, written in black felt pen on a badly stuck piece of cardboard, were the words -

NOW KNOWN AS ERIC E. EVIDGE

Next to this was an entry-phone device which I used and Gus duly let me in.

A dusty hallway opened up to reveal a number of rooms, all but one with their doors closed. Gus ushered me into this room nearest the entrance. He seemed to be the only occupant of the premises. He sat down at a desk on which were piled masses of what appeared to be police witness statements. I took the chair opposite, which was the only piece of furniture other than a small table set against a wall on Gus' right-hand side. Sheets of white paper were piled next to an ancient typewriter.

'Got the briefs right here,' Gus said taking two sheets from this pile. He folded them both longwise, scribbled the name of the case on each and tied them up with pink ribbon. 'There you are…'

It was no more than I expected but irritation got the better of me – why had I needed to come all this way, when I could just as easily have written out the briefs myself in the Temple?

'Gus,' I said petulantly. 'I've acted for your firm in a number of cases now. Why is it that you never provide any information about them – not even what the defendants are charged with!'

'Yeah, sorry,' Gus said insouciantly, 'the clients tell me about their cases, of course, and I do make a few notes but never seem to find the time to include them in the brief. It's all here though.'

He pulled open a drawer and produced two empty cigarette packets, examining the back of each with care.

'Easiest way of jottin' things down when you're in the pub. You see, I tend to see most of the punters in the Princess Alexandra, across the road at lunch time! Let's see… ah, both your blokes are charged with receiving lead from a church roof on separate occasions. They're both going not guilty. Bought the lead cheap from a man in the market, never thinking it might be stolen. Now, you've got everything you need to know.'

So why not put it in the brief then – the words were on the tip of my tongue but I bit them back. Gus was one of Leslie's closest buddies and I couldn't possibly offend him. Instead, I changed the subject completely.

'Gus, I have a query. You now call yourself, Ernest E. Evidge. Why the change of name at all and who *is* this chap anyway?'

Gus cleared his throat, hesitating before he spoke.

'Well, Harley Ball's the only remaining partner, you know. Mr. Flood died years ago. Harley doesn't come in the office much because he works mainly from, oh, abroad. Anyway, he's due to appear before a disciplinary tribunal for failure to keep proper records but I'll soon get that sorted as I run the firm in reality. Because of that slight problem, we thought a complete change of name might be in order.'

'So Ernest E. Evidge is a wholly new partner then?'

Gus looked a bit sheepish.

'Er… not exactly. We've borrowed the name, you might say, from history. Ernie Evidge was a well-known solicitor at Bermondsey Police Court in the 1950s. Defended all the local villains. Then he retired – well we think he must have done, because he just disappeared.'

I looked incredulous. 'You mean you never attempted to seek his permission?'

'Oh, Harley said he would never have minded. Probably be right chuffed actually. Harley had worked for his firm for a bit as an assistant solicitor, you see, way back when.'

Gus wasn't able to provide any more information and it was only after I was placed on the Director of Public Prosecution's supplementary list that I eventually learnt the full facts. It all came out after the conclusion of a trial a while later.

The case concerned the robbery of the cash takings of a shop whilst it was being transported to a nearby bank. The officer in charge of the case was a detective sergeant, coming to the end of his career after years in the Flying Squad. He was called Parch; a somewhat inappropriate name as he possessed a remarkable thirst for alcoholic beverages.

After the case had ended (with a conviction), he suggested we adjourn for a 'good drink', in a little pub he knew in Mudchute, opposite the local police station.

'We'll go on down there in my motor and take the weight off our feet in the Snug which is strictly reserved for Old Bill.

The landlord sees to that. The main bar gets the locals and our snouts too, but we'll avoid them today. I'm off duty now.'

The Oak and Acorn was a gloomy Victorian pub with a chilly, cavernous public bar which smelled of stale cigarettes and beer. Tucked away inside however, was a cosy little bar with a real fire in the grate and comfortable leather chairs. An unmarked door led into it which, from the outside, gave no clue to its existence. A small hatch on the side of the wall was where drinks were dispensed.

It was one o' clock by then and we didn't depart until ten in the evening. We drank pints of 'light and bitter', later accompanying them with a succession of shots of bourbon, to 'sweeten the taste of the beer' as Parch put it.

Official closing time (in those days, two-thirty in the afternoon) made no difference to the flow of alcohol. The hatch did actually shut for a few hours but the landlord simply proceeded to leave a full bottle of bourbon for our delectation. At five o' clock, it opened again and we continued to consume more beer.

That day, I heard more tales about the police, in particular the CID and the Flying Squad than I have ever heard before or since.

Parch was a mine of information about villains in the past, and how the Flying Squad and the Serous Crime Squad used to catch them. As his tongue loosened, he freely admitted 'verballing' suspects although, according to him if properly done, it would never look too obvious.

'The old-time villains accepted verballing as a matter of course. So did the judges – it was all a game really. Nothing gave the cons more sport than slagging off Old Bill and the verbals provided the ammunition.'

As the afternoon wore on, a variety of police officers, none in any semblance of uniform, wandered in for a drink and a chat. I remarked as to why it was that only detectives seemed to frequent the bar.

'Plod and plainclothes coppers never did mix well, including where they drink although the Commissioner has now changed all that. Thank God, it won't affect me.'

Recently, the new Commissioner of the Metropolitan Police had introduced a rule that there should be much more interchange between the CID and the other branches of London's police force. Henceforward, all detectives were required to return to uniform before being promoted.

We drank a great deal and it was about quarter to ten, (the squad car , giving us a lift, was due to arrive at ten), when Eric E. Evidge came back into my mind. Taking another swig of bourbon and lighting my umpteenth cigarette I asked Parch or Arnie as I was now calling him, if he'd ever heard of the mysterious solicitor.

'Ernie Evidge? Well, that takes me back, that does. He was the regular defence brief down Bermondsey Police Court in the – let me think, late fifties, early sixties time. I was a Temporary Detective Constable way back then stationed at Leman Street police station.'

He paused to light another fag himself and proceeded to recount the following story –

Ernie fell out with Mickey Markoff, you see. Screwed up an alibi for Mickey's younger brother, Lex who got a ten for a GBH and Mickey was really hacked off. Ernie was a fat, fruity geezer always shouting the odds but after that he lost his bluster. We all reckoned he might get a cutting off Mick but in the end it was much worse than that…

Ernie just disappeared one night, walking his dog out Hampstead Heath way. Dog was later found abandoned but no Ernie. He just vanished and no body was ever found either.

Mickey Markoff ran a protection racket out at Hoxton at the time. He wasn't a big boy – kept in with likes of the Krays by doing a bit of enforcing – but he was a vicious bastard nonetheless. Known as Mick the Machine – the cutting machine because he could slice a face up like a hot-cross bun within seconds. Lex was his brother – the heavy. He was as thick as two short planks and built like a brick shithouse but Mickey was bright enough for the two of them. He'd been in the Russian Army during the War and somehow escaped to England bringing his kid brother with him.

One day, a member of their gang came in to see us. I was very new then in the CID and just sat in with the guv'nor, a Detective Chief Inspector. The guy was called Lenny Large. He said that he had some information implicating Markoff in Ernie's murder and disappearance. Told us that a few weeks back, Mickey had kidnapped Ernie up on the Heath and later had him shot through the head down at some garages near the Docks. Lenny insisted that he'd had nothing to do with wiping Ernie out himself but had assisted in the disposal of the body. Apparently three of them took the corpse to where they were building the Bow Road Flyover and tipped it into the foundations, pouring liquid concrete on top…

Well, Lenny said he wanted to turn Queen's evidence and do a deal. He'd had no part in Evidge's murder and he wanted out. Rumours were going round the underworld that the Director of Public Prosecutions might be prepared to drop cases against known villains if they testified for the prosecution against their kind. So he was offering his services. You can imagine that my guv'nor was very interested in all this and we took a full statement off him there and then. Next step was to try and recover Evidge's body so Lenny took us to this building site.

When we got there though, he began to look all nervous as if he was changing his mind. Maintained he couldn't tell us which end of the flyover it actually was. The upshot was that we couldn't find the spot. It wasn't helped either by most of the support pillars being up by then. We had to go back to the station and tell the Detective Chief Superintendent who said that without knowing the exact place to look, he'd never get authority to dig up the whole bloody thing. Leastways, not to begin with. Still, he sent the papers to the Director but time ran out…

Only days later, Lenny's body was lying face down in the Thames Estuary. He'd been shot. The Evidge file was closed after that. Lex died of a heart attack and Mickey retired to Spain, I believe.

'Did Evidge leave any family?' I asked.

'He had a wife but no kids. The Guv'nor felt obliged to tell her that they'd received information about what had happened but she didn't seem that concerned. Sold their mansion in Hampstead Garden Suburb within weeks and bought herself a pub in the country. I went down there after a bit to tell her the enquiry was closed. She was a right merry little widow – having the time of her life and obviously not grieving over old Ernie!'

Thus the mystery of Ernest E. Evidge was resolved and thereafter, I always reflected on his sad fate whenever I drove over the Bow Road Flyover – a kind of memorial in its own way of a functional if not religious kind.

EIGHT

'There you are,' Andrea shook out my pin-striped trousers so I could clearly see the neat patch which she had sewn in the crotch, 'the best thing I can do in the circumstances. Darling, don't you think though that it's time to buy another pair of trousers? One set simply isn't enough.'

Shaking my head, I examined my wallet. I had ten quid left to last me for the rest of the week and a pair of second-hand pin-striped pants would cost me eight pounds at Moss Bros. Extending my wardrobe would just have to wait.

'No can do. I've just about got enough money to pay my travel expenses and eat during the day.'

Andrea sighed. 'Well, if you say so. I could lend you a fiver, of course – we can use up the rest of that bacon for supper and have baked beans for the rest of the week.'

'No, sweetheart, that wouldn't be fair. After all, you've just bought me that marvellous coat.'

Being December, I was truly grateful for this garment. The ex-RAF issue raincoat which Andrea had purchased by mail order for five pounds had arrived only that day. It might be on the small side but it was warm, comfortable and ideal for trudging about in all weathers to the far flung courts where I seemed to be spending most of my time. Tomorrow was no exception; I was attending Beccles Juvenile Court situated somewhere in the wilds of Suffolk.

I gave my wife a kiss and added wistfully. 'You've contributed enough to our budget already. Not exactly glamorous, is it, being married to a barrister?'

But Andrea, bless her, was too busy with the practicalities of life to comment. Katie and Winston were mewing persistently for their dinner so she hastened to feed them. In the meantime, I opened another bottle of our cheap sherry. As well as cheering us up, it helped with the heating (of the bodily sort) too – the one bar electric fire doing very little of either.

The next day, the journey back from Beccles to King's Cross station seemed to last forever. The slow train stopped everywhere and I rapidly became bored with staring at the flat, uninteresting countryside. Reluctantly, I opened my mail.

It had arrived just as I was leaving home at about seven o'clock that morning and I hadn't had the time nor the enthusiasm to read it as yet (not that I really wanted to anyway). Indeed, my gut churned as I examined the familiar envelopes; one from the Inland Revenue, another from the Customs and Excise and a third from the bank.

The proceedings in court that morning hadn't improved my mood either. Sam Aaronson was a sixteen year old boy who was charged with burglary of a dwelling-house and possessed numerous previous convictions for similar offences. The lad had been adopted at birth by his diminutive father, a greyhound-track bookmaker from the East End of London. Apart from not having an honest bone in his body, young Aaronson was actually a likeable lad with a wide smile and good manners. His father had made certain of that even if he had failed utterly to keep him on the straight and narrow.

In the event, the court committed the boy to the Crown Court with a view to Borstal training for his latest crime. It was realistically the only disposal but the person I felt really sorry for was his adopted dad. A small dapper man with a large nose and gentle brown eyes, he always wore an enormous chequered cloth cap straight out of the 1930s. He seemed to come from another era altogether – softly spoken and deferential – like a chipper cockney character from an early Ealing Studio film.

'Esther and I longed for a child, sir, not bein' able to 'ave one ourselves, like. So when the orphanage told us about Sam goin' spare so to speak – well, we just had to 'ave 'im. He was a luvverly baby, so 'e was.'

Indeed, Sam Aaronson had grown to be fortunate in the looks department. Being of mixed racial stock, he was a handsome blend of the best elements of his unknown parents; one of whom was of African origin. Regrettably, his morals were another matter altogether. He just didn't think there was anything wrong in burgling other peoples' homes.

'Esther died when 'e was twelve. I tried to keep him out of trouble, sir, I really did, but 'e soon fell in with a bunch of wrong 'uns.'

So now poor old Aaronson had lost his son as well as his wife. The lad had been sent to the Crown Court in custody in which state he was likely to remain for the next two years – the duration of the sentence.

I turned back to my mail. I was expecting the tax and VAT demand, of course, but the letter from the bank really worried me. Had I not carefully calculated that I was just within my overdraft limit?

Dear Mr. Courtley, (The letter read).
The current balance of your account stands at £612.70 overdrawn. Please arrange funds to adjust this figure so it falls within the agreed limit.

Yours sincerely,
P. Tinby, Manager.

How did dear Mr. Tinby expect me to 'arrange' funds when

there were simply no funds available to arrange? Accordingly, an 'adjustment' in those terms was an entirely mythical concept. Now, perhaps if he had agreed to increase my limit to £1000?

Sod him! I thought, as I crumpled the letter in a ball and threw it out of the window of the train. That made me feel, temporarily at least, a lot better.

However when I got back to chambers, it was time to confront my clerk.

'Leslie, old chap, I'm absolutely desperate for funds. I need at least a couple of hundred to keep me afloat.'

'I've got two bits of good news, Sah!' He was waving a piece of paper at me. 'I 'ave 'ere a cheque for two hundred and fifty nicker from Braspers and what's more -'

I stopped listening being totally fixated on the cheque. Braspers were paying up at last! I was positively beginning to drool.

'- you're off to court tomorrow in...'

'Just give me that cheque, Leslie!' I gasped. '...and I'll go anywhere, however far-flung it is. I'll even go back to Beccles Juvenile Court!'

'Germany actually Sah! A place called Bad Zur Linde. You've got a court-martial there starting the day after tomorrow defending a soldier charged with criminal damage. Unless that is, you'd prefer the Juvenile Court. There's a shoplifting defence of an eleven year old going in Bexley. One of the other guv'nors can always go to Germany in your place if you like?'

I'd learnt to button my lip by now and simply shook my head.

'Good. Off to Germany tomorrow then. Here's the brief. There's a business class ticket in there and you're due to arrive at Hanover Airport at five o'clock tomorrow. Captain Simmons, the defending officer will be meeting you.'

I nodded and began to examine the brief. It read as follows:

BRIEF FOR DEFENDANT:

R. V NO. 2783745 SAPPER R TOBBIE.

Instructed by: Lt Col F. Took
The Directorate of Army Legal Services.
Metropole Building, Northumberland Avenue
London WC1.

A bundle of prosecution papers were enclosed. Attached to them was a card which bore the legend: *With the compliments of the prosecutor, the Director of Army Legal Services.*

'Some mistake here surely?' I asked Leslie. 'This is a defence brief but the instructing authority seems to be the prosecution...'

'Army do things in a funny way, Sah! British soldiers who are court-martialled in Germany are given civilian barristers to defend them out there. It's all processed by Franky Took of DALS in the prosecutor's office in London. He contacts a defending officer who introduces you to the client and you take it from there. One hundred and fifty smackers on the brief, refreshers of seventy-five quid and forty for every day spent out of the United Kingdom. It's got to be better than schlepping down to a juvenile court for fifteen pounds surely?'

With that proposition, I certainly agreed.

* * *

The Braspers cheque having been safely banked, Andrea and I were back in the Steak House in Dulwich.

'I bought three pairs of pin-stripe trousers today, darling.' I said. 'The chap from Moss Bros gave me a discount, twenty pounds the lot.'

Andrea nodded and ever practical returned to our budget.

'That leaves two hundred and thirty pounds out of the

Braspers' money which takes you below your overdraft limit – the balance is about one hundred and twenty, I think.'

'Every reason to celebrate then. Let's have a couple of ports.' I called for the waiter.

'Is that wise?' Andrea said.

'Darling girl, our financial problems have receded. The bank manager will now know that funds are coming in at last – let's just enjoy ourselves!'

It was only when I woke the following morning with a hangover that I remembered. The tax demand and VAT bill still had to be paid – and would wipe out any credit in an instant. Moreover, the minicab I had ordered to take me to the airport was an unwarranted extravagance!

I shrugged these worrying thoughts off with a sigh – the whole thing would simply have to wait until after Christmas.

NINE

'Try the Herforder, sir.' Captain Ned Simmons, my defending officer, suggested as we sat down on a plush seat inside the bar. 'I don't think you'll have any complaints if you like your beer.'

I didn't demur and half expected him to depart to fetch the drinks as he would have done back home, but instead an extremely pretty waitress appeared at his elbow to take our order.

Ned murmured. *'Zwei glas bier von Herford, bitte'* and I took the opportunity of taking in the surroundings.

Earlier, Ned had met me at the airport and whisked me off to the barracks on the outskirts of Bad Zur Linde. After I had unpacked my things in a guestroom at the Officers' Mess, he'd suggested that we go into the town to eat. 'There's a rather snug bar I know – where they serve good food too.'

So now we were sitting in what was the equivalent of an English pub – except that it was infinitely superior in every way. Sparkling clean stain-glass windows looked out on the town square from a well-appointed interior with plenty of space between sets of tables and chairs. English and Irish hunting prints adorned the walls and a wood fire burnt cheerfully in the grate. Somewhat disconcertingly though, skeletal trophies of a variety of small animals also featured in clusters over the walls.

'Hunting in the deep German forest is very popular with the locals.' Ned noticed my concern. 'Hence the rather gruesome exhibits!'

The young waitress brought over two foaming glasses of beer. I sipped mine appreciatively; the cool liquid immediately hitting the spot.

Ned leant forward. 'Sir, I didn't just bring you here for a social visit. We could have eaten in the Mess. I have an ulterior motive – I want you to see where the incident actually happened.'

I nodded, reflecting on what I had read earlier.

My client, a young sapper, was charged with destroying an advertising display in Bad Zur Linde town centre in the early hours of the morning. Allegedly, he and his mates having consumed vast quantities of strong German beer in a local bar, congregated in the town square and then proceeded to overturn the small caravan which housed the display. A German plainclothes policeman (following his Alsatian, Bruno) had given chase and apprehended my client; the others making good their escape.

However, the information supplied to me from this witness (one Herr Dolf) had aroused my suspicions. It came from a translated German police report and seemed unsatisfactory. According to Herr Dolf, on arrival at the scene, a group of youths were running away including my client who was then seized by the seat of his pants by the dog. The report also suggested that the policeman had actually witnessed the crime being committed but now having seen the square for myself, I wondered. My client denied that he had been in company at all that night and had been in a bar drinking on his own. He had wandered down to the town centre on his way back to barracks only to be waylaid by the dog.

Snowflakes gently settled on the steep red-tiled rooftops surrounding the square. Inside the shop windows, Christmas trees sparkled with light illuminating beautifully made nativity cribs and displays of hand-crafted wooden toys. Trudging about the scene of the crime, I was distracted for a moment. What a truly delightful place Bad Zur Linde turned out to be.

The next day, we assembled at the barracks in a room set up as a court. A board of army officers, in full uniform, had been appointed to decide the facts whilst a judge advocate (sitting in the middle of them) presided over the proceedings in the same way as a crown court judge.

I had made up my mind that I wanted a reconstruction of the scene which the court-martial should witness for themselves. Where was Herr Dolf actually located when he first saw my client? Did he see him at all or did he assume he was part of a group because of the dog's actions?

The events had taken place in August when it was still dark so a late December afternoon was an entirely proper time to have a 'view' as a visit to the 'locus in quo' is known in court terminology.

So later in the day, the board of officers were assembled rather self-consciously in the middle of the square where the caravan had once stood. Their highly polished Sam Browne belts and medals accentuated their smartness which caused passers-by (good German burghers doing their Christmas shopping) to cast them curious glances. Not since the Second World War had uniforms been so splendidly displayed. Once the greatest proponents of uniforms, the Germans discouraged it now as it only served to remind them of their militaristic past.

The court orderly, also smartly attired with a striking red sash across his chest, handed the board members mugs of steaming *gluewein* (hot mulled wine spiced with ginger) bought from the Christmas market. Herr Dolf had also attended but vanished up a side-street shortly after arriving. All I wanted to know was where he was actually positioned when he first observed my client.

Several minutes passed, and the winter weather continued to close in. Appropriate refreshment was now being served to us all. The judge advocate and I stood together with the court recorder, dictaphone in hand, gratefully sipping our mugs of the hot spicy liquid.

The major conducting the prosecution, now somewhat flustered stood at the edge of the square anxiously scanning the side-streets for his witness. How that individual could have seen any activity at all when he was nowhere near, remained a total mystery.

Meanwhile, I savoured the wonderful atmosphere bestowed by the German celebration of Christmas. Most towns hold a fair at this time of year, with rides and carousels for the *kinder* and stalls selling gifts and food. How much better it was to be imbibing Bad Zur Linde's cold clean air than trudging my way down Newington Causeway on my way to Inner London Crown Court with a bitter December wind agitating the dusty litter round my feet. I didn't even feel self-conscious because I had removed my barrister's wig and wore an overcoat to cover my gown and bands.

Herr Dolf suddenly appeared at the side of the square. He looked like plainclothes police officers do all over the world. Short and pugnaciously built, with a shaved head, his black leather jacket stretched with difficulty over his frame. He was gesturing emphatically at my harassed opponent.

'*Mein hund… er komt,hier!*' was all I was able to hear.

I was longing to cross-examine him now, but couldn't do it there and then. It would have to wait until we all returned to the courtroom.

An hour later, I began my cross-examination through the services of an interpreter.

'Herr Dolf – explain why when you were told to stand at the point where you imply you saw the caravan being overturned, you vanished up several side streets?' I enquired.

The stolid German plod looked puzzled.

'I did not have to see it – I found it on its side. That is not in dispute, I believe.'

'I must accept that – but nonetheless you could not have seen my client running away, could you?'

'No – that is true,' Herr Dolf nodded, 'it was my dog, Bruno, he saw your client running away.'

'Your *dog* saw my client running away?'

'But of course, I let Bruno loose to chase after him.'

'You mean you let him loose – and he chased after somebody – how could he pick out my client? He's a dog not a witness!'

'I am the witness, of course.' Herr Dolf patiently explained through the interpreter, 'and I heard the sound of the caravan overturning earlier. Bruno heard this also. I let him go, he rushed into the square and caught your client. The others were still running. Quite simple.'

I stared at him open-mouthed.

'But how did you know that my client was running away at all, when you never actually saw this for yourself?

'Bruno is a highly trained dog – he knew. I rely on him at all times. He never lets me down. *Ach* – he acts as my eyes and ears!'

Further questions were pointless so I sat down. The witness was purporting to positively identify my client through his dog! He had simply released the animal when he heard the noise of the caravan overturning. The most he actually saw was some other youths running. My totally innocent client had been brought to the ground by Bruno – who could hardly be expected to distinguish between any of them.

'Now that we've reached the end of the prosecution's case, we'll adjourn for the day.' The judge advocate glanced at the clock. It was quarter past six. Herr Dolf's evidence had been followed by a short police interview in which my client denied all complicity in the crime.

What a speech I planned to make the following day! In the shape of making a legal submission of 'no case to answer', I would be doing this before the judge advocate and court members in the hope that they would simply chuck the case out without the necessity of hearing my client.

In my rather spartan room back in the officers' mess, I sat late that night sipping a glass of duty-free malt whiskey purchased at the airport. I was going to make a submission to beat all submissions! Fond as I was of dogs with every confidence in their reliability generally, since when has man's best friend been allowed to identify anyone? The Teutonic plod's evidence was really that of his dog. It was simply outrageous!

The following morning, I was all fired up to make a resounding speech and the notes to which I was about to refer waxed eloquently on the humorous aspect of the situation.

'German evidence falls far short of our exacting standards! My wretched client has been caught up in the metaphorical jaws of injustice as well as the physical gnashers of the dog.'

The judge advocate, eyes twinkling benignly behind his pebble glasses, politely motioned me to sit down as I rose to my feet. He looked as relaxed as ever; I had discovered that court-martials were conducted in a very civilised manner. What other judge would ever be sipping *gluewein* whilst engaged in judicial duties?

'Mr. Courtley, we are minded to invoke Rule of Procedure fifty-four and acquit your client straightaway.'

This legal rule enabled a court to actually dismiss a charge at any time after the conclusion of the prosecution's case. Unsurprisingly perhaps, they had formed their own judgement about the reliability of the police officer's evidence. But it stole my thunder – deprived me of my moment of glory. Nothing is worse than hyping yourself up to make an oratorical address which will result in a magnificent result only to have it snatched away through the operation of a legal technicality.

Who knows? I might have gone on to make legal history. *Dogs can't give evidence!* I might have thundered in the Court of Appeal. *Faithful and loyal animals, dogs may well be,* but *competent witnesses, never!* I could have submitted in the House of Lords. I might even have written a text book – *Courtley on Canine evidence.* But it was never to be.

TEN

Mr. Justice Bedivere-Jones was a strange beast in an unfamiliar jungle. Perched behind the long bench of the main court in the Chancery Division, he was small and rotund. Indeed, everything about him was circular; round spectacles, rounded wig and an egg-shaped body – not that those comical qualities made him jolly for a moment. He was crisply terse when he spoke, and utterly humourless at the best of times. However, winding-up petitions and jokes were poles apart anyway, so perhaps it was just as well.

I looked around the court and wondered how I had ended up here at all, instructed to wind up a number of companies one Monday morning in the spring. There was a simple answer to that – I was attempting to expand my practice, as making a living out of crime was a continuing struggle.

Quite simply, I was doing too many *yardos*.

Yardo was the slang term used for a brief to prosecute in the Magistrates' courts as instructions were issued on behalf of the Metropolitan Police Solicitors based at New Scotland Yard. This often entailed trudging off to far-flung courts in the Metropolitan area.

The good thing about this type of work was there was a lot of it, but a distinct disadvantage was that all appearances, be they for remands, adjournments or full trials were paid at exactly the same rate – £10 a throw. Thus there wasn't much incentive to prepare cases much in advance – as I found to my cost a week before when I arrived at the Dagenham Magistrates' Court.

The problem arose because I arrived half an hour later than I had intended. I anticipated getting there at half past nine and mugging up the case before being called on. Unfortunately, there were delays on the tube and I pitched up instead at three minutes to ten.

Never mind, I thought. My case was a contested trial of three youths accused of burglary of a warehouse. The matter was estimated to last two hours. Accordingly, I was confident that the usual practice would prevail and a number of guilty pleas would be listed first.

'Special court set aside for your case, sir,' the usher said as I gave my name at the entrance. 'Clear start, sharp at ten!'

Now a potential embarrassment arose. I couldn't ask for time because that would mean admitting my predicament. After all, wasn't I supposed to have read the brief the night before? Improvisation was required but I knew what I had to do – keep my nerve and bluff.

On the dot of ten, I waltzed into court to be confronted with three male Justices of the Peace impassively waiting for me to open the case.

'Sirs, good morning (no self-respecting barrister ever called lay magistrates, 'Your Worships'). This is a case of -er, (I glanced hurriedly at the charge sheet)-burglary involving these three defendants. The evidence is plain enough and requires no comment from me at this stage. I'll simply call Police Constable (I glanced down once again at the list of witnesses) – Butler who will give evidence of the alleged offence and tell you all about it.'

And me too! I thought as the witness began recounting his tale.

This wasn't my finest moment in court, I admit, but then I didn't much like prosecuting anyway. Somehow, it wasn't compatible with my vision of being the 'Great Defender' rescuing the innocent from the jaws of injustice.

It was time to call upon my old college pal, Barry Caterman who worked for a firm of solicitors in the City. So, one evening when Barry and I were having our regular weekly drink in a pub just off Fleet Street and we were well into our third pint of Light and Bitter, I broached the subject of briefs. In those days, there were strict rules about touting for work but that didn't stop me from making a tentative enquiry.

'I know you don't touch crime, Barry but is there any kind of advocacy work you might be able to send me?'

Barry took an appreciative sip of his beer and pondered.

'We do a fair bit of industrial tribunal work but it tends to settle at the door of the court. At the end of the day, it's really all about financial calculations.'

Maths never having been my strong point, I looked doubtful.

'Tell you what though – a colleague in the firm does a lot of company law stuff which includes winding-up petitions. You know, closing down firms when they've gone bust, that sort of thing.'

I still looked doubtful. The trouble was that I didn't know the first thing about running companies, much less about winding them up.

'It's all completely straightforward. Routine unopposed stuff. You just bob up and make the application in court and earn yourself a tidy sum. Benny, the clerk who processes them, marks the briefs at a hundred quid a time. Moreover, they usually come in batches, quite often as many as four. I'll have a word.'

So a week went by, and now there were three of us ensconced in the same pub. Benny turned out to be an enthusiastic drinker too so we were all set up to enjoy a good evening.

After taking a long pull from his first pint of lager, Benny rummaged inside his briefcase.

'First things first, gentlemen. I'm always pleased to do one of Mr. Caterman's pals a favour, and so the firm's booked you, Mr. Courtley, for Monday week over the road in the Chancery Division. I've agreed the fees with your clerk. £100 apiece and five cases. Not bad for a morning's work. So before really hitting the beer, just you take a butcher's at the little nuggets!'

He handed over five slim briefs neatly tied up in green tape. All of them were set out in exactly the same way.

In the High Court of Justice
The Supreme Court of Judicature.
Chancery Division.

Brief to Counsel. Charles Courtley esq.

Re: Lorrimer Lucky Charms (Souvenirs) Ltd.
Application for a winding-up order.

GULLIBETT'S,
NUMBER 4, TWISTING LANE
LONDON EC2.

The green ribbon round the thick cream paper made them stand out for a start. As a criminal hack, my briefs were generally tied up with white (for prosecutions) or red (for defence), tape. I began to read the particulars of the first one but the details, involving as they did the collapse of a souvenir shop near Westminster Abbey didn't grab me. More interesting was the brief on behalf of a firm called Vigour Therapeutics (England)Ltd.

Much of the commercial jargon was beyond me but the essential facts were obvious. This company had traded for a short time in potency pills and had been spectacularly unsuccessful. A number of disappointed customers had sued the company and now its creditors were closing it down.

'Got the general picture then, sir?' Benny was watching me. 'My firm always acts for the creditors. You never get anybody on the other side opposing the applications. We do these sort of cases by the dozen, situated as we are in the City.'

The beer slid down very well that evening, and optimism as well as alcohol surged through my veins. Five hundred quid for a morning's work… if I could do that every day, I'd be making two and a half thousand a week. That was well over a hundred grand a year! After quaffing my sixth pint, I began to think there might be potential in doing more of this sort of work.

Of course, the reality was that I had no idea how to set about making this kind of application. What did you actually need to say in court? – bearing in mind that I had never been anywhere near the Chancery Division in my life. If the judge actually asked me to explain anything, I would be well and truly stumped.

But now at last I was here, in front of Bedivere-Jones who was about to start his list. Earlier, I had thought that I might be called on first but thankfully, I was spared that ordeal.

I had arrived at court and anxiously scanned the list of cases hanging outside the door. All five of my cases were at or near the top of the list!

'Oh, God – I must speak to the court clerk as soon as possible,' I muttered to myself, hurrying inside the court's precincts. Just at that moment, a woman came through the judge's entrance at the back. The wig perched on top of a large grey bun confused me for a moment but then recognition dawned. It was dear old Melanie Anstruther, a good friend of mine from Bar School. She had come to our profession late in life after rearing her children and ditching her husband; a dreary accountant who had treated her as a domestic drudge. Now, she had become a legally qualified court clerk. Seeing her was like finding an oasis in the desert.

Melanie gave me a broad smile. She was a real sweetie who had given us youngsters much emotional support as students.

'Charles! Fancy seeing you in the Chancery Division! Now don't tell me, you're trying to get your case on first!'

'Oh goodness, Melanie, you couldn't be more wrong. That's exactly what I don't want!'

I told her my problem, whereupon she gave me a reassuring smile.

'Don't worry, Charles. The list is wholly interchangeable. We'll be calling the Inland Revenue applications first as usual. They tend to do most of these cases anyway. It'll be ages before you're on.'

The day began and I sat in the back row of Counsel's benches trying to be as unobtrusive as possible. Seated in the front row was Lucius Polp who was doing the applications for the Inland Revenue. My pen was poised. Every phrase he uttered was about to be faithfully recorded by me in my notebook. Copying him was the only way I could get away with this exercise.

'My Lord, I appear for the applicants, the Inland Revenue… *Blah! Blah! Blah.* Accordingly, the lists are negative, the share register is nil and I apply for the usual order.' Polp intoned each time.

The judge sat impassively occasionally glancing down his spectacles with their magnified lenses, which made his small eyes goggle rather disconcertingly. He never queried anything and repeated the same mantra at the end of each application in a slight Welsh accent.

'So be it – application grant-ed.'

A half-hour went by and then an hour. This was dead easy, I thought. Anybody could do it, including me. With my word-for-word prompt in front of me what could possibly go wrong?

Lucius Polp was a tallish, spare man with a thin face from which jutted a beaky, aquiline nose. His voice resembled the unwrapping sound of parcel paper but its very dryness blended with the aridity of the proceedings. I couldn't ever see him make an impassioned plea on behalf of a murderer at the

Old Bailey – but why should he worry? I noted that he had a fee of £250 marked on every brief. He must have had at least a dozen laid out on the bench in front of him.

Watching him, the actor in me began to stir. I rather liked the way he uttered – *the lists are negative* – using his right hand to emphasize the point by throwing open his fingers towards the floor. What rather spoilt it was his tendency to incline his head at the end of each application like a parrot pecking at his seed tray. I suppressed the urge to giggle; something in the Chancery Division which would be akin to farting in church.

When my turn came with Lorrimer Lucky Charms, I exuded confidence from every pore. I sailed through that and three other applications. A cool £400 so far! Now for Vigour Therapeutics Ltd. So hyped up was I that I felt the urge to giggle again. How could anybody be so foolish to buy these ridiculous pills in the first place, (this being long before the advent of Viagra). To hell with it I thought, I'd change the wording this time.

'My lord, the share register is zero, and the lists are nugatory. I apply for the usual order.'

I sat down. Now, I'd earned my £500.

'Mr. Courtley?' I was startled. The judge wasn't supposed to say anything at that stage.

'I have before me a lett-er written on behalf of the Inland Revenue. According to this, the lists are not negative or nugatory as you choose to put it, do you follow?'

I didn't follow at all. In fact, I hadn't got a clue what he was talking about. Hurriedly, I looked through my brief. No correspondence about lists at all. Now what was I going to do?

Bluff, of course.

'Yes, My Lord. Perhaps Mr. Polp, who appears for the Revenue today, may be able to help…'

The judge turned his attention to Polp and raised his eyebrows slightly.

'My lord, I am not instructed in this matter as one would

70

have expected my learned friend to have known from the outset, as he brings the application. However, as *amicus curia*, perhaps I can assist to the extent of reminding your lordship of the well-known authority of *Podger versus Clotbill*. It is a matter which the applicants should have resolved earlier applying the *ratio decidendi* of that case and bearing in mind what was said *obiter* by Lord Justice Diderick in the leading judgement.'

The judge's eyes, hard as pieces of coals, goggled at me once more. Now, I knew exactly how a wretched rodent must feel when a hawk is about to pounce from the sky. To mix a metaphor, I felt a fish out of water daring to trespass into the hallowed hunting grounds of real lawyers in the Chancery Division, whose knowledge of authorities such as *Podger v. Clotbill* would be second nature.

'Remind me, Mr. Courtley – of Lord Justice Diderick's defining principle in that case and why the applicants or those who instruct you, have not submitted the proper affidavits and certificates to rebut any assertions implicit in the let-ter from the Inland Revenue?'

A sense of unreality came over me. Momentarily, I forgot where I was and what I was supposed to be doing. The judges' voice rolled over me and I felt detached from myself. The court-room began to grow dark.

I was near to fainting when I felt a tug on my gown which, thank God, brought me back to my senses.

'Bev's playing silly buggers at your expense,' hissed a voice. 'He's in a sadistic mood today. Just ask him to put you to the back of the list whilst you talk to your solicitors.'

'Perhaps I can crave your lordship's indulgence,' I gabbled. 'and ask for the matter to be heard later after the other cases.'

The judge's small eyes glittered now as well as goggled. With malice too. I thought I detected a faint twitch to the lips which was the judicial equivalent of a smile. Slowly, he shook his head.

It was Melanie who saved my bacon.

71

Graciously, she rose to her feet whilst I stood dumbfounded, swaying slightly. She turned to the judge and whispered something which I failed to hear. Then she turned and faced the court.

'Now, we will deal with the applications involving the Customs and Excise. Mr. Brook, who appears on their behalf is very anxious to get away I understand.'

She smiled at the barrister who had just spoken to me. Bevidere-Jones glanced at the clock and grunted. A minute or two passed as Melanie handed up another set of files. Brook, with a sigh of relief, began mustering his own papers. He was a grizzled, dour chap but he turned to me sympathetically.

'He'll take you last now. If you can't get any sense out of your solicitors, just ask for the application to be adjourned until the next winding-up day.'

Benny had told me that he wouldn't be attending court himself and I simply didn't dare to leave court and try and phone his firm – so I was stuck.

Minutes later sweating profusely I staggered back to the robing room, to find Brook packing up his kit.

'You can't fool old Bev, dear boy. He can be a real turd at the best of times and you were lucky that Melanie was with him today. He had you well and truly by the short and curlies when he asked you about the Clotbill case!'

I shuddered at the memory of it all. Eventually Bev had adjourned my case but with costs against the applicant.

'For wast-ing the court's time – the paperwork must be in ord-er.' He remarked caustically.

Benny looked gloomy when the three of us met next time for a drink. Distinctly apprehensive, I was the first to buy the first round, hurriedly plonking a pint of lager in front of him.

'My principal's none too happy about that award of costs Mr. Courtley,' he complained. 'The least you could have done was to have asked the judge to reserve them pending the final disposal of the case.'

Benny, my friend, you don't realise how quickly I wanted to get out of that place.

'Sorry and all that…' I said lamely.

'Of course, company law is not really your line, is it?' Mournfully, Benny took a long pull from his beer.

He was right of course, and I avoided the Chancery Division like the plague from then on. Still, I didn't feel as guilty as perhaps I should have done. Brook had become quite chatty after our encounter in the robing room and informed me that solicitors charged clients at least £400 for every application, which normally involved just filling in forms and ticking boxes – thus they made a very good profit. In future, as far as I was concerned, Benny and his principal were welcome to it!

ELEVEN

'Any questions, Sir Fred?'

My leader heaved himself to his feet; his tyre-like paunch jutting out in front of him like the prow of a ship. He sighed and I wondered for a mad moment whether his bulk might deflate like a balloon.

Sir Fred Borler, one-time Solicitor-General in a long-forgotten government, was thickset and fat with a large moon-shaped face. This made him look like a very old baby. Ancient he might be, but he still looked magnificent in the black frock coat of a Queen's Counsel with the large material-covered buttons and elongated button-holes, stretching over a matching waistcoat. White 'weepers' (linen wraps) adorned the cuffs and his pristine white bands had a special pleat down the middle. These were only ever worn for court mourning but a minor royal had just died – meriting this additional adornment to the traditional costume. The garb, generally, was designed to make fat old men look rather impressive and indeed it did.

'My Lord no,' was the answer and my eyelids drooped again.

Admittedly, it was a warm day in early spring, but that was no excuse for going to sleep – after all, I was being paid handsome refreshers for doing very little.

Recently, the weather had improved and so had our lifestyle. Now, we were not only able to sit out on the patch of grass outside our basement flat, laughingly called a garden, but also sip Pimms instead of cheap sherry. That was because finances were better too – Mr. Tinby had reluctantly increased the overdraft limit to £1500 and I was being led for the first time in a fraud case.

This was one of the few perks in a young barrister's life – to find himself sitting behind a Q.C. in such a case. Particularly, when the Q.C. had little enough to do and the junior was really only there for show.

The defendants were all charged with a 'long firm fraud' i.e. ordering goods on credit, storing them in a warehouse and knocking them off on the cheap before the ruse was rumbled. Our client was employed as the warehouseman who maintained that he knew nothing about the contents of the building. He had been paid in cash simply to mind the place for a few days and asked no questions. Nonetheless, he was charged with conspiracy to defraud.

Sir Fred's advice to the client was brief but eminently sensible in the circumstances.

'Sit it out, that's what we'll do. I shan't ask any questions, we won't rock the boat or call any evidence. They'll find it damned hard to prove anything and you'll get *orf...*'

Which he did and I was to become several hundred pounds the richer.

I can't say that Sir Fred inspired me with much confidence though – I knew just the person who I wanted to be led by the next time – and he wasn't even a silk!

I'd first met Dan Rydehope in Tom Tug's – the ancient inn situated near the Temple's stairs which had once led down to the river. The set up there was not particularly comfortable nor was the decor either smart or chic. Blotchy prints of vineyards in France adorned the walls and black barrels dispensing Tom Tug's own brands of sherries and ports were heaped high behind the bar. The manager, who was indistinguishable from a barrister in pin-striped trousers and black jacket floated round the premises always looking important but actually doing little, leaving the chore of serving the customers to the waitresses.

In those days, Tom Tug's was the haunt of senior barristers, journalists and their editors and I didn't go in there very often – it was just too expensive. Tonight was an exception – Rex Huggins had just been made a judge and was having a final celebratory drink at the famous watering-hole.

'Now that I'm a judge, I shan't be coming here anymore. Once you're on the bench, you just don't, you see.' He said.

I nodded understanding the convention that once raised to the judiciary, you were expected to steer clear of your former mates. Barristers who became judges ceased to exist in the real world of the law as we saw it – they dropped out of sight. This was particularly poignant, as today was the day that the new silks appointed by the Lord Chancellor had been proclaimed so I couldn't help asking. 'Rex, didn't you ever think of applying for silk?'

My pupilmaster took a swig of champagne and grinned.

'Never for a moment, old boy. My ambition was to put in the time and then get my bottom on the Consolidated Fund and draw a regular salary. I've done well enough as a junior and taking silk was a risk I've never wanted to take. You put yourself forward as the best in a very competitive business and there's no mercy if you don't meet the mark. I wonder how many of this lot will survive.'

Glancing around the room, I suddenly realised that among the clientele were a smattering of patrons dressed in frock coats and frilly stocks; the formal dress of all Queen's Counsel.

'Brand new leading counsel, Charlie. Sworn in earlier in the day before the Lord Chief Justice. Well, it wasn't for me but one day you might well be one of them.'

Perchance to dream, I thought. As Rex was paying for the champagne, we had consumed the best part of a second bottle by now. Squiffily, I pondered the singular professional life I had embarked on.

A barrister's life is a strange one. There is no rank structure or promotional ladder. The old saw you are only as good as your next case, is a well-worn cliché but it happens to be painfully accurate. Reputations can be destroyed overnight. Yet barristers are as vain as anybody else so they crave recognition too. Taking silk is about the only official mark of it.

Then Daniel Rydehope walked in.

'I'm amazed he's come in tonight of all nights,' Rex said. 'Never mind the new silks, he's the chap I would have defending me if I ever got into trouble, rest assured of that.'

Dan's reputation as one of the best defenders in the business was known throughout the Inns of Court. Vaguely resembling Winston Churchill, he dressed much better than the old statesman in a beautifully cut, double-breasted chalk stripe suit with a matching waistcoat.

His appearance certainly caused a stir. There was a distinct hush for a start as the regulars looked up uneasily.

'Evelina Scarrow in his chambers was given silk this time. Dan is much senior to her in call but was turned down once again despite that,' Rex informed me.

Scarrow the Shriek, as she was rather unkindly known to us had a hack prosecution practice down in Wiltshire. The nickname came from her sharp, shrill and penetrating voice, which induced headaches in judges and persuaded defendants to plead guilty simply to escape the torture of cross-examination – so, at least, went the story.

'Her appointment is the final insult to Dan. To apply again would be pointless. The Lord Chancellor will never bestow silk on him now,' Rex growled.

Hence the slight but perceptible hush as Dan made his stately progress in the direction of the bar.

'Dan my dear chap, please do join us?' Rex held up a hand in welcome.

Dan possessed a broad face with deep-set brown eyes over heavy bags. Close-up, he looked less like Winston Churchill, indeed more like a cross between Alfred Hitchcock and an amiable toad.

'My dear chap, meet my ex-pupil. We're having a final drink to mark my becoming a judge – so join us in a glass of champagne!'

'Thank you – I had heard of your elevation. Sorry to see you go.'

He removed his overcoat and performed a fine piece of theatre which I remember quite distinctly to this day.

He was a pipe-smoker, and now indulged in the wonderful ritual known to lovers of the pipe throughout the centuries. No doubt it all began with the American Indians who first discovered the glories of tobacco in the dim and distant past. First, he took a bulky leather pouch from his pocket and laid it on the table. Unzipped, it revealed three large pipes secured by loops. Then he selected a bent pot, filling it methodically from a large tin. Afterwards, he took out a shiny lighter which produced a whoosh of flame. Finally, he puffed away until the bowl began to glow reassuringly.

Rex filled a spare glass with champagne.

'I have to say it's a disgrace that the Lord Chancellor gave it to that bloody woman – and not you!'

Later I was to learn that Dan hadn't been helped in his application by the fact that he once served as a detective sergeant with the Metropolitan Police. Ex-coppers weren't regarded as being entirely respectable in those days. Moreover, he frequented a rather louche drinking club in Soho which had at one time figured in a police corruption scandal some years before.

I couldn't help wondering whether Dan might feel embarrassed by Rex's forthright criticism. Perhaps he would simply shrug it off.

Then he uttered the immortal words so well-known to anybody who has ever followed the history of film.

'It won't affect my practice – solicitors brief me in leading cases anyway. Quite frankly Rex, I don't give a damn.'

This immortal line was hardly original having come out of the screenplay of *Gone with the Wind* but it fitted the moment perfectly. What style the man had!

Rex and Dan reminisced for a while about the case which had first brought them together; a murder trial in front of Judge 'Bugle' Dickson (a war veteran) in the 1950s.

'Aptly named, that old bugger,' Rex chuckled, 'ran his court like a parade ground – if you as much as shuffled an aching buttock whilst he summed up, he'd roar – *my court is not to be treated like a stable!'*

Dan nodded calmly, puffing away at his pipe. After a while, he finished his champagne and rose to leave. His sang-froid never faltered for a moment as he strode past the new silks. That represented the true glory of the man, I thought. This was the leader for me when the next chance came.

The feeling of well-being in all departments of my life continued to grow. A few days later, Leslie told me that Braspers was sending me a multi-handed car 'ringing' case in a few weeks time. Immediately, I persuaded him to contact Dan Rydehope's clerk and to my joy, Dan was available to do the case. Then a large cheque rolled in for the long-firm fraud.

That justified another slap-up dinner in our local Steak House. I had a couple of surprises for Andrea too.

'Darling girl, I've ordered that bed from the catalogue we were looking at the other night.'

'Can we afford it?' Andrea seemed doubtful.

'We certainly can now that I've been paid for the fraud.'

'Well, as long as it's the cheapest.'

'The best is never cheap, my sweet. In fact, it's the most expensive. Six foot by six with a doubly sprung mattress to be exact.'

'But that costs a fortune!'

'True – although I've only had to put down a deposit for now. Delivery next week and monthly payments for a year.'

'Can you meet them? It's not as if you receive a regular salary.'

'Oh, our financial position can only get better now – what with another big case in the pipeline.' I said airily.

What I didn't tell her was that surreptiously, I had also bought a car which was parked just up the road; a six year old Vanden Plas 1300. Kitted out in leather and walnut, it was the next best thing to a Rolls-Royce!

Andrea was so impressed by the smooth ride home that she only enquired how I had managed to pay for it when we reached home.

'Charlie, what deposit did you have to put down to purchase this car?'

'Ah, I didn't actually. I paid cash on the nail, you see. Only £650...'

TWELVE

'Now look here Mr. Courtley!'

Judge Blewstone was getting angry and excited, throwing himself about on the Bench, cuffing his notebook and slapping down his white gloves in front of him. He was one of the few circuit judges I knew who religiously brought that part of his ceremonial kit into court.

'It simply will not do! Your client got off the wounding with intent charge because he maintained his testicles were being squeezed causing him excruciating pain. Now, I see from the medical report that he doesn't possess testicles at all! This is quite preposterous and intolerable!'

I couldn't help but facetiously agree.

'Your Honour is right and indeed the lack of that particular part of his anatomy must make life intolerable if he wants to indulge in sexual intercourse.'

Blewstone was on the point of exploding.

'That is an impertinent remark, Mr. Courtley. It is the misleading of the court which is intolerable as well you know!'

'I hope Your Honour is not suggesting that I had any foreknowledge of his medical condition and kept it back deliberately.' I protested.

Blewstone continued to glower but said nothing more.

My client, Danny Stoke described himself as a 'painter and decorator' but I suspect that he had never done any such thing in his life apart from, perhaps, daubing graffiti on a prison cell wall. In truth he was a minor villain who attached himself to more significant criminals to 'help out' when needed for a specific dishonest activity. However, he was breezy and cheerful by nature and I couldn't help but like him.

One particular afternoon, he was 'minding the shop' as it were, at a crooked motor dealer's yard in Dagenham. Known to be ever ready with a 'slap', (a criminal euphemism for a violent blow usually with a weapon), Danny was the ideal person to greet any unwelcome visitor to his 'employer' for whom he provided 'security'.

A man named Sid called round to collect a debt and inevitably, the meeting between him and Danny wasn't a friendly one. Moreover, more than a slap was administered on this occasion with Danny picking up a handy screw-driver and jabbing it neatly between Sid's ribs, almost killing him.

Danny's account at trial of what had happened was quite simple. Unwilling to be fobbed off by the former's admittedly impolite blandishments, Sid had threatened 'to do him over good and proper', and to demonstrate his aptitude in that regard took hold of Danny's private parts twisting them in such a way as to cause excruciating pain. Accordingly, the latter seized the screw-driver in such a fashion as to cause Sid, somewhat carelessly, to impale himself on the object. The jury half accepted Danny's story and the upshot was that he was convicted on the basis of wounding Sid only, being reckless as to the consequences of his actions and not with intent to do him grievous bodily harm.

Judge Blewstone, the permanent judge at Bentleigh Crown Court took a grim view of the case, particularly as Danny who came from the East End of London had numerous previous convictions for offences of violence. The case was only being tried in the sleepy Essex town because their court was taking work from its overburdened London counterparts and I suspected the judge didn't much like metropolitan criminals anyway.

Threatening a long sentence to protect the public, he

decided to adjourn the case to obtain a medical report- 'which will help me to assess the considerable risk which your client seems to pose to everybody,' he had barked.

The medical report revealed nothing more psychologically about Danny than was known already – namely that he was a small-time villain who had been prone to violence since the age of ten and abused both alcohol and drugs copiously. However, one significant surgical issue did come to light – Danny had no balls. They had been removed a year or so earlier after he was found to be suffering from testicular cancer.

During the trial itself, there had been no hint of Danny's sad condition. His guttural voice wasn't particularly high-pitched but then years of booze, fags and cannabis had undoubtedly hoarsened it.

Now we were ensconced in the cells whilst, on the orders of the judge, I enquired whether he could proffer any excuse for misleading the court.

Danny looked at me indignantly.

'What's the old bugger so upset for? I may 'ave lost me wedding tackle but it still 'urt like 'ell an' all when I was grabbed! Sensitive area, innit? Anyway, he twisted me todger-you ask that blahdy judge 'ow 'ed like that done to him!'

Somehow, it didn't strike me as a good idea to go down that particular route.

'No, Danny – we will just have to grovel because you didn't tell the whole truth, now did you?'

A look of deep puzzlement crossed Danny's face. Of course, I should have known better. Telling the truth is an alien concept to most criminals as you might expect.

'Blewstone will fume like fury...' I was thinking aloud, '...but in the end, it probably won't much affect the sentence he actually passes. He can't add on the years just because you were less than frank as to the paucity of your genitalia.'

'*Pors* – I dunno wot you on abaht guv'nor. I'm just missin' me family jools and that's 'ard, that is! '

Returning to court, I endeavoured to explain the situation as neutrally as I was able. Blewstone listened in frosty silence.

'Your counsel tells me and I must accept it, that you had not told him of your medical condition. Nonetheless, you misled the jury gravely in a material particular – I quote from my note.

'Sid was grabbing my crutch and squeezing hard. I was in agonising pain.'

This was too much for Danny who couldn't help interrupting the judge's flow.

'So I blahdy was, your 'onour. Balls or no balls, it still 'urt like 'ell!'

Blewstone's head flew up and we all expected a bellow of fury. Nothing emanated though and he shut his mouth again. Without engaging in an animated discussion with Danny about crutch-grabbing, (of which, presumably, he had no previous personal experience), there really wasn't much he could say.

Having composed himself, he continued.

'You are very fortunate indeed that I am not able to sentence you for perjury. Regrettably, in the circumstances, I shall have to confine myself to two years imprisonment. Take him down!'

'That whole scenario was really quite funny,' I remarked to my elderly opponent later in the robing room. 'Did you see the local reporter scribbling away in the public gallery throughout? The case will probably get in the papers, don't you think?'

'Oh, I'm sure it will. Together with your name too, I expect.'

'That will be good. A bit of publicity never hurts after all.'

The old chap cast me a disapproving look.

'Joe Blewstone doesn't like his court turned into a laughing stock, you know. He's been the senior judge here for many years and is well respected in the community'

'So is Danny in *his* community I believe, even though that's the underworld and not the County,' I retorted glibly. 'Anyway, it's not as if I deceived the judge on purpose.'

My opponent looked at me levelly.

'Knowing Joe, he'll give you the benefit of the doubt on this occasion but I wouldn't push your luck again!'

What a pity it was that I didn't heed that advice as I was destined to be in front of Blewstone again a few days later. The storm erupted on the last day of the trial as I was making my speech.

'Stop this now!' bellowed the judge, banging his fist down on the bench.

Thoroughly puzzled, I ceased addressing the jury in mid-sentence and gaped at him like a fish. It was pretty unusual for any judge to interrupt counsel's closing speech to a jury.

'Members of the jury, would you be so good as to leave the court please? Thank you – Mr. Courtley, I note that the shorthand-writer is not present at the moment. What I have to say to you must be on the record so I will wait until she returns.'

With that he swept out of court.

Somewhat confused, I turned to my opponent – the same elderly chap as before.

'What have I done to upset him this time?' I enquired.

'Don't you realise, old chap. I warned you not to chance your arm with Joe again. We'll have to wait for the short-hand writer to come back as she's probably gone shopping in the town but, in the meantime, think about it!.'

The delay made me sweat anxiously and I cast my mind back over the case.

The problem was that it was by no means straightforward. My client was accused of snatching a woman's handbag in a local park at dusk. The charge was robbery because he shoved her to the ground in order to grab the item. She never formally identified him but he was the obvious suspect as he was found wandering aimlessly by the police near the scene of the crime. Moreover in interview, he made a number of remarks which would have been very incriminating had he been entirely normal – (which, in fact, he wasn't; his mental condition, according to accepted medical opinion, being unstable to say the least.)

So I decided not to call him to give evidence. Such a course was risky even though the judge was obliged to tell the jury that there is never any legal requirement for a defendant to go into the witness box. Nonetheless, any reasonable jury is bound to speculate as to why an innocent man should be reluctant to enter the box and deny his guilt.

I believed what I said in my closing address to that jury was perfectly reasonable. The defendant had given an account to the police and though he might have shilly-shallied a bit, basically he denied the robbery or indeed being anywhere near the woman at all. Because in English law no-one is required to prove their innocence, I suggested simply that there wasn't much he could add to what the jury already knew. This was the particular comment which had so outraged Judge Blewstone as I was soon to discover when he stomped back onto the bench later in the afternoon.

'You told this jury that sworn testimony from the witness box would not help them in the case and that your client's answers to the police were sufficient. It is outrageous to suggest that such evidence is of the same quality as testimony in court which can be tested in cross-examination!'

'I can't accept that criticism, Your Honour. He doesn't have to prove anything in our criminal jurisdiction.'

After all, the judge was perfectly entitled to point out in his summing-up later that when a defendant declines to go into the witness box, he does nothing to rebut the assertions made against him. In the meantime, I was justified in telling the jury what my instructions were – that if he didn't want to give evidence, that is always his inalienable right.

'What you said was quite reprehensible nonetheless. Accordingly, I shall be discharging this jury from delivering a verdict in this case. It won't be re-listed until I have written to your head of chambers to whom I shall refer the matter immediately.'

Well, at least the old sod's not actually reporting me to the Bar

Council for professional misconduct! I thought defiantly as I made my way back to the robing room. Surely, Tufton Crump would back me up in due course anyway but I decided, in the circumstances to seek my opponent's opinion too.

'Courtley, the way you chose to express yourself was just too casual. Of course, the defendant doesn't have to prove anything and isn't obliged to give evidence in his trial – but to suggest that he couldn't add anything useful from the box to what he told the police – well, that's plain wrong isn't it? His evidence would have backed up his denials of the crime which I could then have tested in cross-examination. Joe may be more of a stickler for the rules than some but he has got a point!'

Stickler or not, he's still a pernickety old pedant, I thought but refrained from saying it. I would just have to wait and see what Tufton's verdict would be and in the meantime, it might be better if I returned the brief to someone else. Being hauled over the coals judicially is not a very edifying experience personally and the poor old client deserved a fresh start!

THIRTEEN

I didn't have long to wait before I found out Tufton's reaction to the complaint. A week later, Leslie pushed a brief into my hand.

'It's your lucky day, Sah! Got yourself another junior brief, you 'ave. Tomorrow down at London Sessions. Defending the dripping diamond on a handling rap – £100 on the brief – not bad for just sittin' behind Mr. Crump. He's in chambers at the moment so go in and have a word.'

Tufton was defending an old client by the name of Lou Quell who was engaged in the jewellery trade and had, over the years, been arrested on several occasions for handling stolen goods.

Tufton chuckled as he turned over the pages of his brief.

'Comes back to me time and time again, does Lou – but then I've always managed to get him off! Sails very close to the wind but never actually capsizes, you might say.'

'Why does Leslie call him the dripping diamond?' I was curious.

'Ah, that's because he tends to ring chambers up directly to find out whether I'm available – and always says, *it's the dripping diamond here*. Sales puff, you could call it. It's the name of his shop, you see – which knocks out quite good stuff really when it's legal. When it's not, he calls upon me to defend him. With some success over the years although I say so myself.'

'What happened this time?'

'Over-extended himself by attempting to sell this...'

He produced a photograph of a solid gold ring with an enormous diamond set in the middle.

'Worth five grand apparently but Lou was selling it for seven hundred and fifty quid. A copper's nark tipped off the police and then they discovered this...'

Tufton showed me another photograph. Inside the ring read the inscription – *E.L with all my love R.S.*

The police had apparently traced it straightaway to the proceeds of a burglary from a house in Chelsea. *E.L* were the initials of the rather rich victim.

'So what's our client's answer to the charge?'

'Oh, bought it off a stall in Petticoat Lane one Saturday. Market Overt, dear boy, or to put it into villain's lingo – don't ask no questions and you won't be told no lies! I'll get him off at half-time, I expect. Particularly, as we're in front of Judge Cecil Rummage who just happened to be my pupilmaster whilst still at the bar in back in the 1950s. Moreover, it's not often that they see a silk at Sessions and a member of Parliament too!'

Tufton leant forward and tapped his nose.

'It's all tactics, you see – ah, that reminds me.'

I gulped. Now the time of reckoning had come.

'I received a letter from Judge Blewstone, yesterday. Ticked you off good and proper, didn't he? I've written back saying I shall do the same but not for the reasons he thinks...'

I perked up. 'You don't reckon that I misled that jury then?'

'I can't go quite that far but Blewstone's a pompous codger and what you say in your closing speech should be sacrosanct. However, only stand your ground if you're absolutely sure you're in the right otherwise apologise like mad, grovel even; it will impress the jury. Remember what I said a minute ago. Tactics is what matters in court. You'll see that when we appear in front of old Cecil tomorrow.'

'Good day to you, Mr. Crump and your learned junior. I understand that you are representing the defendant Quell in a private capacity.'

'That is indeed so, Your Honour,' Tufton rose to his feet from counsel's row where we sat together, and bowed.

'Mr. Quell is not legally aided hence the attendance of both of us today. Before the jury are brought in, might I enquire as to Your Honour's well-being?'

(Tufton had informed me earlier that the ancient judge had recently been ill.)

'Thank you, Mr. Crump. I am very well at present. Indeed, it is a delight see you once again at London Sessions after such a long time...'

'The old boy's purring already.' Tufton whispered to me as he rose again.

'The feeling is mutual, Your Honour, remembering as I do the many happy times that I appeared before you in the past.'

'Ah, but never before as *leading* counsel.' The judge drooled before turning to the prosecutor.

'Mr. Banks, please proceed....'

There wasn't much challenge to the prosecution evidence so the half-way stage of the trial was soon reached. When he made his submission of 'no case to answer' to the judge, Tufton was on good form. He may have been physically short and rather puny but he possessed a magnificent bass voice flavoured with that slight Welsh lilt which always added resonance.

'Evidence! Where can it be found in this case?' To emphasize the point, he cast his eyes around the court seemingly searching for it. 'The prosecution can't deny that my client Mr. Quell bought the ring from a stall selling such things in a well-known London street. I invoke the ancient Common Law doctrine known throughout this good land for many centuries past – Market Overt! Can any man be accountable for an item sold freely from such a source? Is there not an irrefutable presumption that it is lawfully for sale? Where is the proof that Mr. Quell – a man of business himself – knew the ring to be stolen?'

The prosecuting barrister, a nervous young man, was obviously overwhelmed by the eloquence of leading counsel.

'Well... we nonetheless maintain that on his own admission, he paid a low price for the ring. As a jeweller, he must have known its value was much greater than £750.'

'M'learned friend clearly doesn't know his law,' Tufton waved a hand dismissively at his opponent, 'as Your Honour will with his wealth of experience. I know and trust that you will reaffirm the ancient maxim and justice will once again triumph!'

There was silence. Tufton had excelled himself. Rummage sat mesmerized for a moment and then announced.

'Mr. Crump has defined the law correctly and accordingly, I have no hesitation in stating that there clearly is no case to answer.'

Later that day, Tufton and I sat sipping port on the terrace of the House of Commons after a delicious lunch at his expense – or more accurately, the taxpayer's; the prices on the menu being extremely low. The cold spring weather had suddenly been replaced by a spell of warm sunshine which sparkled over the river. Observing a number of political celebrities mingling on the terrace and full of excellent claret (specially bottled for the House of Commons by an exclusive French vineyard), I felt good – enjoying the reflected glory as it were of the distinguished company.

My reverie was soon shattered. A flustered House of Commons messenger appeared at our table closely followed by Leslie.

'Mr. Crump, sir. This gentleman insisted on interrupting your luncheon. He says he has a brief for Mr. Courtley which he needs to give him as a matter of urgency.'

'Missed a case in the list, Sah! Trial in front of Lord Sheckleworth at Middlesex. Just along the road from here. Should have started an hour ago at two o' clock.'

'Well there you are, *boyo*.' Tufton's Welsh lilt became more pronounced under the influence of alcohol. 'Duty calls – and it will be the perfect opportunity to apply what I told you earlier. The clerk's cocked up by missing a case in the list and Hub can be pretty unpredictable at the best of times whether at the Bar or on the Bench.'

Of course, I had heard of Lord Sheckleworth – Queen's Counsel, head of chambers and a recorder of the Crown Court. Hubert Sheckleworth (always known as Hub), came from a rich brewing family; a leading member of which had allegedly bought the original peerage back in the 1920s. A pre-war playboy lifestyle had been replaced by a harsh war which ended in a concentration camp. A fluent French-speaker (Hub's mother came from France), he had gone to ground as a spy after the German invasion of that country and only been discovered towards the end of the Second World War. On the point of being shot several times, his experiences had reputedly caused his hair to fall out overnight. I cast my mind back to an incident which had happened during pupillage…

One lunch-time, a tall stick-like figure had approached myself and another in the Old Bailey Bar Mess, dressed in the rounded waistcoat and tails of a Queen's Counsel. He was smiling, although as I learnt later that didn't necessarily mean that he was in a good mood. Smiling was all a part of his cultivated aristocratic manner and the beam rarely faltered.

'You young chaps must be pupils.' He perched his bony behind on a chair next to my companion; a pupil called Ned from another set of chambers.

'Come to the Bailey to see how the law works in the real world, have you? We apply it rather differently from the way they teach it in college, I'll be bound!'

Hub's broad grin, revealing yellowing teeth, lit up his

sallow face whilst he drawled; using the mock-cockney vernacular of the upper classes of the 1920s.

I decided to be bold. Our pupil-masters had left the building for the day; their business concluded. Ned and I were at a loose end.

'Perhaps, we could come and watch you, sir?'

Hub wagged an admonitory finger at me.

'Never call a barrister, *Sir*, dear boy – bad form an'all. Surnames or first names always between members of the Bar.'

'Oh, so sorry – Lord Sheckleworth,' I spluttered.

'Call me Hub, most people do.'

Nonchalantly, he filched a slim cigarette case from a waistcoat pocket. I watched fascinated as he extracted an oval cigarette and lit it, using a pink-tipped match scraped casually down a grey pin-striped trouser-leg.

'I'm makin' my closing speech in Court Five.' He turned to go. 'Prosecuting a murder as it happens, come and watch if you like.'

Ned and I looked at each other and nodded in agreement. This was our opportunity to hear a closing speech in practice, rather than having to endure the artificial ones demonstrated during lectures as law students.

Hub stood before the jury in one of the new courts at the Old Bailey (which resembled a drawing room) with comfortable bucket armchairs pointed and tipped at every angle. Green leather-topped tables, replacing counsel's old-fashioned benches floated on an aquamarine sea of carpet.

He waggled his shoulders vigorously as he rose to speak resembling a thoroughbred limbering up for action.

'Members of the jury – the defendant maintains that he never murdered the victim but it's as plain as a pike staff, he obviously did! '

Hub's beam swept round the court-room like a lighthouse; the tone of his voice raised to a high pitch. Shoulders still waggling, he said no more and resumed his seat.

The jury returned a guilty verdict within twenty minutes. Saying so little couldn't have worked better. What a lesson in advocacy from a master – but what, on earth, would he be like when he graced a court as a part-time judge?

These were my thoughts as I entered the ornate edifice of Middlesex Crown Court situated at the other end of Parliament Square. The long since abolished Middlesex County Council had decided to build their Quarter Sessions court in such a way that it would match the Houses of Parliament opposite. It was a Gothic extravaganza!

Spotty Nick (from my instructing solicitors) was waiting for me in the lobby with news both good and bad.

'The judge is dealing with some bail applications at present. So he's not ready to start our case just at the moment.'

'Thank God.' I muttered, remembering that I hadn't even perused the brief as yet. I flopped down on a convenient bench and began to read.

Bargery was a recidivist charged with burglary of a warehouse containing electrical equipment and storing it in his daughter's house. The daughter, unwilling to take the rap for receiving the stolen property, had blown the whistle on him. The defendant denied any responsibility maintaining it was the daughter's boyfriend who committed the burglary. As a result, much of the case hinged on the daughter's credibility.

I grimaced looking down at the list of the client's previous convictions. They ran to four pages. By challenging her evidence, these convictions were bound to be revealed to the jury.

Nick might only be an outdoor clerk but he was a perceptive sort of chap and read my mind.

'Bargery will expect you to go for her whatever the consequences, Mr Courtley. I ought to warn you too, he's a real bastard of a client.'

'Thanks, Nick.' I could tell that it was going to be that sort of an afternoon.

The client sat in the holding cells in the bowels of the court, peering at me through a pall of pungent blue smoke, emanating from the squalid roll-up which seemed to grow from his lower lip. Age about forty-five, but looking at least ten years older, his moon-shaped face was etched with the lines of the resigned old con. His pallor was a true prison hue, grey and dirty pink combined. He was an old lag who had lived more of his life in prison than out. After apologising for being late, I got straight down to discussing his convictions.

'You know what these mean, don't you, Mr. Bargery?' I felt I had to explain his predicament although he probably knew more about the law of criminal evidence than I ever would. 'If I attack your daughter's credibility by accusing her boyfriend of being the burglar – the two of them being in cahoots – your form will go in.'

'I'm innercent,' he said in the wholly unconvincing way of the perpetually guilty, 'stitched up wan' I? She done the burglary with that little scrote, an' stored the stuff in 'er 'ouse. I was just lodging there between stretches in the nick like – that's the truth of it. Easy to blame me wiv me record an' all.'

'Well yes, but the jury are going to wonder, aren't they? The stolen goods which the police found were electrical after all… and your last eight convictions were burglaries from high street stores which sell that kind of thing.'

'I'm not goin' guilty, got it?' Bargery was becoming truculent. 'I want you to cross-examine that slag of a daughter real hard when she goes in the box.'

The fact was that Bargery wanted a few days out of Wormwood Scrubs prison and to indulge in a measure of self-entertainment at public expense. Going not guilty wouldn't do him any harm as he expected a long stretch of imprisonment anyway with his criminal record. The reality was, I suspected, that all three of them had played a part in the crime. Bargery and the boyfriend were the burglars and the daughter's house was being used as the receiver's den – with her full knowledge.

In the event, the police having raided the premises at dawn; the day after the burglary, only the absent boyfriend had avoided apprehension.

Minutes later, I was facing Hub in court. He looked totally in place in the venerable courtroom panelled in dark oak with stained-glass windows. Court Number One was the perfect backdrop for him sitting as he was under the royal coat of arms.

Tactics! There was no excuse for being late so I intended to be totally frank about it. I would simply grovel and put the full blame on my clerk.

'Very sorry not to have been here at two, Your Honour. My clerk missed the case in the list and I've castigated him for it already.' I lied.

Hub's smile turned into a sympathetic grin.

'Mine does it all the time too, Mr. Courtley – perfect they ain't but how would we ever manage without them, eh?'

The trial began and unlike most television courtroom dramas, plodded tiresomely towards its inevitable conclusion.

Then, almost at the end, Hub received a note from the defendant complaining bitterly about me. According to him, I hadn't cross-examined his daughter vigorously enough and was useless anyway. He wanted to sack me and thought the most effective way of doing it would be to address the judge by way of a note passed through the dock officer. Needless to say, I was caught completely by surprise.

Hub sat on the bench holding the note between finger and thumb as if he'd picked up a soiled tissue from the floor.

'I have received a missive from the defendant, Bargery. Usher, hand it to Mr. Courtley please for him to read.'

Hub gave me a moment to do so before turning to the defendant.

'Bargery,' his habitual smile had turned to a glare. 'It's pretty sneaky to write to the judge complainin' about your barrister without even tellin' him you're going to do it!'

Bargery rose in the dock, pushing his glasses down his nose;

no doubt imitating the countless lawyers whom he had occasion to observe over the years. He began to address the judge in true barrack-room lawyer fashion.

'Your Lordship,' he whined, "ow can I get a fair trial with this brief here who don't try hard enough. Me, an innercent man too – facin' a long stretch in prison. I know that I got form, guv, but beggin' your pardon, you gentry don't know what it's like being banged up twenty-three hours out of twenty-four...'

Hub's smile returned but this time it was enhanced with glee.

'Ah, but that's where you're wrong, Bargery – very wrong! I've been in prison too. For some time! Banged up just like you and there was no remission of my sentence! Now, dealin' with your note. I think that Mr. Courtley's been doin' a splendid job for you. If you sack him, you know, you'll have to conduct your own defence from now on. I ain't going to allow you to change your counsel and start again!'

A young barrister's confidence is easily dented in the early years of practice and a judicial boost to it works wonders. I wasn't sacked and redoubled my efforts – even if it was to no avail. Bargery and his daughter were rightly convicted in the end, yet the inevitable sentence of imprisonment was pretty short by contemporary standards. Hub didn't believe in vengeful sentences on old cons.

I left court that day with mixed feelings. Hub was known to be idiosyncratic in his likes and dislikes of counsel and I felt I had made a good impression. On the other hand, being almost sacked by the client was not an encouraging experience. As it turned out, that event didn't matter very much – Nick told me his principal wouldn't hold it against me.

'Mr. Brasper thinks Bargery's a right pain in the proverbial and wishes he'd go somewhere else.'

As for Hub – little did I know then how important his support might become in the future.

FOURTEEN

The spell of sunshine didn't last and another gloomy Sunday dawned with temperatures right down in the fifties. To cheer us up, Andrea prepared a delicious Shepherd's pie in our ancient oven. Washing that down with lashings of Bulgarian plonk, I broached something which had been much on my mind.

'I think we need a holiday after all that's happened. There's a place called Playa El Toro advertised at our local travel agents. It's a new development built just a mile away from Benidorm. Special rate for a month in their Hotel de Luxe – £150 all inclusive for two weeks.'

You might ask how I had the money for this venture. Well, I didn't – but the VAT money was temporarily available and Leslie had told me that Eric E. Evidge were finally coughing up!

'Chambers are taking a firm line, Sah! Either Gus gets Harley Ball to settle all outstanding fees or we report the firm to the Law Society.'

Reluctantly accepting my assurances about the money, Andrea still had her doubts.

'Are you sure that this place will be alright? Some of these new resorts which they advertise as being cheap can be pretty dodgy.'

'Sun, sangria and sand is what we need, darling girl. Let's live a little – I'll book it tomorrow.'

Before we went, I duly sent the VAT cheque to the Customs and Excise even though I knew it would push my bank balance well over the overdraft limit. I was going to take a gamble.

'When the Evidge cheque arrives for me,' I asked Leslie, 'could you pay it straight into my bank account?'

'Will do, Sah – Gus tells me that Harley just needs to sign it and then it's on the way.'

Placing my hand on a convenient table, I muttered.

'Touch wood, or I'm in real trouble.'

So we were all set to have a wonderful holiday- except, of course we didn't. Playa El Toro, meaning 'Beach of the Bull' was a misnomer not only because there were no bulls in evidence; indeed the stony beach was inhabited by stray dogs instead but the gritty sea, far from being aquamarine in colour as described in the brochure, was coffee-coloured caused by an underlay of mud.

Moreover the food, in the inaptly named Hotel de Luxe was execrable and we were reduced to taking our meals in a nearby beach stall whose main fare seemed to be beef burgers. Our appetite for these didn't improve either when we were told that Pedro, the stall-owner, organised the culling of the dogs on a regular basis when his meat supply began to diminish! Our week of torture over, we were only too glad to get back home to our flat in Peckham and the company of our two cats but there was another shock in store. A threatening letter from Mr. Tinby awaited me, accompanied by an up to date bank statement which indicated that no cheque from Evidge's had been paid in. I rang the clerks straightaway.

'Leslie, what about that cheque?'

'I'm sorry, Sah but Harley never sent it in the end.'

'For God's sake man, I need the money!'

'Bad news, I'm afraid. Harley Ball's gone to Brazil with the contents of the firm's client account and isn't expected back. He's left Gus in the lurch too – owes him a month's wages.'

At least Gus got a job with Braspers almost immediately

whereas I had to face Mr. Tinby once more. On this occasion, the atmosphere in his office was distinctly frosty.

'You're asking me to increase the limit once more, Mr. Courtley. How can that be justified?'

Knowing what to expect, I had thought long and hard about what to say.

'Ever bigger cases in the pipeline, Mr. Tinby. Indeed, I can quote you one recent example – a privately paid case – being led by my head of chambers, Tufton Crump QC.'

Tinby was looking down the list of credits on my bank statement which were minimal compared to the debits marked in red.

'On there, you'll see the entry where the brief fee was paid in – £100 for one day's work.' I continued airily. 'Now, that's only because the case lasted a day when it was anticipated to take a week. What it shows though is how my practice is developing. Incidentally, I'm being led in another big case very soon...'

Tinby rapped his fingers on the statement for a few seconds.

'Alright – another £500 but only for six months and then your borrowing must remain below the previously agreed level.'

So June hadn't been a happy month so far – a non-holiday followed by yet another financial crisis and things were about to get worse on the work front...

Knightsbridge Crown Court (once a fashionable hotel situated near Harrods and converted on the cheap using plasterboard partitions to create ramshackle courtrooms) was hot and stuffy at the best of times but particularly when another hot spell of weather arrived. Court Number Three, on the ground floor, benefited from no natural light whatsoever and was known to be the most oppressive of the lot. Thus I was already sweating profusely when I ventured into the presence of Saul Wolsey, whose judicial abode it was. Saul had the reputation of being haughty, quite common in judges of those days but was also known to be disdainful in a cruel patronising way. At our first meeting, I suspected that I wasn't going to like him and so it turned out to be.

Of course, we young barristers had all heard about Saul. As well as being a hack prosecutor in London, he had also been for many years a back bench MP from the Shires, hot on law and order, and thus elevated to the Circuit Bench via the old-boy network and not through any judicial merit.

I was defending one of two defendants who were charged with theft and receiving stolen property respectively. My client – the receiver (named Arnie) – had only one real concern and that was not to go to prison if at all possible.

In order to try and avoid it, he had intimated that he would plead guilty and give evidence against the thief who was contesting the matter. Despite many previous convictions for dishonesty, he hoped thereby to sustain only a suspended prison sentence.

Unfortunately, a complication arose on the day it was listed. The thief (named Reg) jumped his bail so didn't appear. Nevertheless, the case stayed in the list for my client's plea to be taken anyway as his solicitors had informed the court of his intended plea in advance.

The case was duly called on and Saul came into court. He was a scrawny man with a lined, thin face. Broken veins on his cheeks indicated that he was a boozer as well as a smoker; habits which were betrayed when he spoke throatily in the customary upper-class drawl of the time.

'Mr. Courtley – as I understand the position, your client intends to enter a guilty plea, is there any reason why the indictment cannot be put to him today?'

'Ah – I would ask that course to be deferred in the absence of the co-defendant.' I suggested tentatively.

There was a problem. Arnie didn't want to plead guilty there and then, because he would undoubtedly lose his bail and be remanded in custody until Reg was arrested. My client had articulated his concern eloquently enough to me earlier.

'I wants a bender now, guv, not some bleedin' time in the future when Reg gets nicked!'

This was the difficulty. The judge would only sentence Arnie at the end of Reg's trial whenever that might be. Instead of being locked up for only a couple of days, Arnie might be remanded in custody for weeks!

Meanwhile, the judge was pressing the point.

'Why should the entry of a plea by your client be delayed? Your solicitors informed the List Office that he would be pleading guilty after all.'

I was placed in one of the most difficult positions for a defending barrister ever to be in – where his responsibility as an official of the court conflicts with the duty to his client which, of course, remains paramount.

'He will not be pleading guilty today. I ask for the whole case to be taken out of the list until the apprehension of his co-defendant.'

Saul ogled me from the Bench; a sarcastic sneer on his face.

'Before I rule on that application surely I am at liberty to enquire – are your instructions that the defendant is, in fact, guilty?'

'I cannot answer that.' I said defiantly. 'Your Honour knows that such instructions as between client and counsel remain privileged.'

'You speak with two tongues, Mr. Courtley. The court will not be trifled with in this way. I...'

He was cut short by his clerk who rose below the bench with an urgent message. A jury was about to return with a verdict in a multi-handed case which Saul had been trying. After guilty verdicts were returned, that case resumed for sentencing to proceed. Due to pressure of time and the judge's other commitments, my case was released from Saul's court back to the List Office who simply stood it out for the day.

Relieved, I made my way to the Green Man, a small pub

hidden away in the depths of Harrods. There I sat sipping an ice-cold lager and munched an expensive turkey sandwich – their speciality – meditatively. Thank God, I'd escaped from him, I thought. He was the kind of judge who liked to put defence barristers on the spot – knowing full well that some of our clients, conversant with the criminal process, expected a certain manipulation of the system for their benefit.

It's an odd thing in life that once a problem occurs, it often crops up again within a short time. Sure enough, a few days later I found myself instructed to represent the front man engaged in running a 'dirty book' shop in Soho. At the time, the prosecution of pornographers in London tended to be somewhat arbitrary depending on whether certain high-ranking Metropolitan police officers in the Porn Squad had been paid off or not.

My client was a fresh-faced young man in his early twenties who earned £100 per week (not a bad wage in the 1970s), as the 'manager' of the outfit. Quite who employed him was obscure as he was paid in cash weekly by a man he knew only as 'Joe'. Nonetheless, my instructions were quite simple – he intended to plead guilty to various charges under the Obscene Publications Act and took full responsibility for the illegal material sold from the back of the premises; 'soft porn' being openly for sale in the front. The penalty would apparently cause him no problem provided it wasn't imprisonment. He could easily meet a large fine despite the fact that he was currently unemployed – no doubt 'Joe' would oblige!

There was however one significant problem. The defendant had been prosecuted only a year beforehand for the same thing – running another dirty bookshop not far away – and been given a conditional discharge for two years. The present offences meant that he was in breach of this order.

Expecting the prosecution to have full details of the background, I was somewhat surprised when the officer in the case handed me the defendant's Form 609 (the police record of previous convictions). There was no mention of any earlier wrong-doing whatsoever.

'Clean as a whistle your boy, sir,' the rumpled old DS from the Porn Squad told me with what I discerned to be the faintest of winks, 'never been in any sort of trouble as you can see.'

Somehow his effusiveness didn't seem quite genuine.

Although this information was very good news for my client on the face of it, it put me, as his counsel, in a very awkward position. What does a defence barrister do when the prosecution are unaware of a very relevant aggravating feature which figures in a particular case, but which is starkly set out in the defence instructions?

The rule is actually quite simple. A barrister is not obliged, indeed bound not to, reveal any information against his client which might prejudice him but equally he mustn't mislead the court either. I could mitigate generally on his behalf but be completely unable to make the obvious point – that he was a man of good character – and critically – that he was somebody hitherto unconnected with any sort of pornography.

Arriving at Knightsbridge, I cast my eye down the list and my heart sank. It was Court Number Three again and, sure enough, Saul was the judge!

It wasn't until I began to mitigate that I realised just how hard my task was going to be. In essence, I was unable to say anything about my client's background because I couldn't stress the obvious point – that he had no previous convictions! Moreover, his future prospects were pretty vague too; casual work in one capacity or another was about the extent of it.

Nor did Saul help either. He was the sort of judge who kept his face blank at all times save for a perpetual supercilious smirk and a contemptuous expression about the mouth. Straight away, you were aware that there would be no reaction to what you actually said. I began to waffle horribly (not taking Saul in for a moment) – as became apparent in the following exchange.

'My client has been seeking work, Your Honour. Indeed, he informs me today that he has been offered a job as a –'

' – painter and decorator, perhaps?' Saul finished the sentence for me.

'Yes, as it happens. He frequents a public house in his locality and a friend – well, perhaps more of an acquaintance really – a man called Kevin -'

' – whose surname no doubt, you will now tell me, he doesn't know.'

'Er...indeed so, Your Honour. However, the job starts next Monday when he hopes to meet up with Kevin at a local café and who will accompany him to the location.'

All a bit vague you might think, but this was often the only, somewhat limited, material at one's disposal; criminals tending to lack imagination in what they fabricate for the benefit of their lawyers. Of course, it wasn't always Kevin who so conveniently offered work as a 'painter and decorator' – sometimes, he might be called Des or Ron instead. On occasion, a badly typed 'letter' from the prospective employer would be produced too – but not this time.

'Let's get to the point, Mr. Courtley. Have you anything to say about your client's background?' Saul cut me off in mid-waffle.

'Well, he has in the past worked in the building trade and also as a barman. In that respect, his record has always been good.'

'In *that* respect,' Saul seized on the word, 'meaning that this has not always been the case then?'

'I cannot take the matter any further and simply rely on what is stated in police records.'

'You speak with two tongues, Mr. Courtley...'

Saul had said it *again*.

'I don't think I can add anything further in the circumstances.' I concluded lamely and sat down.

Feeble as my mitigation was, I nonetheless expected the

punishment to be a pecuniary one having been reliably informed that this was the normal tariff. Saul, however, took a different line and duly sentenced the defendant to six months imprisonment.

My client wasn't best pleased. His reaction to my efforts on his behalf was one of the worst I was ever to experience.

'What's your game then?' he asked none too politely when I appeared at the cells. 'I thought you was prosecuting my case not bloody defending!'

Muttering that he could always consult another barrister about an appeal, I left without further ado, and as is the way of these things put the whole sorry affair behind me. After all, most of the time, I just went from one case to another often on a daily basis. On this occasion though, it was to come back to haunt me with a vengeance.

A week later, Bill Champney, a senior barrister in chambers called me into his room. Bill was an amiable chap, a former journalist, noted for his *bon viveur* lifestyle and robust advocacy who was quite prepared to take judges on if he felt it necessary in the interests of his clients. Perusal of a brief by him would often lead to gales of laughter and derisory comments as to the merits of the case, whether prosecuting or defending.

On this occasion though, he was glancing at the brief in his hand with a furrowed brow and there was nothing humorous in his manner.

'Remember a porn case you did at Knightsbridge, old chap, in front of Saul Wolsey? Well, I have a brief here from the Registrar of Appeals to represent your erstwhile client before their Lordships. I've been reading the transcript and it appears that the prosecution didn't know about the defendant's previous conviction. It seems that the copper in the case chose to conceal it he's since been arrested for corruption together with other porn squad officers.'

The unhappy scenario of that case returned to mind.

'It's true about the prosecution not knowing about the

conviction but it was referred to in the instructions from the solicitor. Consequently, it was very difficult for me to mitigate as I couldn't make the otherwise obvious point that he had no form.'

Bill tapped the papers in front of him.

'Hmm...anyway, in the interim, the Registrar has received up to date details of antecedents so the Appeal Court know the full score now. That, I'm afraid, could pose a problem – let me quote what you actually said at the trial.

'I... blah, blah, blah... simply rely on what is stated in police records. That tends to imply, doesn't it, that he didn't have previous convictions – contrary to your instructions?'

'I suppose so,' I gabbled. 'But Saul put me on the spot – as you can see from the context.'

'Nonetheless, you shouldn't have said it, Charlie. The Registrar has picked up on it and their lordships may require an explanation.'

'Oh, God what will they say?' I gulped.

Bill stroked his chin thoughtfully.

'I'll explain that Saul caught you off-guard and put it down to your relative inexperience. That may suffice although I might have to call you at the appeal to back it up. The case is due to be listed at any time in the next few weeks by the way, so be prepared.'

I worried about it for a day or so and indeed the niggle was always present at the back of my mind. However, as it turned out, the work of the following weeks didn't allow much time for distraction into areas not of immediate concern.

FIFTEEN

The day the Maltese car-ringing case started was turning out to be one of the worst of my life. His Honour Judge Wintringham was trying the case in the cavernous gloom of Number One Court at the Old Bailey and an altercation was taking place between him and my leader, Dan Rydehope, engaged in a substantial fraud case in the same building and hoping that he could lead in both cases at the same time.

But Wintry, very much a stickler for the proper procedures, was refusing to play ball. 'Your request cannot possibly be accommodated,' the judge's voice might be reedy but it resounded with authority, 'and I will not allow counsel to conduct different cases at the same time even when a junior is constantly present in both cases. Accordingly, you will have to discharge yourself altogether from this matter, Mr.Rydehope and Mr. Courtley shall conduct the trial alone.'

'My lord,' Rydehope protested,'my junior is a very able young barrister but does not possess the necessary experience.'

'Nonsense – I note that your client is last on the indictment anyway. 'Tail-end Charlie' is the common term at the Bar, is it not? Mr. Courtley's first name appears to be Charles so it seems that the gods favour this outcome.'

A sycophantic titter broke out which certainly wasn't shared by me.

Our client was one of twelve defendants all engaged in a

substantial conspiracy involving stolen cars. He was an elderly chap – once a professional burglar – who still dabbled now and again in crime just to keep his hand in. It was alleged that he stole a couple of cars down in Kent, which together with many others landed up in Malta. The evidence against him fell within a narrow compass as most of the trial involved those responsible for the identity changes to the vehicles in transit.

As it turned out, the judge's prediction turned out to be entirely correct. In most of the evidence, my client wasn't mentioned at all and I was required only to cross-examine a couple of witnesses. It became increasingly clear that in the scooping up of the larger fish, a mere minnow (my client) had been netted. Keeping a low profile would pay dividends and meanwhile I could revel in my leading role – a pupil from chambers having been drafted in to replace Dan – to act as my junior.

They say all barristers are frustrated actors and I confess I played the part of a leader too. I would sweep into court as the judge entered as I'd seen all the QCs do, and often I lingered over coffee in the Bar Mess after lunch leaving my junior to start off the afternoon. In practice, many days went by when I wasn't required to open my mouth at all, save simply to say – *no questions, My Lord* – but, boy, did I make the most of that!

I even took time out to attend a memorial service at nearby St. Paul's Cathedral for a distinguished judge (not that I ever I knew him personally but it flattered my ego). Dressed in pinstripes trousers, black jacket, and waistcoat adorned with my grandfather's fob watch, I felt really good as I popped out of court for a hour or so in the middle of the working week.

With not much to do, I was able to see some of the other leaders in action. One of them was a celebrated silk called Ritchie Hamm, a straight speaking Scot with a gruff voice which projected well in court. On meeting him, you might have mistaken him for a humourless sort of fellow due to his grim mouth and dour expression. Yet when he spoke, his face came alive; the down-turned mouth transformed into an engaging grin and eyes sparkling with mocking merriment.

He delivered a brilliant speech for one of the principal defendants making the most of the material available. His client, a man called Borg (soon known as 'Uncle Tonio' on account of being considerably older than most of the defendants) was alleged to have played an important advisory role in setting up the fraud.

Hamm's tactics were brilliant. Contrary to public belief, the best advocates keep their mouths shut most of the time but when they choose to speak, it counts. Eloquently, he suggested that Uncle Tonio was in reality the joker in the pack far too stupid to be any kind of moving force in the conspiracy. Above all, his speech was funny; the jury were in stitches and the acquittal later became inevitable.

The time was fast approaching for me to address the jury. I asked Ritchie for his advice as he sipped a sherry in the Bar Mess at the conclusion of his own speech.

'Say something which just sounds original -' he said, '- and don't bother to refer to the facts of the case at all. The jury are sick to death of the details and the judge will have to go through the whole damn thing anyway when he sums up. How about citing a quotation, make a literary allusion – something of that sort, lad?'

Which I duly pondered upon. Browsing in the Bar library, I found a biography of the great defender of Edwardian times, Sir Edward Marshall-Hall. Leafing through it, I came across a quotation which, to begin with, seemed wholly apposite if adjusted to meet the context. Sir Edward was defending a prostitute charged with murder in 1894 and uttered these immortal words on behalf of his wretched client; downtrodden since birth.

Look at her, gentlemen of the jury, look at her! God never gave her a chance – won't you?

But turning the matter over in my mind, my enthusiasm

waned a trifle. Perhaps it was a bit too flowery. After all my client, seemingly content to have spent his life engaged in crime, was hardly wretched or downtrodden! I went home and perused a book of quotations I had to hand instead…

The next day I stood up in front of the jury positioning myself as near to their box as I could. I was nervous and only too aware of the rows of fellow barristers beside me, and the members of the public staring from their gallery upstairs. Poised to start the speech, my hands trembled just a fraction. It wasn't just the nerves – I had a slight hangover as well caused by one too many glasses of red wine the night before. But then that would give it an added vibrancy; a spontaneity which only jangling nerves can bestow.

By this time, all my senses were heightened. I could smell the mustiness of my gown and feel the sweat prickling the forehead under my wig. The leather aroma of the court furniture filled my nostrils. The judge, jury and the whole court became like a formal photograph of old; frozen and fixed in time.

The wig and gown acting as a kind of armour, I drew comfort from their physicality by pushing the wig firmly down over my head and drawing the gown close to my body.

I started the speech quietly and without drama but then gradually built up the tempo. After making the usual comments about how every man is innocent until proved guilty, I concluded with a flourish.

'Ladies and gentlemen, a miasma of suspicion droops over this case like a cloud. But, as the poet Tennyson said – '

I lifted my hand slowly and dropped it, palm cupped, towards the jury box.

– *there lives more faith in honest doubt, believe me, than in half the creeds.*

So, as the case against my client requires there to be proof beyond all reasonable doubt, you must acquit!'

Which, I am very glad to say they duly did.

Dan Rydehope stood calmly puffing his pipe outside Court Number Twelve at the Inner London Crown Court. Four days had passed since my triumphant acquittal and my feet hadn't quite touched the ground. My only regret was that I hadn't seen my chosen leader in action.

'Are you in Cardie?' Dan asked.

'That's right – I'm for the defendant. You're not prosecuting are you?'

'On this rare occasion – yes. I do so about once a year on average.' Dan informed me wryly.

My confidence might have been boosted but the task ahead would now be a real challenge. Dan was reputed to be one of the best cross-examiners in the business – and he would soon be testing my client's ludicrous defence!

Ray Cardie wasn't just fat. He was huge; a mountain of flesh which began just underneath his small head in the place where a neck should have been but wasn't. Instead, a series of Michelin-Man spare tyres began, ending only in a pair of short legs. In fact, height-wise, he was only about five feet three yet in the witness box he resembled a vast impenetrable mound of dough.

He was the steward of a working men's club, charged with the theft of beer from his premises in South London. The level of dishonesty had to be pretty extensive for the police to be involved as it was accepted that a certain amount of 'ullage' would always be written off – this was, supposedly, beer washed away as normal spillage from the pumps as well as a proportion of bottled beer breakage. All stewards tended to inflate these quantities to a degree; that was an accepted perquisite of the job but the allegation against Cardie went way beyond that in this case.

Early in the new year, a large consignment of beer (some £5000 worth in fact), was delivered at lunchtime to the club premises. It then vanished without trace.

There was no dispute that the brewer's lorry had made the delivery on the day and a substantial number of kegs were left in the club's yard. My client held the keys to that and the stockroom, although a spare set were always retained by the club's treasurer.

The prosecution were faced with one small evidential difficulty. The delivery driver, who had actually presented the receipt invoice for signing, had now left the brewer's employment and could not be traced. However, there was never any suggestion that he had made off with the consignment himself. Indeed, a delivery docket was produced, found in the club, with a signature on it which the prosecution maintained was Cardie's. The latter stoutly denied this to be the case and indeed the signature only amounted to an unidentifiable squiggle. Still, the circumstantial evidence pointing in his direction was overwhelming.

He duly gave evidence and denied that he had signed for the kegs, maintaining that at the time he was visiting the local betting shop, (of which he was a regular customer). It was true that he was expecting a delivery that day but wasn't surprised when it didn't turn up, stating that the brewery were notoriously unreliable. As to who else might have purloined the beer, he simply had no idea.

Dan drew himself up to cross-examine, fixing the defendant with that level Churchillian stare. I held my breath waiting for the destruction of the witness to begin.

'Mr. Cardie, you state that apart from the treasurer, no-one else other than you held keys to the yard and stock room, that is correct?'

'Yep.'

'...And on the day of delivery, that gentleman was holidaying in Majorca?'

'Yep.'

'We know that someone signed the docket confirming the delivery so who could that person have been if it were not you?'

'Dunno.'

'No-one else apart from your good self had the opportunity to steal the beer – all one hundred kegs of it. You took delivery and misappropriated the lot, didn't you?'

'Nope.'

Each rapier-like thrust was met by the same response. Cardie was looking quite comfortable in the witness box by now; stolidly wedged in a backwards position with his enormous stomach pushed forward. He never allowed the prosecutor to shake his composure for a moment.

The jury having retired, Dan and I repaired to a pub just across the road from London Sessions for a spot of lunch. Sipping a whiskey and soda, my companion glanced at me through a cloud of aromatic pipe-smoke.

'Cross-examining your client, Charlie, could be compared to kicking lard in a plastic sack! Every blow simply squelched into his vast morass. I got absolutely nowhere with him.'

'But he was awful in the witness box – the jury are bound to hate him.' I retorted.

'Take it from somebody who usually defends, my boy. He was brilliant – dogged denials like that without any qualification often does the trick.'

Which for the second time that week, it did. The jury duly returned with a not guilty verdict.

SIXTEEN

Having arrived too early, I walked briskly out of Spandau Barracks and made my way to the old prison. Rain fell steadily from the leaden sky, adding to the murkiness of the atmosphere already made smoky from the workings of the coal-fired industries in the east. The air was bitter to breathe and smelt of tar.

The prison loomed blurrily before me like a haunted castle in an old horror movie. I glanced nervously at the large signs written in Russian, English and French – starkly stating that entry to the fortress was strictly forbidden and that the taking of photographs was banned. Staring at the thick bolted door in front of me which was never opened, I thought of the old man incarcerated in there since 1945; Rudolf Hess – Hitler's one time deputy. Sentenced to life imprisonment, now the sole occupant of this dreadful place, he was guarded day and night by English, American and Russian troops.

Shuddering, I returned to the barracks for the six o' clock conference arranged with the client. His court-martial was due to take place the following day in Berlin.

A substantial proportion of British troops remained in the suburb of Spandau – still part of the British sector of occupation. After the War, the Russians had taken the eastern part, and the Americans, French and British divided up the rest. The Signal Regiment, which had requested my good self to represent one of their soldiers, was part of that contingent. At one time, their expertise had been vital in keeping an eye (or rather an ear) on the activities of the Soviets but, by this time, their role had become insignificant. It is a fact of life that soldiers become easily bored when under-employed, and that's when trouble starts, particularly after the consumption of alcohol. This, then, was the backdrop to the case of Regina versus No. 7690278 Signaller Barry Fogg.

The actual court-martial was held in a truly fascinating place; the hexagonal room used for the fencing competitions in the pre-war Olympic stadium. That was where the British had set up their Brigade Headquarters when the city was divided. The room fitted the bill very well. It was capacious and allowed for a large bench to be built at one end where the military officers and judge advocate sat. To get to it, you walked up the main staircase, between walls still adorned with nude pictures of Aryan youths (a chilling reminder of Nazi propaganda), and walked past offices which had changed little outwardly since 1936.

The Olympic complex as a whole had escaped the bombing and included the international amphitheatre where Jessie Owens had run so successfully, much to the disgust of the Nazis. Now restored to its former grandeur, then its infrastructure was crumbling away; weeds sprouting in the unkempt grass of the central arena.

When Signaller Carmen Ignatius arrived at Spandau barracks in the middle of the previous year, it caused a bit of a stir. She was a vibrantly attractive Trinidadian girl with a fun-loving personality to match. Most of the male signallers couldn't help but fall for her. Signaller Fogg was one of them and genuinely thought that she reciprocated his interest. At the summer party held in the gardens of the barracks, he consumed a great deal of heavily fortified punch and allegedly groped her at the side of the refreshment tent as she returned from a visit to the loo.

There were conflicting accounts of what had happened from a number of witnesses on both sides. Signaller Ignatius (and her friends) maintained that the defendant grabbed her breast and attempted to kiss her, whilst pushing his knee between her legs. On the other hand, Signaller Fogg (naturally enough called Foggy) and his mates disagreed with that account fundamentally. According to them, Ignatius had also been drinking heavily that night and was flirting outrageously with everyone. What had occurred here was a consensual clinch resulting from a tacit understanding that they fancied each other.

The differing explanations as to what had happened in this case was classic in its way. None of the witnesses could be called impartial and their evidence was coloured by what they thought of either party. Some undoubtedly regarded Ignatius (nicknamed Iggy naturally) as a tease whereas others didn't like Foggy very much. He was a Uriah Heepish sort of character with the reputation of sucking-up to his Commanding Officer.

It soon also became apparent that both the complainant's and defendant's recollection of events were patchy, affected as it must have been by the prodigious strength of the fruit punch. No court could ever be sure, one way or another, as to what had really happened. Perhaps not surprisingly, the defendant was acquitted.

The case only took a day and I was free to return to the hotel where Andrea and I were staying.

When Leslie had told me that I was doing a court-martial in Berlin, I decided to take my wife with me for a much-needed break. The poor girl had been under considerable stress as three of her favourite patients at the hospice had died over the same weekend.

'Change of scene is what you need, darling girl.' I said. 'Come and join me in West Berlin – it's a really fascinating place – a kind of oasis in the middle of a communist desert. Some fantastic shops too. A bit of retail therapy will do you good don't you think?'

Andrea thought about it for a moment. 'Yes, that does sound a marvellous idea but I'd like to do a bit of sight-seeing as well. Contrary to what you men seem to think, we women don't just live for shopping, you know!'

I stood corrected. 'Well, let's just hope the weather will be fine. It is the end of May after all.'

Unfortunately, it rained incessantly for the next few days.

Concerned about expenditure as always, I booked accommodation in a cheap hotel – the *Gasthaus Brandenburg Tor* – which described itself as being very near the city's enduring symbol; the Brandenburg Gate.

Indeed it was, in the sense that it overlooked the infamous Wall, covered by graffiti, which had divided the city since the early 1960s.

On arrival, Andrea looked through the window of our bedroom and grimaced at the bleak view. The whole area was starkly lit by floodlights strategically placed on watchtowers within the eastern zone of the city.

'Not exactly a cheering sight,' she remarked.

'True, but we are very near the famous gate, can't be more than a minute or so away from here.'

'Well, why don't we go and see the whole thing then?'

Which we did after consuming a meal of *bratwurst und kartoffeln* at a local *imbiss* – and what a sight it proved to be!

A sharp wind blew rain in our faces as we ascended the steps of the observation platform overlooking the wall on the western side. I mused about its origins. Built, it was claimed, to keep the capitalists from being able to contaminate the purity of the model *Deutsche Democratische Republik*, it was in reality a barricade to keep their wretched citizens from escaping. West Berlin amounted to a small island marooned in a sea of communism; cruelly cut through the middle by a wedge of hideous concrete. Several times, the Russians had almost breached the dividing line to gobble up the territory which they claimed belonged to them so there was constant tension in the air.

Only yards away, the enormous gateway loomed over us as we stared up at the four-horse chariot of the goddess of victory on the top.

'So this is the nearest we get to it then?' Andrea enquired.

'From our side, yes. How close they allow you to approach from the east, I don't know...'

'Can't we visit the east as tourists?'

'Well... I've not thought about it really. I believe that you can purchase a visitor's visa for the day. I'll make some enquiries if you like.'

Andrea shivered. 'Perhaps we can go when you've completed your case and the weather improves. Meanwhile, I've decided I will sample the shops after all. Where did you say that famous department store is situated?'

'The *KaDeWe* near the Kurfurstendamm and darling,' I squeezed her hand, 'spend a bit of that money – buy yourself a dress or two whilst you're at it.'

An elderly aunt of Andrea's had recently died and left £200 in her will. Being naturally cautious, Andrea had wanted to preserve the whole of it as a back-up to our precarious financial position but this was a far better idea.

After the court-martial concluded, I asked my prosecutor, an affable, open-faced chap called Major Jerry Blanford about the possibility of going into East Berlin.

'U-Bahn is the best way, old chap. The line takes you to the Friedrichstrasse station which is the official crossing-point to the east. Mind you, there's usually a long queue at the border for visas – the *grenzpolizei* are not known for either their charm or speed.'

'We'll chance it anyway.' I said. 'My wife's with me on this trip and we're staying on for a few days so we might go tomorrow.'

'Wait a minute. Why don't I take you over the wall myself- an escorted military visit to the east. That's a far better way! We can go and have a meal at the Moscow – East Berlin's best restaurant where all the Warsaw Pact diplomats go. Food's terrible but the Crimean shampoo is just about drinkable! How about me picking you up from your hotel at seven o' clock tomorrow evening?'

'Well thanks – but don't we need permits to go over?'

'Don't worry about that, old chap. Just make sure you've got your passports. I'll explain everything when we meet.'

At eight o'clock the next evening, a sleek blue Mercedes drew up outside our hotel and Jerry Blanford stepped out. We received a shock. He was dressed in full military mess-kit which included a black bow tie, a clutch of medals and a scarlet bum-freezer jacket bound by a grey satin cummerbund. We were thrown for a moment; were we supposed to be wearing evening dress too?

'Part of the courtesies agreed between the allied commandants on the formal division of the city in 1945.' Jerry explained. 'All officers are entitled, as of right, to enter the neighbouring occupied zones at any time. However, the British General Officer Commanding of the British Sector ordained that, at night, all service personnel would have to wear formal attire. As guests though, that doesn't apply to you.'

The car wound its way through some streets until it reached a long central avenue – the Strasse des 17 Juni – which led us towards the Brandenburg Gate once again. Before reaching it however, the car turned sharp left a couple of times before entering Friedrichstrasse.

'Checkpoint Charlie is at the end,' Jerry observed, 'but there's another sharp turn to the right before you actually approach it. In the early days, somebody crashed through the barriers in an armoured car from the other side and successfully escaped! Anyway, let me explain the drill on this side of the border. We will be stopping at the Allied checkpoint first. We get out to sign our names in the register and then are given a form explaining our rights and obligations in the east. For instance, if we don't return to the checkpoint within six hours, a contingent of British soldiers will form a search party and come looking for us. If we are unlucky enough to have a car accident, we must insist on seeing a Russian officer. On no account are we to explain our visit to the *Grenzpolizei* or *Volkspolizei* – the East German authorities. The allied government of Berlin doesn't recognise that the DDR has any legitimacy.'

Minutes later, we crawled through the barriers on the western side and the car came to a halt in the centre of a courtyard. Arc lights blazed from the rooftops. A red light barred further progress. A few metres away, two parallel, railway-crossing type gates led to the east. At this point, the wall rose to form an overhanging square arch.

'If there's an emergency, metal grills descend in two separate places blocking access totally. Sirens begin to wail too. If there is a suspicion that an unauthorised person is trying to cross, then it's bound to go off! Let's hope that doesn't happen now,' Jerry said airily.

We didn't feel reassured as the minutes ticked by.

'Don't worry, the guards always keep you waiting. That's part of a deliberate plan to be as awkward as possible…'

Finally, the light went green and we crawled up to the barrier. A uniformed guard peered in the passenger side of the car where I was sitting and then gestured for me to wind down the window. Jerry touched my arm.

'No – keep the window wound up! They're not entitled to ask you for any identification as you're with me. All you need to do is to show your passport through the window!'

Rather nervously, I did so and the guard, corpse-like in the harsh white light of the lamps, gestured with a finger from side to side.

I began to sweat. 'What's he doing that for?'

'Just show him the last few pages. He's just checking to see if you have any interesting visas. If you've been to a communist country, for instance, they might want to question you. That could be a bit awkward. I take it that you haven't been behind the Iron Curtain before, have you?'

'No...' Then I remembered. 'Oh God, I went to Prague in 1967 when I was a student and the visa's still in there!'

My hands shook as I turned the pages.

However the guard, after examining the document, seemed satisfied and after repeating the performance with Andrea, the journey continued.

The transformation in the city was dramatic. Whereas in the West neon lights blazed garishly lighting up the buildings amongst a constant buzz of traffic, now the streets were dim and shabby and apart from the odd Trabant spluttering away, there were no cars at all, except for the large black ZiL limousines reserved only for high-ranking members of the Communist Party.

As the car bumped along the cobbled roads, I observed that the signs directing the traffic out of the city were for places only located in the communist world – Leipzig, Dresden, Warsaw, Cracow and naturally Leningrad and Moscow. On a whim, thinking about what Andrea had said, I asked Jerry whether it was possible to approach the wall from the eastern side.

'We can try...' The latter remarked and turned the car sharp left down a side street. A dead end lay ahead with roadblocks and sentry points. Beyond, the whole area in front of the wall (which was devoid of any buildings) was lit by arc lights. The wall itself glowed with luminous paint.

'Tell you what old chap, I dare you to get out and see how near you can walk.' Jerry laughed.

Unimpressed by his sense of humour, but not wanting to be thought a wimp, I left the vehicle and pretended to amble nonchalantly towards the barrier. A guard, Kalachnikov at hand, stood impassively waiting for me, whilst his companion spoke urgently into a telephone situated inside a sentry box.

Jerry, half-out of his side of the car by now, sounded less flippant.

'Seen enough, old chap? I'm not sure its a good idea to hang around for too long. The guards might get a bit itchy.'

I headed back to the car as quickly as possible.

'I ought to have told you that the entire wall on this side of the border lies in No-Man's Land – where the citizens aren't allowed to go except the guards.' Jerry added.

'I wish you'd told me that before,' I muttered under my breath.

When we reached the restaurant in the Alexanderplatz, I noticed that there were many more cars in evidence than in the neighbouring streets. Indeed, the place was pretty well full when we entered, containing a number of booths in which swarthy thick-set men sat in ill-fitting lounge suits accompanied by brassy women.

'Welcome to East Berlin's most fashionable restaurant. Pretty well the only restaurant really if the truth be told. Ah, I see there's a free table in the corner – let's grab it whilst we can. The clientele here are mainly party representatives of the eastern bloc countries as I said before – plus a smattering of the DDR's own communist elite. This place is, I suppose, roughly the equivalent of a top notch night spot in London although the entertainment doesn't really compare. However, it's something to be experienced nonetheless as you'll see in a while. Meanwhile…'

Jerry snapped his fingers. '*Ober! – ein flasche Russisch sekt, bitte?*'

A surly bald-headed waiter dressed in a grubby black smock nodded plonking three menu cards on the table.

'Fritz is the senior *ober* here. He's not exactly welcoming but he doesn't have to be seeing that he owes his position to being a long-standing member of the Party. This place is state-owned naturally. Now, let's examine the menu. I'd dispense with any starter if I were you – the service is unbelievably slow.'

A while later, the waiter returned with the wine and a pad and pencil at the ready. I chose the *Kalbfleisch mit Bohnen und Kartoffelen* and Andrea followed Jerry by ordering an omelette.

It took forty minutes before the meal finally materialised. Stringy and tough, my veal obviously came from a very old calf, the potatoes were soggy and the beans tough and stringy.

'I told you the food was pretty bad,' Jerry said cheerfully, 'which is why I stuck to having an omelette. Even the *Ostis* can't ruin that! Fancy a bottle of Romanian red for a change? It's not bad for Iron Curtain vino and it will help to chase the taste of the food away.'

After two or three glasses of the fruity wine, I abandoned the food altogether and it wasn't long before the effect of that and several glasses of Crimean Champagne began to take its toll. By the time the music began, the place had become imbued with a kind of boozy surrealism.

Now, an old man with long flowing hair streaked dirty-yellow in patches, tottered out to a small stage in the centre of the restaurant. He carried a violin and bowed deeply to the assembled company. Then he turned expectantly towards an upright piano next to him. I was puzzled. No pianist seemed forthcoming.

'That's old Gottfried. He'll play some of Kreisler's best known tunes in all probability. It's the sort of music the Germans adored before the War and the Berliners here love it still, sealed as they are in their own little enclave.'

As the old man lifted his bow, I waited in anticipation still wondering when the pianist was going to appear. A moment later, the piano began to play itself!

'Gottfried has to make do with a pianola, you see. Unfortunately, most decent musicians deserted East Germany years ago but at least it gives him some backing and he's a wonderful violinist.'

As the plaintive music began to steal over me, I realised what he meant and found myself observing the other customers more closely. Somehow the scene was reminiscent of one of Georg Grosz's paintings of pre-war Berlin society except that in place of the rich drooling capitalists of that period, there were now leading drooling communists instead.

Gottfried played as if he was still employed (as he had once been) in some grand hotel in *Mitteleuropa* between the wars. Musicians like him, usually in groups of four, would play away in the corner of the saloon whilst older guests sipped coffee and munched *torte* whilst the younger people took up their positions for the afternoon dance...

When the Georg Grosz figures began to blur, doubling into clones, I realised that I needed something to mop the alcohol having drunk far more than anyone else. Round-eyed, I began to examine the dessert menu. Apart from ice cream which I didn't fancy, there was *Frischen Obstsalat*. This seemed reasonably innocuous. Meanwhile, the others contented themselves with coffee. When the fruit salad finally arrived, it seemed to taste all right if a trifle watery.

As we drove back to the checkpoint, Jerry suggested that we visit the Tomb of the Unknown Soldier housed in the Neu Wache – a temple-like building not far off the Dom; the great cathedral of Berlin. A number of young, East German soldiers stood guard in front of the entrance. With their coal-scuttle helmets and greatcoats, they reminded me uneasily of their *Wehrmacht* predecessors. I had sobered up by now but was left with a distinct feeling of queasiness coupled with a niggling ache in my gut. Was it just the after effects of the alcohol or could it be something more significant? Things weren't helped by the aroma of drains which seemed to permeate the whole area...

'You probably noticed the smell of sewage back there,' Jerry remarked as we continued the journey, 'which is due to lack of clean water, East Berlin's real problem. The communists were so anxious to block the sewers to stop people escaping that the water supply has been adversely affected!'

Oh God! I thought. That – (obviously not so fresh) – fruit salad! The mixed fruit had tasted fine in itself but what about the accompanying, insipid fluid! I began to sweat aware of an increasingly churning sensation in both stomach and bowel. What if we were kept waiting going back through the checkpoint as long as we had been kept going in?

I just made it to the loo in time some forty minutes later. Still suffering with the gripes, I stumbled into bed.

By contrast, Andrea stood calmly by the window staring out at the view with a rapt expression on her face.

'Very stimulating to have been able to travel to the other side of the Iron Curtain – and to hear that violinist – what a treat! Thank you, my darling for bringing me along – it's done me the world of good.'

'At least that makes one of us.' I groaned making my way back to the lavatory again.

SEVENTEEN

I was back in chambers and the nagging worry in the back of my mind was fast turning into a full-scale crisis of nerves.

'Leslie, that appeal from Judge Wolsey in the porn case – isn't it due to come up soon?'

'Ah, the case of Duggan, Sah – Mr. Champney's case. It keeps being postponed although we're told it could come up any minute. The court 'ave received further correspondence from the prison where the client's being held and he's 'aving a right moan about your conduct of the case.'

'Oh, God, does Mr. Champney know?'

'He certainly does. In fact, he'd like to speak to you about it. Matter of fact he's in his room now.'

Within moments, I was sitting opposite Bill over a cup of tea. The latter reached for the brief and sighed.

'Bad and good news, old chap. The client has written to the court himself complaining that you didn't represent him properly *and* also maintains that he instructed you to reveal his previous conviction saying that he wanted to be utterly frank with the tribunal. Did he, in fact, discuss the conviction with you at all? '

I cast my mind back but was quite convinced that he hadn't.

'No, it wasn't mentioned and what he says is a damn lie anyway!'

'That's as may be but the Lord Chief Justice isn't going to like it.'

'The Lord Chief – not Lord Flaggett!'

'The very same, I'm afraid. Now, don't fret, Charlie. I may not have to call you at all – I'll do my best to avoid it as you know.'

Suddenly, my hands went clammy and cold. The ordeal of having to give evidence had been lurking in my mind for the last week or so but I had never anticipated this.

There were a wealth of stories circulating about 'flogger' Flaggett, the tough old ogre of a Lord Chief Justice who refused to quit. Appointed a High Court Judge before mandatory retirement was required at 70, he continued to preside although now approaching 80. Although the most senior judge in the land, he rarely sat in the Court of Appeal due to the ability of his brother judges to overrule him. Tough on violence and dishonesty, he was known to be notoriously liberal as far as the new pornography offences were concerned. At one legal dinner he had been reported as saying – *if a man wants to gawp at filthy pictures that is his affair, provided it doesn't involve either children or animals!*

Bill guessed what I was thinking.

'From the defendant's point of view, it's good news of course and will make my life easier. Flaggett's a good tribunal as far as he is concerned. However, in relation to counsel's duties to the court, he's known to be a real stickler for the rules – do you remember what he said at last year's Bar conference?'

I trembled. Yes, I did recall only too well – as students, we had all been compelled to attend his lecture as part of our training.

Our noble profession from whom the judiciary spring – the Chief had pontificated – *requires the highest possible ethics from those who hold the rights of advocacy in court. Thus it is that the judiciary are drawn exclusively from members of the Bar and it is incumbent upon us who preside in the higher courts to be vigilant in the upholding of standards!*

Bill was looking at me sympathetically.

'If he's minded to allow the appeal anyway then there would be little point in having you called at the hearing. However, he may make some scathing remarks about your conduct but we'll take that as it comes.'

At that moment, Dennis appeared at the door.

'I've just checked the daily list, sir. The case of Duggan is in tomorrow. Last matter in front of the Chief in Court Four.'

'Better keep Mr. Courtley out of court then,' Bill said. 'Stay put in chambers, lad and Dennis will contact you if necessary. He'll be accompanying me over the road.'

It was well after four o' clock the following day when Dennis finally called.

'You're in the clear, sir. No need to come up after all but Mr. Champney would like a word when he gets back to chambers – old flogger ain't too pleased with you, that's for sure!'

Bill noticed how miserable I looked as soon as he walked in.

'I suspect that you could do with a drink, old chap,' he said casting me a sympathetic glance. 'We can go if you've picked up your brief for tomorrow.'

On this occasion I had, so off we set.

Knowing Tom Tug's to be one of Bill's favourite watering-holes, I assumed we would be going there but on leaving Tabernacle Buildings, we left the Temple by a side entrance and into a narrow lane just off Fleet Street near St. Bride's church.

'There's this nice little place favoured by journalists. A club actually, but I'm still a member. The Quill and Parchment, it's called. Much better for a private chat – no lawyers frequent it, you see.'

The club was unobtrusively situated in the basement of a modern office block. A gate led down some stairs and to a front door. Inside, a porter, dressed in a resplendent blue uniform ushered us into a rectangular room with alcoves secreted on all sides. On a far wall, pictures of famous journalists including Edgar Wallace and Lord Northcliffe clustered together. Each alcove contained two capacious chairs bound in red and green leather.

We sat down in one of the alcoves and I noticed that instead of wallpaper, front sheets of old newspapers adorned the walls from floor to ceiling.

'The perfect place for a discreet chat.' Bill murmured. 'Fancy a large gin and tonic?' He gestured to a waiter.

I did indeed and the tangy drink soothed my jangled nerves somewhat. Draining his glass, Bill ordered another and leant across the table.

'Everybody agrees that Flaggett is a miserable old sod, Charlie. Yet the public love him – he's forever advocating the re-introduction of corporal punishment in the House of Lords after all. That's how he acquired his nickname 'flogger'- and as the Chief he carries a lot of clout in the legal world. Here's what he said about you in court today. I've written it down.

The defending barrister, an impudent young fellow, employed tactics in this case which could be likened to those of the three-card tricksters so often seen by the side of our capital's underground stations...'

I gasped. These rogues were notorious at the time for conning the gullible out of large sums of money by inviting them to 'spot the lady' – a task which was well-nigh impossible through sleight of hand.

'That's awful!'

'Quite. It certainly won't help you in applying to get on the various lists to prosecute. The Director of Public Prosecutions, the Solicitor for the Metropolitan Police and most of the county forces all have them, you know and it's essential that you extend your practice if you can.'

'Oh God, what can I do?'

Bill took a large swig from his drink and patted my hand.

'Cheer up Charlie. I've thought of a possible way out of this impasse. Now, next week Tufton was supposed to be leading me in prosecuting a murder. He's had to drop out at the last moment so I'm taking over but I shall need a junior to assist me. The case is listed at Bentleigh Crown Court Monday morning in front of Flaggett no less. It's been agreed that I can bring you in. That will go down very well with Flaggett who's pretty prosecution minded at the best of times and, at some stage, I may even be able to arrange for you to have a chat with the old codger.'

The gloom which had enveloped me lifted a little. I felt a wave of gratitude towards this kind man.

'I don't know how to thank you, Bill – what a mess I've made of things – misleading Wolsey in the way I did.'

Bill sighed. 'We all make mistakes, Charlie – the answer is to learn from them. Anyway, to use Flaggett's example, you were dealt a very bad hand of cards – shits instead of aces. A shit of a first instance judge, a shit of a client and a shit in the appeal court! However, that you'll recover I have no doubt.'

Then I experienced a fresh moment of panic.

'You did say Bentleigh, Bill. That's usually Blewstone's domain. What if Flaggett talks to him?'

Bill laughed. 'The third judge you've managed to cross in a short time but don't worry. Blewstone's doing a stint in the county court so he won't be there. Now, pick up the papers from chambers and read them carefully over the weekend. I expect you to help me with my opening note on Monday…'

The following week, the case began and Bill was about to address the jury on behalf of the prosecution. Although it was summertime, only thin sunshine crept in the room through small windows set high up in the court. This did little to alleviate the gloomy solemnity of the proceedings. Lord Flaggett sat stock-still, his face stern and glowering down on us lesser mortals. Clad in red robes and grey bench wig, his grim appearance was accentuated by his glasses – one lens tinted frosted-white to hide a sightless eye damaged in a hunting accident some years before.

So formidable was the atmosphere that I suddenly felt the

lunatic urge to giggle. I clamped my teeth hard down on a ballpoint; successfully suppressing it even though I also recalled a story I had heard recounted in the Bar Mess only that morning about the ceremonial opening of the Bentleigh Assize earlier that month.

Stalwart officers of the Essex Constabulary had escorted the judge on foot from his car to the public entrance of the court building where he was greeted by various dignitaries and the other judges. From there, he was ushered to the bench and the assembly was now complete with counsel of the day already present. The High Sheriff made the usual appropriate comments of welcome, after which Flaggett, bowing deeply, withdrew to make his way to the judge's chambers situated at the rear. Thus he was the first to exit through a blue satin curtain pushed aside with a flourish by the usher. Unfortunately, a small gap lay behind unbeknown to His Lordship and he stumbled badly, just preventing himself from falling flat on his face. It was at this point that a most injudicious choice of language ensued at some volume.

'Bugger!' Apparently dignity wasn't further compromised by anybody laughing but I bet it had taken a bit of doing!

Following the extensive note I had prepared, Bill set out the facts before calling the evidence. The defendant called Sulby, his girlfriend and the victim were all irregular inhabitants of a squat. On the day of the crime, the defendant fuelled by a cocktail of drugs and drink, was searching for his girlfriend (with whom he had had a row earlier in the day). He returned to the squat in a very agitated state and the victim, an aging hippy in his sixties, wanting to protect the girl, attempted to bar his entry. The upshot was that the defendant battered him to death using a hammer kept in a toolbox in the hallway of the building.

None of the basic facts were in dispute – all the defendant could claim in his evidence was that being under the influence of drink and drugs, he recollected nothing.

The point came in Flaggett's summing-up when he directed the hammer to be brought up to the bench by the usher.

'Ladies and gentlemen of the jury,' he growled. 'Witnesses may swear to tell the truth under oath but sometimes tell lies or more often make mistakes in recollection – but *dumb metal*, such as we have here,' he picked up the hammer and shook it, '*never lies!*'

Sitting behind Bill, I was shocked by this biased comment which could only have been made to prejudice the jury as the evidence was overwhelming anyway. Expecting the defence to object there and then, I whispered to my opponent sitting next to me.

'You can't allow him to get away with that – there's clear case-law which states that the judge mustn't be seen to be taking sides!'

The defence junior, a pimply pasty-faced dumpling of a chap called John Voley made as if to tap his leader on the shoulder but then desisted.

'I'll make a note of it for the appeal. Arnold won't want to interrupt the Lord Chief Justice.'

More's the pity! I thought. Arnold Becton, the defence QC had conducted his case in a languid, casual manner and hadn't made much of an effort on behalf of his client as far as I could tell.

The jury were out for only twenty minutes before they convicted. As the trial had reached its conclusion in only two working days, no opportunity had arisen for me to meet the judge.

'Never mind, Charlie,' Bill was in a hurry to get back to chambers for a conference. 'At least old flogger has seen you batting for the right side.'

Just then, the judge's clerk, a solemn, elderly man dressed in a black tailcoat entered the robing room.

Addressing all four of us, now the only occupants, he said.

'His Lordship sends his compliments and wonders whether

counsel would join him for dinner tonight in the lodgings.'

Typically Voley, whom I suspected of being a crawler, was the first to answer.

'Oh yes, please. What a privilege!'

Arnold Becton shook his head.

'I'm afraid I can't. I already have a commitment in London.'

'Unfortunately so do I but Charlie...' Bill grabbed my arm taking me into a corner, 'this is your chance. Flaggett springs this on counsel from time to time when there's no pre-arranged social engagement for him to keep. He gets rather bored on his own – it's not much fun being a High Court Judge on circuit stuck in lodgings all the time especially if you're a widower.'

I didn't really want to go. Flaggett's biased remark in his summing-up (even though I was for the prosecution) had upset me somewhat. Noting my hesitation, Bill looked me straight in the eye.

'Charlie, this is the perfect opportunity for you to apologise. You'll get a good dinner too and transport will be laid on. His car will take you to the lodgings and run you back to Bentleigh station for the last train.'

I nodded reluctantly.

At six o' clock, the judge's Daimler (and his clerk) duly picked Voley and I up outside the courthouse and conveyed us to the lodgings.

'Dinner will be served promptly at seven.' The clerk informed us ponderously. 'His Lordship always eats early when he dines alone and I must warn you that as he suffers from poor digestion, he won't indulge in idle chat during the meal. He needs to concentrate on mastication...'

'What did you say?' For a moment, I wondered if I had heard aright. 'Oh, I see...'

The evening turned out to be as dire as I had predicted. Flaggett obviously regarded our presence as an excuse to drone on about himself. Had we been more senior barristers, he would have been obliged to show a reciprocal interest but, in our case, we were simply there as recipients of his judicial pomposity.

After a very swift sherry, we were ushered into the lodgings' dining room. The judge, dressed in a red velvet smoking jacket naturally sat at the head of the table with us two acolytes on either side.

The dreariness of the whole experience was only alleviated by the excellence of the food which wasn't surprising as the judges' lodgings employed a cordon bleu chef when the premises were occupied. The wine and port were plentiful too – a situation of which I took full advantage.

'Tort and contract law were my specialities at the Bar.' Flaggett began; his good eye fixed at a point above our heads – the frosted glass covering the other glinting disconcertingly in the candlelight. 'Remember the case of *Billington versus Parminger* in the House of Lords?'

'Oh, of course, Judge. The leading authority on negligence,' cried Voley. 'Where the plaintiff found a dead cockroach in her tin of salmon,' he added with relish.

'That's the one – decided in 1937. Very important case which changed the law fundamentally.'

I helped myself to another glass of port and found myself becoming hypnotised by the judge's lower jaw which clacked up and down like a ventriloquist's doll. Was this how one would become in the unlikely event of ever reaching the pinnacle of the legal profession, – a pretentious bore?

Voley, sweat plastering a lock of fair hair to his forehead, naturally lapped it all up – only interrupting the flow by obsequiously remarking at frequent intervals:

Oh, yes Judge! or how fascinating Judge! or how clever Judge!

I was wondering gloomily whether I would ever get the chance to raise the case of Duggan when Voley rose to his feet.

'I'm terribly sorry, Judge but I must go the lavatory – do please excuse me!'

Now was the time.

'Judge, you recently dealt with a pornography appeal. Quashed the sentence of imprisonment but at the same time criticised the original defence counsel's handling of the case. That was me...' I blurted out.

Flaggett's good eye rested on my face for a moment as if I were begging for small change in the street – an unwelcome distraction.

'My policy is never to indulge in discussions about cases which I have conducted.' He said icily.

'But... surely, there are exceptions?' I protested.

Flaggett didn't bother to answer. The good eye was once again staring above my head.

'*The Long Meadow case* in the Chancery Division was my other great triumph. No doubt you will recall that matter from your study of the law of equity?'

I nodded dumbly.

'The doctrine of equitable estoppel was established in that case and I argued it all the way to the House of Lords. A remarkable achievement although I say so myself.'

'Oh yes indeed, Judge. How wonderful to be making new law in that way!'

Voley had made an unwelcome re-appearance. So that was the end of any attempt to apologise. What really began to bug me (so I laid into the port even more) was Flaggett's total indifference as to how his judicial comments might affect a young man's career.

He continued to reminisce with Voley hanging on to his every word and under the influence of the port, I began to long for an opportunity to prick the balloon of verbosity. Then I recalled one particularly notorious murder case in which he had appeared for the defence.

'What about Janice Weller, Judge?' I interrupted. 'One of the last women to be hanged. That case was hardly your greatest triumph, now was it?'

Janice Weller had killed her husband. Her defence to the murder charge was limited to a possible alternative finding of manslaughter on the basis of provocation. However, the law prior to the Homicide Act 1957 restricted this defence only to a loss of control which occurred immediately before the act of violence perpetrated and not cold calculated rage which had built up over a longer period. Weller had set out to kill her husband after years of abuse, arming herself with an air rifle which she used to shoot him in the head whilst asleep. So when she admitted this in cross-examination, in strict legal terms, no defence was available to her. Nevertheless, any barrister worth his salt would have striven for a sympathy verdict – juries could, and often did in capital cases acquit against the weight of the evidence and despite the directions of the judge. Flaggett chose to make no closing address at all. Many thought his conduct was inexcusable. As a defending barrister, you should always say something on behalf of your client however hopeless the situation seems to be and here Janice Weller faced losing her life.

'I understand you actually declined to make a closing speech.' I added recklessly. Voley stifled an exclamation.

Suddenly I felt completely sober, appalled by how aggressive I must have sounded. I expected Flaggett to answer back with a biting riposte.

Instead, he reacted like so many defendants do when convicted of serious crimes which they undoubtedly have committed yet convince themselves afterwards that they weren't at fault. Sometimes this amounts to a total denial of a crime but often it is no more than a concentration on some minor aspect of the case. In this way, the human mind absolves itself from true responsibility by a process of self-justification.

Before uttering a word, Flaggett stood up and made his way to a sideboard where a cut-glass decanter of whiskey stood. He poured himself a large measure and stood looking out of the window which faced the lodging's trim garden. With his back to us, he spoke in an undertone.

'When I visited her in prison to discuss a petition to the Home Secretary for mercy, she didn't want to be reminded of what she had done. Instead, she asked for cosmetics and curlers. She needed these in Holloway so she could dress her hair and make up her face. She was very proud of her looks, you know...'

He turned and looked at me directly, his good eye watering a little.

'I fulfilled my duty to the client and most importantly to the court. Nothing could have saved her,' he added gruffly.

The evening soon finished with Flaggett bidding us a terse good night. Minutes later, Voley and I were back in the Daimler on our way to the station.

'Cripes, Courtley!' My companion was still in shock. 'By mentioning that case, you really embarrassed old flogger – talk about putting him on the spot!'

Which probably won't help my career in the long run. I thought ruefully. Yet I didn't regret it for a moment. Sometimes, a persistent biter deserves to be bitten in turn!

EIGHTEEN

A few days later, Bill and I were lunching at the Quill and Parchment enjoying their fine carvery. As we tucked into our roast beef, washed down by a bottle of burgundy, I told him of the dinner at the lodgings.

'You certainly chanced your arm there, Charlie – bearing in mind that you're not exactly in Flaggett's good books as it is. Still, it probably did the old fart a world of good.'

'Even so, it won't exactly help in getting on any of the prosecution lists, will it?'

'Not in the normal way, no. You have to write in formally and then they take soundings from all the High Court Judges. However, I've got a piece of good news which could make things a lot easier in that regard. The Director's people were quite impressed by the work you did in the Sulby trial and Basil Tapner is willing to give you a test to see how you manage on your feet.'

This was good news indeed. Basil Tapner, a legal executive, was the DPP's principal representative at the Central Criminal Court and was responsible for briefing many barristers for the prosecution directly. An enormously fat man with a thick black beard, he spent much of his time cloistered in his office sallying out on occasion to sit behind counsel for short periods.

'You know the Director's set-up at the Bailey, Charlie. Apart from Treasury Counsel who prosecute there full-time, there's also a supplementary list of approved prosecutors. I'm on it and Tapner could put you on it too – that would be an enormous boost to your career.'

'How does the test work?'

'Well, you get little notice of it. Indeed, the idea is to spring it on you to see how you deal with things on your feet – on the spur of the moment. Of course, it wouldn't be a full-blown trial – just something to put you on your mettle. So be warned.'

The next few days were taken up by a domestic crisis. Andrea's elderly father had fallen ill again and her mother was unable to cope due to her own severe rheumatism. Taking a few days off, I drove Andrea down to Saltdean where they lived so we could both help out with the chores.

After visiting the hospital and going to the supermarket in the middle of the week, we returned to the house just as the phone rang. It was Leslie.

'About tomorrow, Sah! Basil Tapner's just rang. He wants you to oppose a bail application – in the Stromkarl case.'

Walter Stromkarl was allegedly the head of a group of crooks charged with conspiracy to rob. Banks all over the country had been systematically pillaged and it was said of the gang that business had been so profitable that they were able to enjoy luxurious alternative lifestyles in Spanish coastal resorts.

At that time, the expansion of the economy meant that the country was awash with cash; easy to nick if you possessed the necessary know-how and, of course, the brazen determination to take it by force. Credit cards had not yet appeared and most business was cash-based requiring the transfer of vast sums of money.

As the principal defendant, I suppose I expected Stromkarl to look like a villain but the chap who was hustled into the dock eventually accompanied by half a dozen prison officers, was a disappointment. He was a shortish man wearing a dark suit, a nondescript tie and sporting black, thick-rimmed spectacles fashionable at the time. He looked wholly inoffensive and could easily have been mistaken for a bank clerk himself.

Indeed, he lived in a respectable area in Surrey with his wife and two children and was renowned as a keen golfer. So keen in fact that he had risen to the position of captain of the exclusive club where he regularly played. His fellow club members regarded him as a splendid chap with a low handicap; always ready to stand his round at the 19th hole and never enquired as to what he actually did for a living (*not quite the thing, old boy*) and assumed that he was just 'something in the city.'

His counsel Dan Rydehope had been instructed to use his best endeavours to spring Walter legally by getting him bail. Unimpeachable members of the 'great and the good' were prepared to stand surety in large sums to guarantee his attendance. Indeed, these same pillars of the community – a vicar, a retired admiral and a Justice of the Peace – would also, in due course, be providing him with a cast-iron alibi for the time of one of the robberies.

Rydehope (as I expected) waxed so eloquently on this particular point that I was almost persuaded myself that Stromkarl's alibi was genuine but, in reality, the latter was a cunning individual who, in his capacity as a regular golf-player, had planned his alibi well in advance. Accustomed to playing most days at a certain time, he was able (through his solicitors) to persuade his friends that he must have followed the same pattern on the morning of the robbery – simply by adjusting the time a bit.

The truth, of course, was that Dan Rydehope didn't stand a hope in hell of getting bail for his client as a 'supergrass' was preparing to put him and many others in the frame.

For security reasons, the case was being tried in the ramshackle and confined West Court building which that morning was guarded on all sides by armed police officers. Moreover, Wintry (who was notorious for never granting bail) was the judge.

However, with the rather sinister-looking figure of Tapner in the back of the court, I felt I had to make an impression.

'Bail is vehemently opposed by officers of the Robbery Squad.' I proclaimed. 'It is alleged that Stromkarl is guilty of preposterous crimes and there is every reason to suppose that not only would he intimidate witnesses but also flee the land making his way to a safe haven in the Iberian peninsula.'

'There is no need for counsel to indulge in hyperbolic verbosity.' Wintry said crisply. 'I think, Mr Courtley, you are referring to the fact that the defendant owns a villa in Spain.'

Feeling a pompous fool, I subsided with the mere mutter of a *yes, M'lord*.

'Notwithstanding,' Wintry continued acidly, 'bail is wholly inappropriate in a case of this nature and will be refused.'

As I left court, I almost collided with Basil Tapner whose huge bulk was blocking the doorway. Much to my amazement, he was grinning.

'Like that word *preposterous*, Mr. Courtley – at least, you were original.'

He turned away before I could reply.

Days later, I was told by Leslie informally that I'd been placed on the Director's supplementary list – and swiftly learnt from my first case involving Detective Sergeant Parch just how differently the police saw the administration of Justice!

NINETEEN

The chocolate box certainly didn't live up to its cosy description. It was the colloquial expression for the new court added to the Inner London Crown Court main building sometime in the 1960s. Cheaply built, badly lit, malodorous and uncomfortable, it was prefabricated in a hurry but remained in use years afterwards with a new coat of paint. The breeze-block walls had been painted cream with brown dividing lines to give a mock Tudor effect. The sickly result accounted for the name.

So here I was one sultry day in autumn prosecuting my second trial on behalf of the DPP.

'*Fuck off, you honkie ras-clot bastards,*' I said solemnly to the jury, causing a sharp intake of breath from the bench, '-is what the defendant said to the police officers when they stopped him in his car on Balham High Road.'

Lindy Backford, my deliciously pretty opponent, didn't turn a hair but, as I had somewhat maliciously intended, Bevidere-Jones (used to his ivory-tower existence in the Chancery Division) was really shocked.

The fact that he was trying a serious criminal case at all came about because of a combination of circumstances as indeed did the location. Being August, the Central Criminal Court's main building in the City of London had been closed down for temporary refurbishment and the few listed cases transferred to Inner London instead. The senior resident judge should have been trying this case but due to a nasty car accident the day before, he wasn't available. Desperately, the listing authorities had cast about for a judge to take the matter and tentatively suggested it to Bevidere-Jones. The only reason he was available was because he happened to be the duty High Court Judge for the long vacation. Perhaps bored with sitting in his bachelor flat in Lincoln's Inn (sallying out to read only if the weather was fine in the private garden reserved for the Benchers or dining at his club) he readily volunteered to try the case. After all, to a *real* lawyer, criminal work posed no problem – apparently that had been his instant reaction when asked.

What he couldn't have anticipated however was being dispatched to London's grottiest court – the chocolate box. Unfortunately, Number One Court where he would have sat was also closed for the duration. Asbestos had been discovered in the ceiling and plasterers had been called in to rectify the problem.

In the 'box', the dock and the bench were built at the same level. The chairs were made of black plastic and the tables of a similar material but with a cheap wood veneer. This was far removed from Bevidere-Jones' usual abode in his 19th century oak-panelled court in the Chancery Division surrounded by a wealth of leather-bound law books – a fact Lindy Backford touched upon as we drank coffee together in the Bar Mess. She looked absolutely lovely that morning with her shining blonde hair, cut in a pageboy style, setting off her innocent brown eyes and bow-shaped mouth to perfection. She also swore like a trooper and was known to be a tough opponent.

'Bloody hell, Charlie,' were her first words to me as she sat down lighting a cigarette. 'Why the fuck have we been sent to that shithole to do our case?'

I explained the problem and told her about our judge.

'Oh, for Crissakes! Not some namby-pamby from the Chancery Division. Quite apart from anything else, he won't understand the sodding lingo, now will he? Actually, Charlie…'

Lindy cast her most exquisite smile at me.

'Won't you exclude all that ras-clot stuff? It's terribly prejudicial and doesn't really take your case very much further, does it?'

I grinned. Defence counsel's tactics. Something I had often done myself to get an important piece of prosecution evidence excluded.

Tapping my fingers on my carefully prepared opening note, I shook my head.

'No can do, Lindy. You know it's all admissible although you can always have a go at Bevidere-Jones to exclude it.'

'I shan't bother. Those High Court buggers tend to know their law unfortunately...'

Lloyd Delroy was a black drugs-dealer going about his normal business in south London, one night a few months before. The prosecution's case was, that as part of the tools of his trade, he carried a pair of very sharp knives in the back of his car, as well as a large bag of cannabis resin. Lloyd didn't argue about the drugs but he was upset about the alleged possession of the knives.

According to the police, they introduced themselves in a somewhat informal manner using phraseology which is habitual between policemen and known criminals.

'Come on, Lloyd – you're nicked! What about these cutters then? Tools of the trade are they?'

Now this little piece of opening evidence, dutifully recorded in a policeman's notebook, caused Lloyd much distress, particularly as he was supposed to have replied. 'Bleedin' right – when punters don't pay, you gotta show them a bit of steel!'

Naturally he denied saying any such thing to the police, maintaining that he had been 'verballed' and also, according to him, no knives had been found in the car anyway. They had simply been 'planted'.

Matters were to get worse. Lloyd resisted arrest and

apparently kicked out, breaking a policeman's jaw in several places which led to a serious allegation of inflicting grievous bodily harm with intent (as well as the possession of offensive weapons, namely the knives.) According to Lloyd, however, he received a beating from the police at the station in the form of punches and kicks leading to substantial bruising and dental damage. The police, for their part, maintained that he had struggled to release himself from lawful custody and his injuries were entirely accidental. Regrettably, these were caused by an unfortunate collision with an awkwardly placed cell-door, the sharp edge of a desk and, on another occasion, with a fall, face-first onto a policeman's hard boot (which caused a chipped tooth.)

The language didn't improve either. According to the police, Lloyd couldn't string a sentence together without using the 'f' word liberally, as well as other West-Indian profanities. In contrast, according to Lloyd (and naturally denied by them), the police called him a scrote, a bleedin' spade, and other insulting things relating to his race. Eventually, this all led to a pained judicial intervention by Bevidere-Jones.

'Mr. Courtley, Miss Backford – I am unable to comprehend some of the expressions used. For instance, the terms – *ras-clot* and *scrote.'*

'Your Honour, *ras-clot* is a word used in West Indian parlance to describe the passing of menstrual blood. It is meant as a term of abuse. *Scrote* is an abbreviation of the word 'scrotum' – also, designed to be a term of abuse in that shortened form.'

'Oh dear, oh dear – such pro – fan – ity! Still, we have to endure it, I suppose – although, Miss Backford, you must find it particularly distressing to hear such expletives!' (Clearly, such language was not commonplace in the Chancery or commercial courts.)

'Oh, not at all, Your Honour – it's all part of the job,' my opponent said airily. Indeed in cross-examination, Lindy went on to re-iterate every term of abuse with evident relish.

The case turned out to be a classic battle between a black defendant and officers of the Metropolitan Police, who were accused of fitting him up. Lloyd denied that he had kicked the officer at all maintaining that the latter had slipped and cracked his face against the bumper of Lloyd's car. The case was contested forcibly by Lindy who demanded access to all relevant police records and accused the police of conspiracy to pervert the course of justice. Everything went before the jury, including the defendant's extensive criminal record and an admission by him that he was, in fact, a drugs-dealer, but one who never resorted to violence and viewed 'cutters' with abhorrence.

As part of his case, he called a number of witnesses including a girlfriend and other members of his fraternity. They vouched for the fact that he was a much loved and popular peddler of hash who provided a valuable service to the area's disenchanted black youth (at least in their view). According to them, the drug laws were totally ludicrous and all he was doing was making a living from a trade which had been declared illegal by interfering politicians.

Nonetheless, Lloyd and his pals had to admit that they didn't like the police and accepted in cross-examination that they were wont to describe them in the somewhat unflattering terms already described.

Throughout all this, Bevidere-Jones sat hunched in his chair; his head almost touching the bench. For much of the time, his mouth remained half-open as if he needed to ingest more oxygen to cope with the strain.

Finally, it was his turn to sum up. The first part was never going to be a problem. He was a good lawyer and criminal law to him was quite simple. Summarizing the evidence, however, was quite another matter.

Repeating the numerous obscenities whilst going through the evidence was obviously going to be hard for this devout Chapel Welshman so when he began, he had a plan in mind.

'The police and Lloyd Delroy have made counter allegations about the exchange of foul language at the time of the arrest. Dis-gusting, vul-gar and filth-y words were used. I do not intend to repeat these obscenities. Henceforward, I shall simply substitute the word *blank* instead. I feel sure that you, the jury will understand.'

Perhaps they did, and all credit to them for that. They sat solemnly enough through the rest of the judge's oration. But Lindy Backford and I found it very difficult indeed to keep a straight face. Our trial was fast becoming a parody of Terry Wogan's show – 'Blankety-Blank' – as the following sample will show.

'The defendant has told you that he never said - *blank! Blankety-blank* to the police. Indeed, they said to him. 'You're nothing but a *blanking-blank*, you *blanking blanker!*'

Lindy and I were almost chewing our notebooks by the end in an attempt to suppress our giggles.

After the jury had duly convicted and Bevidere-Jones had sentenced the defendant to four years in gaol, it was half-past twelve. As was so often the case at the conclusion of a strenuous trial, I felt drained and in need of diversion. A reasonable lunch (as Rex Huggins would have called it) seemed an ideal thing in which to indulge. Moreover, I felt little inclination to go home early. Andrea's stay down in Saltdean had been protracted by her parents' infirmities and she wasn't due back for at least a week.

'Fancy a spot of lunch in the pub across the road? They've tarted up the place recently and put on a varied lunch-time menu. It will be my treat as I managed to trounce you!' I felt in a teasing mood.

Lindy laughed showing off her perfect teeth and pert pink tongue.

'I've got a far better idea, Charlie. Why don't we go up to Jenna's instead – they owe me a favour, you see.'

'Jenna's Trattoria' in Covent Garden had just opened to rave reviews from food journalists but was known to be very expensive.

'I represented them before the Magistrates' last month on an application for a drinks licence and they promised me a free meal for two...'

Bearing in mind the precariousness of my financial situation, it didn't take long for me to fall in with the idea.

'Who am I to resist?'

On arrival at Covent Garden, parking proved to be a problem but Lindy had the answer.

'Just leave the keys with the head waiter, he'll sort it out.'

The new trattoria certainly lived up to its expectations. Their speciality – pumpkin, walnut and blue cheese *gnocchi* was first class particularly when washed down by a bottle of *Chianti Classico*.

Afterwards, the head waiter lit our glasses of *sambuca*; the blue flame emphasizing the softness of Lindy's features. Suddenly, I desperately wanted to make love to this girl. My hand reached out across the table to touch hers.

'Has anybody told you recently just how ravishing you are?'

'Charlie!' She giggled. 'You naughty man – chatting me up now when just this morning we were spitting at each other!'

'That was just work.' I decided to become bolder. 'Let me drive you home, Lindy.'

'There's no need for that – I only live in Henrietta Street just round the corner.'

'Better still. We can walk there then. Shall we go?' I added breathlessly.

But Lindy was looking over my shoulder. I turned to find a handsome woman dressed in a smart grey trouser-suit looking at us with eyebrows raised.

'That's your free meal, Lindy darling – as I promised. Now, it's time to take you home.'

I frowned, my attention returning to Lindy who swayed slightly as she rose from the table.

'Oh, Charlie... I'm so sorry to have led you on like this. I just had to take advantage of Jenna's – that's her, behind you – offer of a free meal and bringing another woman would have made her so *awfully* jealous! Do stay and have some more drinks if you want – it'll be on the house. When you're ready, the car will be brought round for you. Nice to have done business with you, sweetie.'

The two women, hand in hand, swept out of the place. So that was it – they were an item!

Although by now I should have had just a coffee, I decided to take full advantage of Lindy's offer and drank several *grappas* instead. Then I made the fatal mistake of driving back to chambers...

TWENTY

On the way back to chambers, I broke the speed limit – something I wasn't aware of until the policeman stepped out just as I turned into Middle Temple Lane from the Embankment. He was holding a speed gun (only recently issued to the traffic police) in his hand.

'Doing fifty, you were, sir – in a thirty mile limit area!'

Forty in practice was my first reaction. Nobody really complied with the official speed limit in London but I realised then that I had probably been going too fast anyway; the result of my frustrating experience in the restaurant.

However, things were to get much worse.

'I believe you have been drinking too, sir. Your breath smells of alcohol and accordingly I require you to take a road-side breath test. Would you please step out of your car and blow into this device?'

Half an hour later, I was sitting miserably in a cold examination room next door to the warrant office in Cannon Row Police Station. The doctor, having drawn a sample of my blood, was filling two separate phials with it. Gloomily, I contemplated my predicament. Almost certainly (although I felt stone-cold sober), analysis would reveal that I was well over the legal limit of eighty milligrams of alcohol in one hundred millilitres of blood. A conviction for a drink-driving offence would probably result in removal from the Director's list as well as my losing my driving licence for a year at least.

After the doctor handed the two samples over, the desk sergeant who was responsible for the legal procedures thereafter, asked me to wait in the warrant office whilst he completed the necessary paperwork. As a lawyer, I knew all about the process and that I wasn't free to leave until the officer had completed the pro-forma which, as well as indicating that I was likely to be prosecuted, outlined my rights as well as giving me the opportunity to make any comments about the matter if I so wished. I would also be informed that one of the samples taken by the doctor would be sent off for analysis to the Home Office Laboratory whilst the other was for me to retain for a private examination.

The sergeant had reached for a stack of forms from a shelf above his desk when a commotion emanated from the door. A grossly fat man with arms covered in lurid tattoos was frogmarched inside by two plain-clothes policemen.

I recognised one of them immediately; it was none other than my boozy copper pal – Detective Sergeant Parch – who only a week or so before had regaled me with the tale of the phantom solicitor – Eric E. Evidge.

'Hellooa, Sir. Seeing you is a surprise – not in bother, are we? George...' He gestured at his companion, 'book this blagger in will you? – whilst I have a word with my friend. Tell the sarge we got Ernie 'ere bang to rights doin' a post office with a shooter.'

Ernie, hands securely cuffed behind his back, shook his head sadly.

'Just wanted a few bob that's all to spend up west like. I only 'ad a kid's gun too.'

'You still waggled a pistol at the geezer behind the counter, Ern. Now then, guv...' Parch turned to me, 'why are you in here?'

I told him briefly. Without saying a word, he made his way to the front desk. The sergeant was in the process of putting labels on the phials of blood which lay on top of the documents relating to my case. Quite calmly, Ernie stood waiting at the side. The other officer had turned away to light a cigarette.

In the corner of my eye, I *thought* I saw Parch's elbow surreptitiously punch Ernie in the side of his stomach. In any event, it caused the big man to double up – his shaven head smashing one of the phials on the desk in half.

Parch grabbed Ernie by the back of his shirt shouting down the former's protestations.

'Sergeant, this prisoner has become violent and is now resisting arrest! He needs to be placed in a cell immediately. Book him in quickly please as a priority!'

'Hang on a minute – I'm in the middle of completing the breathalyser procedure relating to the gentleman over there...'

'That process has now been invalidated due to the misbehaviour of another prisoner – note, you no longer possess two samples of blood as required by law.' Parch sounded confident and authoritative. 'Anyway, police regulations clearly state that a prisoner accused of a violent crime should take precedence over all other matters. You'd better let Mr. Courtley go.'

The sergeant looked puzzled for a moment. He must have wondered how the detective happened to know my name. But the warrant office had begun to fill up with other policemen by now. He shrugged his shoulders and nodded in agreement.

A few days later, I made the mistake of boasting of my near escape to Bill Champney in Tom Tug's.

'It's nothing to be proud of, Charlie. Either this chap Parch deliberately perverted the course of justice on your behalf, or it was just a case of the other fellow Ernie losing his rag. The whole thing doesn't do you any credit however. You could have prejudiced your career in a big way.'

I was still puzzled by one thing though.

'If Parch did punch him – why didn't he complain to the sergeant?'

Bill looked at his watch and finished his drink.

'Old lags like Ernie are used to being assaulted by the police all the time – often for no very good reason. Put it behind you I would – but Charlie, start getting your act together. If you're going to drink, then for God's sake, leave the car at home! Now I must be off and as you know will be on holiday in Italy for a fortnight. In the meantime, there's an ideal opportunity for you to build up your prosecuting practice as I've had a word with Basil Tapner. He's going to send you all the indictments which normally I would be drafting. He has agreed that you can act as my devil.'

This was very good news. 'Devilling' described the practice, common in those days, of helping out a more senior barrister in his work. Bill received regular work from Tapner which included drafting indictments in the more serious cases. Not only would I be paid for the initial preparation, but it also meant that some of the cases would inevitably be returned to me if Bill couldn't do them.

For the rest of the long vacation, I buckled down to work feeling rather chastened by Bill's remarks. Moreover, I felt guilty about letting down Andrea who, poor girl, was still looking after her mother down in Saltdean. I stopped using the car, travelled up to chambers on the bus instead and spent the day at my desk only returning home in the late evening.

I missed being in court though and it was a great relief when, one day, Dennis popped his head round the door.

'Trial down at Middlesex tomorrow, sir. Old client of Mr. Brasper's – who'd like a word about the case...'

I felt that it was high time to be defending again after a month of prosecuting. In fact of late, defence work had declined a fair bit and this was not unconnected with the fact that Ferdy had begun to prosecute for the British Rail Police. Since Le Malle's disappearance to South America, he had decided he wanted to become respectable and in pursuit of this aim, had already been made a recorder (which proved easy enough as the Lord Chancellor wanted more solicitors to be involved in the part-time judiciary). Indeed, rumours abounded that he hoped eventually to become a Crown Court Judge.

'Ah Mr. Courtley,' Brasper's voice echoed fruitily down the line. 'I gather you're representing Purvis tomorrow – a client who's been coming to me for so long that I can't ditch him now despite prosecuting being my main priority these days.'

'No doubt,' I said curtly, not wanting to indulge in irrelevant waffle, 'but is there a specific problem you wish to bring to my attention?'

'Just that our client, Purvis, is a miserable lying toe-rag and the most difficult defendant I've ever had to represent. I've appeared for him many times in front of the Magistrates and he doesn't understand why I can't do the same thing in the Crown Court. Thus I have arranged to come down to Middlesex tomorrow to introduce you – smoothing the path as it were. See you at one o' clock. Trial isn't due to start until two and I'll stay on for the rest of the afternoon.'

I arrived at court to find Ferdy already with the client. The former stood out in the crowd as usual, not just because of the flashing gold rings but also his garish suit – made from a kind of herringbone material interspersed with gold thread – which was matched by a purple tie, itself accentuated by an enormous tie-pin.

'Ah there you are, Mr. Courtley. I've just been explaining to Mr. Purvis here that I can't represent him in the Crown Court as a solicitor but he has in you a most able barrister to do it instead!'

I grimaced. Solicitors who were effusive about your abilities to clients caused embarrassment at the best of times – even more so when those clients didn't get what they wanted later – and this client looked as if he would be hard to please.

Purvis looked remarkably like the late Lord Longford but without the redeeming features of a benign smile and twinkling eyes. Instead his eyes, muddy brown in colour, stared dully at the world; his expression permanently twisted in a leer of resentment. Sprouts of grey-black hair pushed up intermittently from a dome-shaped head which topped a pasty, pockmarked face. A grating whine which passed for a voice completed the ensemble. In short, Purvis looked exactly what he was; one of life's moaning malcontents.

He was charged with stealing goods from the charity shop where he worked; a mean crime entirely in keeping with his general character as an unreliable layabout. The shop had opened in Camberwell and the charity concerned had nobly decided that it should give the long-term unemployed in the area the chance of work.

Accordingly, Purvis was taken on, somewhat unwillingly from his point of view, but having little option due to the authorities threatening to stop the social security that had kept him in relative comfort for many years. In fairness to him however, his criminal record mainly for shoplifting and petty burglary had come to an end about ten years before.

A co-employee, Logan was a much more likeable character altogether. Persistent alcoholism had been his bugbear over the years but when sober, he worked well and was obliging by nature.

Frequently, consignments of old clothes and other discarded household articles arrived at the shop and Logan soon became aware that Purvis was a thief. On the first occasion, he saw the latter take a leather jacket from a pile of jumble and stuff it into a carrier bag left in a storeroom at the back of the shop. Thereafter, he watched Purvis all the time noticing that he continued to thieve on a regular basis. The former remained oblivious throughout assuming that his fellow employee was quite incapable, through drink, of normal observation. In fact, Logan remained on the wagon the entire time.

After a couple of weeks, Logan decided that he should inform somebody of what was going on and chose a particular Saturday when a representative from the charity came in to inspect the shop. The system of accounting was elementary to say the least. No proper inventory appeared to have been kept and the two men simply put cash in the till after supposedly entering a record of sale in a child's exercise book.

On the day in question, the representative appeared just before closing time. As it happened, Logan had seen Purvis remove a coat from a pile earlier and stuff it into his bag. Accordingly, Logan took a Mr. Culver, (the man from the charity) to the storeroom and pointed out the item in Purvis' bag. Culver confronted Purvis who simply said he had purchased it in the normal way but simply forgot to enter the transaction in the exercise book.

Thereafter the investigation was botched to say the least. The police were alerted but no suspicious items were ever recovered. There was a rumour that Purvis might have been flogging goods to a market trader but no proper enquiry as to this was ever made. In the event, the defence to the charge was quite simple. Logan was lying because he had resented Purvis from the start. The former was hoping to become the sole employee in the shop and thus receive better remuneration.

The trial was duly set down before His Honour Judge Onnicks QC. He was an eccentric old fogey whose years at the Bar had been spent in patent chambers so he knew nothing whatsoever about crime – not that that was ever regarded as a disadvantage. Unlike most of his ilk though who normally found crime wholly repugnant and to be quelled if at all possible, this judge wasn't prosecution minded in the least; in fact he rather enjoyed ripping their cases apart just for the fun of it. He was to behave entirely true to form in this case.

Meanwhile, I had to endure Purvis whinging outside court whilst we waited to come on. There were no conference rooms available and Brasper had departed – conveniently pleading an urgent engagement which, regretfully, he had overlooked.

'Diabolical, guv'nor... diabolical to be accused of doin' this terrible thing. Did I not promise Mam after the last bit of bovver that I would never transgress again? Dear little Mam, on her deathbed too when I was nicked, so ill she was…'

With that, he became convulsed with sobs although I couldn't help noticing that his eyes remained bone-dry. I was becoming increasingly nauseated by my client by now and reckoned the jury would be too if he carried in this vein.

'Invoking your beloved departed mother might be going over the top with the jury.' I observed. 'They could just think that you were doing it to get their sympathy, you know.'

'Never, Mr. Courtley – never! Still, if you're advisin' me as a legal man not to bring it up, well I 'ave to bow to your greater knowledge of these things.'

'Let's just concentrate on Logan's unreliability, Mr. Purvis. His evidence is all they've really got against you.'

Judge Onnicks was a small man sporting a black moustache spread thinly over his top lip. Were he not bewigged and begowned, he could easily have been mistaken for a gas-board official – taking into account the clipped, nasal voice which made him sound like one too. Yet his manner belied a keen legal brain for all that.

The trial began and the judge in his neat, precise way began to pick holes in the prosecution's case which wasn't difficult in the circumstances. However, I knew that once the defendant went into the witness box, things could only get worse and so it proved to be. As any criminal lawyer knows, the best witness for the prosecution is always the defendant.

'Mr. Purvis, did you steal any of the items, the subject matter of the indictment against you?'

'Oh, no – Your Lordship – I mean Your Worship – beggin' your pardon, Your Honour. I would never do that. Mr. Logan is so wrong – so *wrrrong!*… it makes me want to weep, it does.'

'Quite so – still Mr. Purvis can you think of any reason why he might want to make up this accusation against you?'

'He wants to run the shop, all on his own like. More pay an' all that…'

I sighed inwardly with relief. If he had just left it that. But, of course, he didn't.

'Your Worshipful Honour – ladies and gentlemen of the jury – I've just got to tell you about my old Mam, my dear old Mam! She was dyin' at the time, she was. Now she's passed over to a more blessed place, Gawd rest her soul! BOO HOO! BOO HOOOOO!'

'Mr. Purvis – I'm sure we all sympathise with you, but the court needs to concentrate on the facts…'

Purvis, however, was just getting into his stride. Clutching his chest, he leant dramatically out of the witness box.

'I would never have done this vile thing to me Mam in her final days. She was so precious to me, she was. Did I not promise her years ago that I would never break the law again… Boo Hoo!'

That does it, I thought sourly. Now the jury knew that he had previous convictions; something which I had been endeavouring to keep out of the frame if at all possible. Mentally, I prayed that a hole would open up in the witness box and he would drop through it never to reappear.

'Perhaps, we could just move on…' I tried to intervene.

'As for that tosser Logan!' He suddenly spat; the flood of tears ceasing abruptly. "He's just a wino tellin' porkies, sod the bastard!'

Suffice it to say that from this moment onwards, we were doomed in the jury's eyes. I could just feel the waves of hostility wafting over from them.

The following day, Purvis was duly convicted despite the judge telling the jury that the prosecution's case was 'wafer thin'. Much to my surprise (and I have to admit, despite being his counsel, sorrow), he was only given a suspended sentence of four months imprisonment. On top of that, he was ordered to pay a contribution towards the costs of the case in the sum of £750.

Well, he had elected for trial by jury; the prosecution would have been quite content for a magistrates' court to deal with it summarily. All in all, I felt he couldn't really complain. Anyway, his beloved *Mam* had owned a flat in Kennington which was rapidly going up in value. Was he not a truly devoted son who had helped his sister to care for the old lady – so bound to benefit from her will surely? When I pointed this out and that he would easily be able to meet the costs when the flat was sold, he exploded in fury.

'That old bag left me nuffink – bleedin' zilch, guv'nor. Everything goes to my sister, see. True I hadn't seen the old biddy in years but I was there when she was gasping her last – bugger her!'

After that, I parted company with Mr. Purvis as soon as I could – understanding just how Ferdy Brasper felt about the man. Not that the latter had bothered to come back at the end of the trial and share in the burden of being the recipient of the wails and moans which were still ringing in my ears as I left the court building.

TWENTY-ONE

'Dobstowe – where the blazes is that?' I enquired of Leslie as he handed me my brief.

'Along the coast from Felixstowe, I believe Sah – in Suffolk. It's a sizeable port in its own right too. There's been a fair bit of publicity about the place recently. A lot of dockers were arrested for nicking stuff – in fact, you're defending one of the thieves.'

I was intrigued. I fancied getting my teeth into a decent defence brief after the unhappy experience of the Purvis case. Glancing at the indictment, I noticed the charge was one of conspiracy to steal involving three defendants. Returning to my room, I began to read the prosecution witness statements which revealed the following scenario...

My client, Des Lemper, wasn't a docker as such but employed by Dobstowe Docks itself to shift cargo for them when required. As a result, he became friendly with the regular dockers he mixed with at work and saw nothing wrong with being supplied by them with sugar for his tea – replenishing the plastic cup he kept in his cab at frequent intervals. That way, a welcome cuppa was always available.

So it came as a huge shock when, on attempting to leave the docks one day, he found four marked police cars blocking the exit. A burly chap flashed a warrant card and announced that he was a member of the recently set up Dockland Fraud Squad.

'We have reason to suspect, sir, that you are involved in a

conspiracy to steal a substantial amount of sugar, the property of the Dobstowe Dock Corporation,' he said his eyes alighting on Des' cup of sugar by now half-empty as the latter hadn't filled it up that day, 'and I observe,' continued this eagle-eyed sleuth, 'there to be a quantity of sugar in that cup. I intend therefore to seize the aforementioned item as an exhibit believing its contents to be stolen. Have you anything to say?'

Crucial to the case against Des was, according to this policeman, his immediate reaction. Allegedly, he touched his nose with a finger, winked and stated, 'Well, I knows it to be dodgy like – but it's only for me brew on the road!'

In due course, Des found himself indicted with two other co-defendants. The particulars simply alleged that the three defendants had conspired to steal a quantity of sugar, the property of the Dobstowe Docks Corporation.

The police had been keeping observation of the docks over a period of some months and seen two dockers (Des' co-defendants) removing crates from a warehouse. Later, on information received, they raided a lock-up garage in Dagenham and discovered a considerable amount of sugar in crates waiting to be sold. Enquiries revealed the lock-up to be rented by the two dockers who were subsequently arrested and made full confessions.

I looked up to find Leslie grinning at me.

'I've just been in touch with the list office in Dobstowe. Your judge, Sah for the week is no less a personage than Ferdinand Brasper, Solicitor of the Supreme Court sitting as a recorder.'

'Ferdy! I wonder what the hell he'll be like when they let him off the leash on the bench. Less flashy, let's hope.'

'Oh Sah, we must keep Mr. Brasper happy. I've been angling for some of that British Rail work for ages…'

'Just as long as he keeps out of the arena,' I muttered. Solicitor Judges had the reputation for being prosecution-minded on the bench – probably as a result of having to deal with villains in their normal work at first hand.

I duly had a conference with the client that afternoon and the trial began the following day.

Ferdy Brasper seemed to have lost his air of joviality on the Bench. Indeed, gravitas was the order of the day. Gone was the purplish suit and many of the gaudy rings; he now wore the classic lawyer's garb of black jacket and pin-striped trousers. His fruity voice was the same although he spoke more ponderously, anxious no doubt to demonstrate what an efficient judge he intended to be.

'Let us proceed without delay please. The defendants should stand for their pleas to be taken.'

When the indictment was duly put to them, Des pleaded not guilty and the others guilty. Sentence was put back until the conclusion of Des's trial when, if he was convicted, all three would be sentenced.

In the absence of the jury, I raised a point concerning the legal admissibility of some of the evidence.

After Des's alleged remark about the sugar in his cup being 'dodgy', Temporary Detective Constable Budgeworth had arrested my client but not cautioned him – that is informing him that he was not obliged to say anything but anything he did say would be taken down and given in evidence. My objection was that this explanation of the defendant's legal rights hadn't been administered before the 'verbal' – so it should be excluded.

'Not cautioning the defendant, Your Honour, is contrary to the Judges' Rules of 1964.' I submitted. These rather vague regulations predated the Police and Criminal Evidence Act by some years and indicated that judges could always exclude evidence in a criminal trial if they thought it had been obtained in any way unfairly.

'Accordingly, this is a classic case for exclusion,' I concluded after reviewing the authorities, 'the prejudicial effect of such evidence clearly outweighing any probative value.'

Brasper, as I anticipated, dealt with my submission in a pompous and verbose manner.

'As a judge, I must consider the consequential importance and significance of the use of my judicial discretion taking into account all the relevant features which appertain specifically to the evidence in this trial. The law, as expressed by the Judges' Rules and interpreted in a number of well-known authorities some of which have been referred to in argument during the course of counsel's speeches – '

Oh, get on with it, I thought. As it was the only evidence in the case against my client anyway, I doubted he would be prepared to exclude it.

'-leads to one conclusion only. The evidence will be admitted.'

Surprise, surprise!

At the appropriate time, I stood up to cross-examine TDC Budgeworth and wasted no time in challenging the verbal.

'Officer, you made your note several hours after arresting my client, did you not?'

'I don't know about several hours, sir. It was within three hours of my return to the police station. In fact, that was the first available opportunity for me to do it.'

'I accept that, but in making it you relied only on your own recollection. Nobody else witnessed this conversation with the defendant, did they?'

'No sir, I was the only officer who actually approached his cab, it's true.'

'And that was because he really wasn't a target, was he? You were on the look-out for dishonest dockers suspected of stealing items from their place of work... so let me deal with what I suggest are inaccuracies in your evidence. For instance, he scratched his nose and didn't tap it!'

'No sir, he tapped it.'

'Come on, officer. This was a December evening – five minutes past six, to be exact as you recorded in your notebook. It was dark in my client's cab too – he had just pulled away! It could have been a scratch surely rather than a tap?'

'Police officers are trained to observe, sir. I know what I saw.'

'You could be mistaken though,' I countered. 'Admit that at least!'

'Quite impossible, sir.'

I sighed ostentatiously taking care that the jury noticed.

'Now, about the detail of the actual conversation you had with my client – there's no dispute about the contents, you see – just who said what! I suggest you didn't say – *I intend to seize the aforementioned item* – meaning the cup of sugar or – *I believe it to be stolen*. Nor did he say – *well, I knows it to be dodgy-like*. You said – *this looks dodgy to me* – and he added and to this extent we agree – *it's only for me brew on the road!*'

'No sir, what's in my note is one hundred percent accurate.'

Truly living up to his name, he refused to 'budge' from this stance.

The farce of it was that so much time was wasted before the Police and Criminal Evidence Act 1984 in having to challenge these ridiculous verbals, (easy for the police to concoct by 'improving' perfectly innocent remarks or by downright fabrication) which required hours of cross-examination; otherwise bad-tempered judges would bellow – *that wasn't put!* – if defendants disagreed with police evidence when they found themselves in the witness box. It all went back to the basic rule that the defence case always had to be put to the prosecution witnesses in advance.

Nonetheless, it couldn't be denied that the evidence against my client was pretty thin. On the basis of the one verbal, he was supposed to be part of a broad agreement to steal sugar together with his co-defendants. There was no other link between them whatsoever.

The case continued apace and lunchtime came. I left the courtroom and espied my opponent puffing a Turkish cigarette through a holder.

'Where's the Bar Mess then?' I enquired.

Giles Crossett blew a perfect smoke ring and smiled.

'No such thing here at Dobstowe, dear boy. We're not at the Old Bailey now. However, I know of a nice little pub just off the waterfront where they serve real ale and I can recommend their Ploughman's which comes with a very good Stilton. Will you join me?'

One of the delights of the Bar in those days was the camaraderie of fellow barristers when not in court. I readily agreed and we travelled there in his midnight-blue Bristol smelling deliciously of leather and tobacco.

Although we had never been against each other before, I knew that at one time he had been a very busy junior prosecuting the Director's cases at the Old Bailey. This whole affair seemed a bit of a come-down for him. As if he knew what I was thinking, he explained.

'I grew tired of living in London and moved the entire family to the country. My wife set up a riding stables business and I help her to run it. My clerk still sends me work in Suffolk and Essex so I keep my hand in. The rest of the time,' he grinned, 'I relax, if that is an apt description of spending more time with the children!'

In due course, we were comfortably seated on a padded bench inside the pub. Crossett sipped his pint of real ale appreciatively.

'About the only compensation of coming anywhere near the Dobstowe *palais de justice*,' he observed, 'is this pub and its locally-brewed beer.'

I agreed. The court building had only recently been converted from an old warehouse and done on the cheap so its facilities were minimal. An upsurge of criminal work had required the creation of a further court centre in the area so the whole thing had gone up in six months flat.

'Bad luck, old chap, about not getting the verbals excluded but no doubt you'll have a go at trying to get the whole thing chucked at half-time?'

'Possibly,' I wasn't going to elaborate.

In fact, I felt pretty confident about the success of my submission of there being 'no case to answer' at the end of the prosecution's case. Des's verbals in themselves didn't make him guilty of a criminal conspiracy. There was no suggestion that he was connected to his co-defendants who had pleaded guilty in any way at all. Merely stating that his daily quota of sugar might be a bit dodgy couldn't be enough surely? Crossett's eyes twinkled at me as he finished his pint.

'Leaving me in suspense, are you, old lad? Well, we'll see what this new recorder makes of it all.'

I duly made my application at quarter past four in the afternoon. Not surprisingly, Ferdy indicated he would rule on it the next day.

Not long afterwards, I made my way down to the train station to go back to London – to be presented by what was a typical problem at the time. 'Unofficial strike action at Liverpool Street means that there are no through trains running to London this evening, sir,' the ticket collector told me, 'but you can still get there by picking up the fast train from Ipswich. There's a stopping service due up there in about three minutes.'

As this train drew in, I became aware of a familiar puffing figure hurrying in the same direction. 'Ah hello, Courtley – confounded nuisance about the train eh? I suppose we're both heading for London but best keep apart as I am your judge after all!'

'Yes indeed.' I was thankful enough not to have to share his company.

On embarkation, the train chugged its way slowly down the line and then both of us had to rush for the connecting train at Ipswich station. As it had made several unscheduled stops from Norwich already, second class was packed. Seeing that the first class dining-car was virtually empty, I entered it deciding that I would treat myself to their Afternoon Tea Special.

Thankfully, I flopped down on a high-backed seat which

ensured some privacy. Doors slammed and then I heard puffing which sounded only too familiar in the next section just behind me. Moments later came a muffled exclamation.

'My Lord – how delightful to see you.'

'Brasper! What brings you to this neck of the woods? Trying to get one of your regular villains *orf*, are we?' A gruff voice answered.

'Oh, no, no, no – I'm sitting, My Lord. They've made me a recorder, you see.'

'Good grief!' The words rang with disbelief.

'Yes – one of the few solicitors to have been so created - indeed, I'm conducting my very first jury trial at the moment.'

This was definitely going to be a conversation worth eavesdropping particularly as I knew instantly who Brasper's companion was. No less than the Lord Chief Justice himself – 'Flogger' Flaggett. I was all ears but I wondered whether I was to be disappointed. There came only the rustling sound of a newspaper and then complete silence. Flaggett probably hoped he wouldn't have to talk to Brasper at all. I wondered where the great man was headed but then recalled that he was sitting in Norwich Crown Court trying a murder. He was probably going up to town for an official engagement.

'My lord, I wonder whether I might crave your indulgence for a moment on a point of law?'

'Well, if you must.'

'A submission of no case has just been made by the defence...' Brasper waffled on for a good two minutes before being cut short.

'Don't allow it – simple as that!'

'Ah – thank you Judge – my thoughts entirely. Naturally, I shall have to give reasons for my decision.'

'Forget all that rot. Just say that there's a case to answer. Giving reasons could lead to problems in the Court of Appeal if you get them wrong. Moreover,' and he let forth an evil chuckle, 'even if there is no case at the half-way stage, you can be sure that there will be one by the time chummy gives evidence – that's because the best witness for the prosecution is generally the defendant. Never forget that basic principle Brasper!'

'Ha, ha Judge – what sterling advice if I may say so.'

Had I not seen an example of this myself recently in the case of Purvis? But to hear it so cynically put by England's most senior judge caused me to boil with indignation. I had heard enough. Having lost my appetite, I left the carriage prepared to stand for the rest of the journey, feeling utter disgust for the hard-bitten old bugger.

After chewing it over for a while, I made up my mind. I wouldn't call Des to give evidence and defy the jury to convict of conspiracy! This would amount to no more than a defendant exercising his fundamental right – to simply sit back and challenge the prosecution to prove their case without any assistance from him – but it was nonetheless a risk. A natural reaction would always be; what does he have to hide if he really is innocent? Yet I did have some good points to make. Because the police were busy investigating other aspects of the conspiracy, no formal interview with Des had actually taken place on his arrest. He had been released on bail and by the time such an interview was arranged, he had, as he was perfectly entitled, refused to answer any questions on legal advice.

The next day, Brasper duly rejected my application in the simplest possible terms.

'I find against you, Mr. Courtley. There is clearly a case to answer and so I do not need to trouble you, Mr. Crossett.' Glancing round, I noticed the latter's eyebrows shoot up but he said nothing. Ferdy sat back and uncapped his fountain-pen with a flourish.

'I take it you're calling your client, Mr. Courtley?'

'No, Your Honour, the defence present no evidence.'

Disconcerted, the judge waved his pen about like a wand. A mixed expression of worry and anger crossed his face.

'Did you inform the Court Clerk of this fact in advance? It could affect the listing of other cases.' He glared at me.

I was taken aback. 'No – I'm not required to give any notice. My client isn't obliged to give evidence after all!'

'Nonetheless, valuable court time costing public money has been wasted. After your speech, I shall have to rise.'

I kept my address short and sweet. What did my client actually have to challenge and where was the evidence that he was involved in any wide-ranging conspiracy? – the nub of the allegation against him.

'Chap's obviously in a panic,' Crossett murmured after Brasper hurried out, 'he didn't anticipate having to sum up until tomorrow giving him plenty of time to prepare it.'

Now, I understood. If my client had given evidence, he would undoubtedly have been in the box for a couple of hours. There would then be two speeches and Ferdy wouldn't be summing up until the following day. In the event, there had only been one speech because it wasn't customary for the prosecution to make a final address to a jury if the defence called no evidence.

When the judge did return two hours later, it was obvious that he had written out his summing-up in longhand. I suppose you couldn't blame him for being careful; it was the very first time he was actually doing it and no wet-behind-the ears recorder wanted to be upset by the Court of Appeal in his very first trial.

At the end of it, he turned to the jury.

'Members of the jury, have you appointed a foreman as yet?'

A bird-like elderly lady, wearing pince-nez perched at the end of her nose, stood up. She looked every inch a retired schoolteacher.

'Madam Foreman, you will be responsible for chairing the discussions about the appropriate verdict and delivering it in due course. I will now invite you to retire.'

'That won't be necessary thank you, Your Honour.'

'Madam, I must insist you leave the courtroom and consider your verdict in the jury's retiring room. Now, if you would just follow the usher...'

The lady peered up at the judge through her pince-nez.

'But why should we? We intend to acquit, after all. That is our right, is it not – under the Common Law of England?'

'Well, yes...'

'So, not guilty it will be. Surely, Mr. Lemper is entitled to that disposal sooner rather than later,' she added reprovingly.

A tittering broke out in the public gallery. Brasper grew red in the face.

'Let Lemper stand for the jury to find him not guilty,' he barked. After my client had been formally acquitted, the former was determined to take it out on somebody – and the person he had in his sights was me!

'Mr. Courtley – in view of the collapse of the prosecution's case in the trial, I put this to you. Why did this matter reach the Crown Court at all? Was consideration given to having an old style committal here? Such a course might have led to the dismissal of the charge against your client much earlier. Why shouldn't I order that he pay a contribution towards his own legal aid costs?'

I was taken aback. An 'old-style' committal, where some of the witnesses were actually called to give evidence in the lower court (once common practice in all criminal trials) was only ever held where the defence specifically requested it so that an application could be made to the magistrates' court to throw the case out. Because such hearings rarely succeeded, they were infrequently held.

I was flummoxed for a moment until I remembered what had happened earlier on! How dare Brasper criticize the way the defence had conducted their case at an initial stage, when he himself had rejected my submission of no case to answer? But I was unable to get in a word as he was now in full flood.

'It is the duty of those of us who only sit on the bench from time to time as well as full-time members of the judiciary, to ensure that public expenditure is kept to an absolute minimum bearing in mind the inflationary times in which we live and the general state of the economy...' (There was much more of this portentous waffle which went on for several minutes.)

I was so angry that I began to eye my copy of Archbold – the criminal practitioner's bible – contemplating what the consequences would be if I flung it at him. No doubt my fledgling career would be abruptly terminated but, at least, chucking it might shut him up!

In the event, such drastic action wasn't necessary. Giles Crossett rose languidly to his feet.

In a firm voice, finely tuned to reproving recalcitrant witnesses needing to be controlled during trials, he said.

'Just one moment...'

Brasper stopped in mid-sentence.

'Your Honour must surely remember that the defence made a submission of no case to answer which you rejected. Moreover – ' He glanced at me and I discerned the slightest wink. '- you didn't call upon the prosecution to reply. Had you done so, you would have known that the Crown did not intend to oppose my learned friend's application anyway.'

Brasper spluttered indignantly but there was no answer to this; he contented himself with a brusque 'oh, very well' – before rushing off the bench.

* * *

'Let's have a bottle of bubbly to celebrate,' I glanced at Andrea's face smiling in the soft candlelight. 'My wife is back, there's money in the bank and plenty more work to come...'

Things were good. I may have made Brasper look a fool but a firm of Dobstowe solicitors had learnt of my success and were going to instruct me in the future. Moreover, now that I was drafting indictments regularly for Basil Tapner, the cash flow position had improved considerably too. Most important of all, I had my darling Andrea safely back. Her father, seriously ill for some time, had made a complete recovery after a heart by-pass operation and was back home permanently.

I raised my glass, clinking it with Andrea's.

'Darling, it's all been a bit of a struggle so far but we're well on our way now.'

More fool me to have forgotten the old saw – pride always comes before a fall – as events were soon to prove.

TWENTY TWO

Isidore, to be brutally frank, was simply a nasty piece of work. With a track record in petty crime, he had become violent; graduating allegedly from simple mugging to the crime of armed robbery of a jeweller's shop with a sawn-off shotgun. To hide his identity, he had worn a balaclava helmet over his head. The gun had never been recovered but the mask had – and been found to contain a sample of his hair in the crown. To top it all, he had made a 'full and frank' confession of everything to the Robbery Squad in interview – which, in this instance, had been recorded contemporaneously although not actually signed by him. These were the facts which confronted me when, one fine day, I appeared to represent him in Court One at the Old Bailey in front of His Honour Judge Cedric Wintringham.

Any defence to the charge was negligible but that didn't mean Isidore intended to admit the charge. On the contrary, he was fighting all the way. It was all a dreadful coincidence according to him – being in the wrong place at the wrong time and then foolishly trying on an abandoned balaclava for size – an item which just happened to be lying in the middle of the street!

But as these were his instructions, I was required to act on them. Where the truth lies is never defence counsel's responsibility because under our adversarial system, it is for the prosecution to prove a defendant's guilt not for the latter to prove his innocence.

For the three days of the trial, I caught a train from Peckham and travelled to Holborn Viaduct station which ran overground to just opposite the Central Criminal Court building. Once there, I partook of a large breakfast in the Bar Mess before ambling down to Wintry's court.

The case was a very important one from the point of view of my practice. I had been instructed for the very first time by a well-known firm of London solicitors – Silverside's no less – who operated from an office in Ludgate Circus and represented many of the big London villains. Moreover I had the redoubtable 'Cuffs' Cuthbertson against me and although an acquittal was hardly expected, a good performance would do me no end of good.

Now I sat in a secure interview room located in the bowels of the building with Isidore and my solicitor's clerk. In appearance, Isidore looked not unlike the late Jimi Hendrix but without the redeeming feature of the singer's attractive, rather zany grin. Instead, his cold expression radiated sullen resentment against all authority particularly the police. There was menace and malice in the very way he spoke. I was glad, in a psychological sense, of the protective armour of my wig and gown.

'I'm obliged to tell you that the evidence is strong, Mr. Isidore, if not to say overwhelming. Admittedly, the gun was never recovered but there's the hair found in the balaclava and your admissions in the police interviews...'

'Fuck them pigs, man! I ain't nevvah 'avin' them verbals, no way – they wouldn't let me 'ave a brief even!'

There was no dispute that he had been refused legal representation after requesting it and that such a denial was, on the face of it, a breach of his rights.

The police could, in some serious cases, deny a defendant legal representation but only on specific grounds laid out in case law. For instance, if contacting a lawyer might lead to – 'interference with or harm to evidence connected with a serious offence' or – 'the alerting of other persons suspected of having committed such an offence' or – 'will hinder the recovery of property obtained as a result of such an offence.'

To give the appearance of legitimacy, the interview was recorded contemporaneously with the police dutifully writing down all the questions and, if my client was to be believed, inventing all the answers which comprised a full and frank confession to the crime. To cover every angle, they even maintained that they had asked him to sign at the bottom of each page and he had flatly refused – all very neat, you might think from their point of view.

By now, Isidore was pointing his finger at me aggressively.

'I ain't acceptin' them lies, see – an' you gotta slaughter the filth, man!'

I suspected that was his principal objective. The length of the sentence at the end of the day was quite immaterial to him.

It wasn't the first time I had come across this particular mentality. Many criminals just wanted to have their 'day in court' and watch the police (seen by them as tormentors) squirm in the witness box.

I took my leave and returned to the Bar Mess for a light lunch. Every so often, I thought wryly, a case posed a real challenge – little did I know then quite how testing it would prove to be!

The case wasn't due to start until mid-afternoon and this didn't exactly help either. I was at my best in the morning and dreaded the timing. The most difficult part of the case was going to be cross-examining the police – and I would have to embark on that well after four o' clock in the afternoon. Moreover, Wintry had decided to sit until nigh on six o' clock every day as he was determined, because of other commitments, to finish the case within three days.

Furthermore, I wasn't in a very happy frame of mind that day anyway because Andrea and I had had a tiff the night before – due to her blessed Aunt Imogen.

'She fell down the stairs this morning, darling and fractured an ankle. Pretty debilitating when you're seventy-eight years old. I have to go and look after her for a while.'

'But you've only just come home! Why can't Vera do it instead? She is her daughter after all.'

'Well – Vera would if I didn't, I suppose but she's so busy with her job. The fact is, as a nurse, I'm really more suited anyway...'

'Is that a good enough reason for leaving me on my own again?' I complained.

'Oh, Charlie, don't be so grumpy! Aunt Imogen was an absolute sweetie to me when I had all that teen trouble with my mother.'

'Well, at least leave me the cats for company.'

'We've discussed this before. They are so much better off with me – quite used to travelling in their baskets nowadays. Anyway, look at the irregular hours you keep – mucks up their routine completely.'

'What about your job then? They'll be getting fed-up with all the time you have taken off!'

'The Matron has been very understanding about it all. She's persuaded my temporary replacement to stay a bit longer.'

'Well, I will just have to bloody put up with it, I suppose. You'd better be off – I see you're packed already. Meanwhile I've got a heavy brief to read.'

'For God's sake, Charlie – I only heard this afternoon. You're not the only person who has a life you know – perhaps, you should damn well try to be less selfish!'

With that, she grabbed the cat baskets and stormed out of the door.

I rang her later from a local phone box and humbly apologised. But I still felt depressed – returning to a cold, empty flat at the end of a draining day at the Old Bailey wasn't going to be much fun. One thing I did know was that the case would be tough-going...

At three o' clock sharp, the jury panel trooped in. I recalled a tactic that Dan Rydehope had advocated over a drink in Tom Tug's.

'Forget about the evidence in a hopeless case. Just size up the jury as people. Try and work out what you think the prejudices of just a few of them might be. Then concentrate solely on that selection. Twelve are just too many. Now, if you happen to have a young black chap and the defence is a fit-up – well, it's possible that he's been stopped in his car for no good reason by a racist copper. That's quite likely in London. On the other hand, you might get a middle-aged matron – who feels sorry for your client and wants to mother him – it's that sort of approach really.'

It was good advice although somehow I couldn't imagine anybody wishing to mother Isidore – even his real mother must have had quite a job!

So I looked carefully at each juror as the court clerk summoned them into the jury box in turn. Names didn't register; only appearances mattered and I would provide appropriate nicknames myself. Nobody stood out until a girl appeared who might have been pretty were she not wearing horn-rimmed spectacles and hid her hair under a black woollen bobble cap. She hardly glanced at the defendant and looked thoroughly bored so I dismissed her instantly. Then a black man with a shock of frizzy hair was called. Perhaps he wouldn't like the police; I nicknamed him *Affro*. He was followed by a trendy-looking chap with shoulder–length blonde hair, wearing a denim jacket and jeans and speaking with a mid-Atlantic twang; I nicknamed him *Heyman*. Finally, I chose an earnest-looking chap wearing a corduroy jacket and clutching a copy of the Guardian who looked worriedly at the dock; I named him *Gardi*.

My initial assessment over, I sat back to listen to Cuff's opening speech.

According to the verbals, Isidore told the police that he had disposed of the gun 'at a mates' but refused to elaborate. So, on the face of it, a denial of legal representation might just be justified on the basis that a lawyer could pass on a message to a friend.

There was a real art in cross-examining the police particularly in the days when verbals were so rife. Naturally, you looked for material from any records which were supplied and might help trip them up but the Robbery Squad were skilled in covering their tracks pretty carefully. Lacking anything like that, all you could do was to challenge them in a convincingly critical way using every actor's trick in the book. All you were really doing was making bricks without straw. It was pure theatre really – done to keep the client happy and keep him out of your hair!

Regrettably, as far as errors in the records were concerned, I hadn't found anything so far.

Detective Inspector Burton was the first officer to go into the box. I made little headway with him. His answers to the court, rebutting my suggestions in cross-examination, were given quietly and firmly. I had to fall back on hot air and little else. We parried and thrust for three quarters of an hour finishing just before the adjournment for the day.

After the judge left court, there was a short delay before the prison officers took Isidore back to the cells. At that point, a shout emanated from the public gallery.

'Hey Izzy, howya doin'? That police pig jus' shat over you, man. Your mouthpiece ain't no fuckin' good. Get rid of him, man. Sack the bastard!'

Isidore, already in a highly charged state, began to shout back but the prison staff were determined to prevent any illicit chat and bundled him out of the back door.

Later in the cells, my client began to sound off at me.

'You didn't give that pig hell, man! I wanted the bastard to squirm!'

In vain, I tried to reassure him that I was doing as much as I could but he wasn't mollified and I left the cells that evening with his fulsome complaints still ringing in my ears.

It was after seven o' clock in the evening when I finally left the court building feeling badly in need of a drink. The Magpie and Stump was the obvious place; just across the road. I was in no rush to return to the flat contemplating a cheerless supper of ravioli on toast. Andrea would normally have left me with a tasty snack to tide me over but her hasty departure (all my own fault, of course) had put paid to that.

The pub was gradually emptying as I entered which suited my rather gloomy mood. In next to no time, I downed my third large Scotch relishing the anaesthetic effect of the alcohol. Barristers, emotionally drained by the effort of sorting out other people's problems often use strong drink to replenish the void. Successful advocacy may be an art but it can hardly be called creative. On the whole, I escaped this trap; Andrea and our two cats providing me with a loving home – but not that night.

By eight o'clock, the pub was empty apart from a couple of office security guards having a swift drink before going on duty and one girl on her own. The barman glanced at his watch and yawned. Realising that the place probably closed early because of its location, I ordered another Scotch and took a closer look at the young female sitting in the corner…

At that point, she looked in my direction and I realised how attractive she was. Large hazel eyes were framed in an oval face about which lustrous black hair fell. I guessed she might be of Spanish or Portuguese origin. She was alone; I was alone. What the hell. Why not chat her up?

Draining my glass, I called across the room.

'You look a bit sad sitting there on your own – fancy a drink?'

She smiled and I noticed the delicious way her mouth curved upwards.

'Why not… Campari soda, thank you.'

Moments later, we were sharing the same table.

'What's a girl like you doing sitting on her own at this time of the evening?' I was too drunk to be anything but corny.

'Oh, you know. Relationship problems. I work across the road as a shorthand writer and got involved with a barrister doing a fraud case. It went on for a few weeks – as did our affair but both finished this morning. He's gone back to his wife in Leeds.' There was a tremor in her voice.

After this exchange, my recollection becomes hazy. I believe I had a final drink (possibly more) and Debbie (she did tell me her name) had at least another Campari. Other than that, I only recall us going our separate ways but somewhere along the line we made a casual arrangement to meet up the next day...

TWENTY-THREE

The following day, I awoke with a foul hangover and consumed with guilt. How would Andrea feel if she knew about my shenanigans the night before? However, I needed to concentrate on the hard day's work ahead of me.

Later, I was in the robing room putting on my wing collar when Douglas Bergson appeared clutching a bundle of papers.

Douglas was employed by the Director of Public Prosecutions department at the Old Bailey as a clerk. Squeezed generally into a suit slightly too small for his fleshy frame, he tended to fuss which made him sweat and led to the pungent presence of body odour. I caught a whiff of this before he spoke.

'Ah, Mr. Courtley – sir! Here's some papers. I should have served them on you before. Unused material in the case of Isidore. You ought to have been given it with the prosecution papers at committal for trial following the Attorney-General's new guidelines.'

Recently, The Court of Appeal had allowed a number of appeals because vital material in the possession of the prosecution had not been disclosed to the defence. As a result, the Attorney-General had issued strict instructions to the prosecuting authorities that, in future, all such material however insignificant it might appear, should be served as a matter of course.

This would include, for instance, any statements taken by the police and not used for the actual prosecution as well as copies of the notebooks of the arresting officers. Even rough notes were supposed to be included although these were easy enough to get rid of in advance!

With almost an hour to spare, I riffled through the bundle hoping to discover any information which might assist in the case. But the Robbery Squad weren't stupid – whatever private notes they might have made about the case would obviously have been destroyed.

Not on this occasion though.

Right at the bottom of the bundle appeared a carbon copy of a booking-in sheet; the original of which had been filled in by a custody sergeant. It simply listed the property which Isidore had on him when he was brought to the police station and wasn't itself significant. The robbery squad officers must simply have been given it for information when they took over the investigation. It was what was on the back which caught my attention. One of them had been doodling…

Questions

Balaclava belongs to you? (Found near scene – forensics will check it out) Where gun? Check Izzy's mates – put in Izzy fingers Welly Peel – we could nick him for aiding and abetting – he's well due for it!

This last part was particularly intriguing.

Wellington Peel was well known to those of us who had dealings with criminals in the South London area. A jovial middle-aged Jamaican, he ran a 'shebeen' (an unlicensed drinking club) in Railton Road which catered for the social needs of the local low-life. In addition, the old rogue was a colourful local character who often appeared on television speaking up for 'black rights' when problems in the Brixton area surfaced. It was an open secret that the police had been out to get him for years but been constrained somewhat for political reasons. However, an excuse, even if contrived, to turn over his place might prove to be tempting indeed. Perhaps that's why the Robbery Squad contemplated verballing Isidore in this way at one point- so as to put Welly Peel in the frame.

My mind was whirring by now. In the end, the police obviously thought better of the idea and decided that it was too dangerous a ploy. Welly might be an unsavoury character but it had never ever been suggested that he harboured guns for robbers.

I checked the handwriting. It matched that of the officer who had actually compiled the contemporaneous record – and that was Detective Sergeant Binns who was to give evidence next. I had real ammunition now and the important thing was to use it at a stage when it could be most effective. Accordingly, Binns needed to be lulled into a false sense of security.

Covertly, I sized him up as I walked past him outside court. He was a square-faced chap with red hair and a bushy moustache of the same hue. He was younger than Burton and probably less experienced.

I hoped to be able to speak to Isidore in court just before the judge entered. However, the gaolers were late in bringing him up so I had no time to inform him that I had a welcome surprise for him in store. Thus the case resumed.

Deliberately, I soft-pedalled Binns so that he would think he was in for an easy ride. It seemed to work as he began to answer my questions with an air of feigned surprise looking at the judge and glancing at the jury - a sure sign of an over-confident police officer.

At the crucial point, I pretended to be particularly hesitant patting my papers as if I had mislaid something.

'Just one last thing, Officer.'

And then the defendant almost ruined the whole thing.

'Hey, Judge! I don't want this geezer to represent me no more!' Isidore had risen from his seat in the dock.

You bastard, I thought and sat down. What did I care after all – he deserved everything that was coming to him!

'Sit down please,' Wintry's thin voice was icy. 'Mr. Courtley, were you aware that your client was going to address me in this way?'

'No My Lord, but if my client so desires... I'm happy enough to be discharged.'

'That I shall not allow particularly at this juncture. Such a request is quite impertinent and wholly inexcusable. Your cross-examination will proceed.'

So it did.

I focussed my attention on the witness once more.

'Does the name Wellington Peel mean anything to you Officer?'

The judge wasn't prepared to let this pass without a judicial aside.

'It certainly does to me, Mr.Courtley. Two distinguished former prime ministers – but then I read history at university.'

The jury tittered and I groaned inwardly. I didn't want to give the officer time to think.

'He's better known, in fact, as Welly... a middle-aged Jamaican gentleman who runs a shebeen in Brixton, is that not the case?'

'Shebeen?' The judge raised his eyebrows.

'Drinking club, My Lord – of the unlicensed variety. Well, officer?'

'Welly Peel is known to the police, My Lord...'

'More than known, surely. The police suspect that Mr. Peel's club is a haven for young criminals, do they not?'

'If you say so, sir.'

'I certainly do and just to confirm it, Welly Peel isn't mentioned in the interviews you had with my client, is he?'

'No indeed, sir. Had he been we would have recorded it. We were particularly anxious to recover the gun if we could.'

'Precisely – that was the whole reason for denying Isidore a solicitor, was it not? Now, by the way, which of Isidore's associates did you actually contact?'

'We're very busy in the Robbery Squad, sir. I can't recall after all this time, I'm afraid.'

'Why then did you conclude that it was high time Welly was nicked?'

The witness looked affronted.

'I'm not sure that I follow your line of argument, sir.'

'I see, so those words don't ring any bells in your memory at all?'

'I'm not sure I approve of the word *nick*, Mr. Courtley,' Wintry chipped in once again. 'Try not to use colloquialisms in place of the proper terminology.'

'There's a very good reason for it in this case, My Lord,' I decided to be bold, – and I insist on sticking to it. Officer, would you now look at this document?'

I produced the booking-in sheet with a flourish.

'That's your writing, isn't it?'

'Yes, it is.'

'You see where you've written... *Welly Peel – we could nick him for aiding and abetting – he's well due for it.*'

'Yes...'

'Now just tell us please what immediately precedes the excerpt that I've just read?'

'*Where gun? Check Izzy's mates- put in Izzy fingers Welly Peel...*'

'Exactly, you were contemplating pretending that my client mentioned Welly Peel, weren't you?'

'No – there's no reference to this person in the interview.'

'Only because you obviously thought better of dragging his name up – perhaps it was just too risky. The fact is that you can't explain these words away, can you?'

D.S Binns was no longer nodding to the judge or jury. Instead, there was a long pause whilst he nervously stroked his moustache.

'I don't know... to be frank I have no recollection of Peel being part of this investigation.'

Tactically, it was time to stop. I had done enough, I hoped, to leave a nasty feeling of suspicion hanging in the air. After requesting that the document be made an exhibit, I resumed my seat.

The prosecution didn't re-examine and the witness withdrew. I noted with satisfaction that his face was now bright red matching the colour of his hair and moustache perfectly.

By now, it was lunch-time and after a quick snack in the public canteen, it was time for a vital conference with the client and Silverside's representative – Tom Worlock. If anybody knew villains, it was Worlock who, as a Detective Inspector in the CID for many years, had dealt with them extensively on the other side of the fence as it were. Although he had retired after twenty-five years in the police, there were rumours that he might have been pushed – apocryphal stories of backhanders abounded. But Tom knew his business and at this point of the trial, that was crucial.

'I wanna go in the box, man – an' slag off them pigs!'

Isidore was nothing if not pithy about what he wanted to do in the trial.

Removing a chewed pipe from his mouth and mopping his beefy face with a silk handkerchief (it was hot in the bowels of the Old Bailey), Worlock banged his fist on the table.

'Now look here, Izzy. We discussed the options when I first saw you after you were charged. The police case, which looked as solid as a block of concrete weighing down a stiff at the bottom of the river, has cracked – this young gent here has rumbled Binns enough to create a doubt. If you go into that witness box, you'll sink yourself for sure and collect a ten or fifteen stretch – think about it, boy!'

I kept quiet leaving it to Tom to do the running. Instead, I was concentrating on what I needed to say to the jury.

Finally, Isidore nodded his head.

'Okay, okay, man – I stay in the dock.'

'Good lad,' Tom rammed the pipe back in his mouth and

turned to me. 'Mr. Courtley, Izzy and me need to talk about other things for a bit – concerning his family and that...'

'Fine,' I was only too happy to leave, intending to use what remained of the lunch break to polish up my speech to the jury.

The plan was to make an impact about really only one thing – the credibility of the police; the lack of which could destroy the prosecution's entire case.

'When there's a general election...' I told the jury. 'We all possess a vote, don't we? But how important is it really – one vote amongst millions? Here in this trial, members of the jury, you hold a vote too but your choice is absolutely crucial. Each one of you must decide whether the defendant is innocent or guilty. His fate is in your hands. You may never bear such a heavy responsibility again in your lives. I implore you to ponder long and hard over the following points.'

For a moment, my eye swept over all twelve jurors but covertly, I sought out my chosen three.

'First, the police evidence is tainted and utterly discredited by Binns' jotting on the custody record which clearly indicates that the Robbery Squad contemplated putting someone else's name in the frame. The stuff of fiction? Or the harsh reality of a bunch of detectives initially thinking about smearing an innocent man and then going on to swear blind that the defendant admitted the crime!'

Affro nodded slightly, putting his head in his hands.

'Second, the police wouldn't allow my client access to a lawyer – can that be fair? Would such a course of conduct ever be tolerated by our cousins across the Atlantic? Yet the American legal system is supposedly based on our own!'

Heyman jiggled a bit as if assessing the merits of the latest pop tune.

'Third, you must be sure of guilt. Any uncertainty about that means that the prosecution are unable to discharge the burden of proving their case. Can you banish all doubt from your minds? Fair-minded and impartial men and women as you are!'

Gardi removed his spectacles a couple of times whilst tapping his newspaper.

After we adjourned, Tom Worlock walked with me towards the lifts.

'Izzy will be well pleased with that speech, Mr. Courtley. I reckon you got three of them on your side.'

'Not enough for an acquittal if it goes to a majority,' I replied.

'But sufficient for a disagreement which is better than nothing – and not bad for what looked like a stone-cold bonker.' He patted my arm.

Under the rules, after a prescribed time on retirement, the judge could accept a majority verdict from the jury either way and which had to be, at least, ten to two. Otherwise, the jury would be discharged and a retrial ordered. However, the really important thing was that Worlock approved of my speech and this might mean Silverside's sending me regular work!

It had been a tiring day and all I really wanted to do now was to go home. Leaving the main entrance of the building, I walked past the Magpie and Stump – only to see Debbie waiting for me outside.

'Oh Charlie – I'm so glad to see you. I need to talk to someone badly!'

I hesitated – having put the events of the previous night out of mind. After all, there was Andrea to consider – but then I caught sight of those gorgeous eyes full of tears – and my will crumbled.

'What's happened?'

'I rang my guy's chambers not believing that he could drop me so quickly. The clerk told me that he'd gone on holiday with his wife and three kids – and refused point blank to divulge his home address.'

We ended up in the Shermont Arms nearby with me commiserating despite my better judgement.

'You see, I just couldn't accept that his decision was final. Particularly, as he bought me this…'

She pulled a gold puzzle-ring off her finger studded with the tiniest diamonds, rubies and sapphires.

'At the time of giving it, he actually told me that he would divorce his wife and never mentioned having children...'

I put my hand over hers for comfort's sake but couldn't help thinking how delightful it would be to kiss her delectable mouth.

'He's obviously a bastard – you're better off without him.'

'Bloody men – always letting you down!' She jerked her hand away. 'Oh God, I've just swept the thing off the table!' She began to sob.

Pushing my chair aside, I explored the floor and retrieved the ring. Debbie was wiping her eye with a tissue. 'I think I could do with another drink.'

'Of course,' I finished my gin and tonic which had begun to taste bitter. Debbie was drinking red wine so I bought a bottle back to the table for us to share.

She began telling me her life history. After her mother's demise in Madrid, she had accompanied her Spanish father to England where he worked as a chef for a number of years. The life insurance policy after his death only two years before, had enabled her to rent a small flat in Barnsbury and pay for a shorthand course at a local secretarial college. After that she took up a job at the Old Bailey.

After a second glass of wine, the room beyond Debbie began to rotate in an alarming manner and I became increasingly befuddled. Now I could no longer concentrate on what Debbie was actually saying but just gazed at her face which waxed and waned in size...

TWENTY-FOUR

After staggering into the alley, I was violently sick. The rain, which was slashing against my face, helped me to find my bearings and I realised that I was somewhere near Blackfriars Bridge. For a moment, I couldn't remember anything but then my memory began to return in patches.

I recalled being half-carried out of the pub by Debbie who was squeezing my arm constantly and telling me not to worry – she would take care of me. I also remembered her saying that she would hail a taxi and take me back to her flat. After that, she kissed me passionately whilst murmuring that she wanted me to make love to her.

Suddenly, I felt an excruciating pain in my groin and it was only when Debbie pushed herself away that I realised what had happened. She had kneed me in the crotch!

Then I lay groaning on the pavement staring up at her – astounded by the furious expression on her face and the explosion of invective – *bastard! I'm going to ruin you…*

The shock caused a surge of adrenaline to course through my body. Hearing someone shout, I staggered to my feet and ran pell-mell down Farringdon Road.

Coming out of the alley, I saw a cab with its 'for hire' sign displayed. By now, I was completely sober and caught it thankful to be taken home.

Once there, I tried to go to sleep but the several cups of

coffee I drank made that impossible at first. My mind churned – why had I become so intoxicated? – even taking into account of having had a skinful the night before – and what reason was there for Debbie's duplicity?

Eventually, I did drift off at four o' clock in the morning awaking finally at nine with a throbbing headache and some soreness in a sensitive area of the body! There was no time, however, to worry about the debacle the night before – I had just enough time to gobble a piece of toast and gulp down several aspirin before setting off hoping that I wouldn't be late for court…

TWENTY-FIVE

I made it to the court-room by twenty past ten. The aspirin had done the trick and I felt much better if still rather sore in the nether regions. Moreover there was no work for me to do that morning and a reasonable result was a distinct possibility. Perhaps the events the night before had been some sort of aberration best forgotten about altogether.

'Cuffs' was waiting for me as I was about to enter the court which was, in itself, surprising. Normally, Treasury Counsel (with special rooms allocated to them for their sole use in the building) made a dramatic entrance moments before the judge walked in. What's more, the former wasn't wearing his usual expression of benign condescension, but was frowning instead.

'Courtley before he sits, the judge wants you to see this…'

He handed me a sheaf of papers. I noticed, at once, that it was a witness statement and jumped to what seemed an obvious conclusion. This was probably an additional statement from the owner of the jewellery shop whose evidence had been read earlier, dealing with the impact of the crime.

'Shan't be needing this surely if it's an acquittal – and that has got to be on the cards,' I quipped.

Cuffs didn't smile.

'What I've handed you isn't evidence in the case. It's information against you personally, Courtley. I suggest you take a minute or two to read it for yourself – in private.'

Moments later, in an interview room, I sat poring over the witness statement spread before me.

STATEMENT OF: LUISA SANCHEZ. Aged 21
ADDRESS: Not disclosed.

This statement (consisting of three pages signed by me) is true to the best of my knowledge and belief and I make it knowing that, if it is tendered in evidence, I shall be liable to prosecution if I have wilfully stated in it anything, which I know to be false or do not believe to be true.

Signed:

L Sanchez.

I am the above named person. Earlier this year, I was summoned to do jury service at the Central Criminal Court for a two week period. I spent the first week in the jury accommodation area and wasn't called upon at all. However, this week I became a member of the jury trying the case of R. v. Isidore in front of H.H. Judge Wintringham.

Normally, I attend a college in North London doing a business studies course. I have lived alone since my father died and am quite a nervous person so I found the whole thing a bit of an ordeal.

At the end of the first day, I felt I needed a drink to relax so I went into the Magpie and Stump pub across the road where I saw other jurors heading although I remained on my own. During the evening, the pub emptied out a bit and I was approached by a young man who I did not recognise at first. He is, in fact, the defending barrister in the case of Isidore – Charles Courtley. Whether he recognised me at this point, I cannot say.

Mr. Courtley was very friendly – indeed, he was trying to 'chat me up.' Thinking that he was probably a barrister because of the location and his posh voice, I have to admit that I felt flattered and responded in kind. However, I began to suspect who he might be so I asked him outright.

'You're Mr. Courtley, the barrister in the case of Isidore, aren't you?'

Mr. Courtley laughed and said that indeed he was. However, that didn't matter at all provided we didn't talk about the case. I thought as a barrister, he would know the rules so we continued to socialise. Frankly, both him and me had rather a lot to drink that evening. He was on Scotch, I remember, and buying me Camparis so that the rest of the evening was a bit of a blur. I do recall some vague mention being made of us meeting up the following day although this was a very loose arrangement.

In fact, I didn't really know what to expect when we adjourned the next day but as I was walking out of the building intending to go up to High Holborn to do some shopping, I saw Mr. Courtley again. He rushed up to me and said that he would love to take me out to dinner. He was very persuasive so I agreed particularly when he re-iterated that we wouldn't talk about the case. He seemed a bit uptight which, at first, I put down to him making his closing speech earlier that day but later it did occur to me that he might be taking drugs. One of the waiting jurors the week before had said that a lot of barristers were wealthy jet-set types who took cocaine regularly.

Anyway, he asked me where I lived and when I said in the Barnsbury area, he suggested we go to a wine bar in Islington which did very good food. However, finding a taxi proved to be difficult (he refused to use public transport) so as we were walking past a pub in Farringdon Road, he suggested having a drink locally first.

I asked for a glass of wine and I think he bought himself a gin and tonic. In fact, he kept going up to the bar and replenishing his drink and, at one point, bought a whole bottle of wine most of which he drank himself. He started telling me about his life –

how tough it was to be a young barrister who, contrary to what most people think, don't earn much to begin with and live a stressful life constantly being sent to different courts. Then he told me of previous cases he'd been involved in and I must admit I found this very interesting. The time passed quickly and I remained completely sober although the same couldn't be said about him. Eventually, this made me anxious as he showed no inclination to leave or sticking to the idea of getting something to eat.

Finally, when he staggered up to the bar one more time, I decided it was time to go home and contemplated leaving him on his own. However, I was worried about what would happen if I left him in that state and decided the least I could do was to put him in a taxi. When I told him of my plan, he did agree although he leered at me suggestively and I did wonder how he would behave when we got outside.

At first, the fresh air seemed to have a bad effect on him and I virtually had to hold him up once we got outside. It was about ten o' clock by now and being the City of London, not many people were about at that time. However, whilst we were waiting for a taxi, he seemed to recover and suddenly became amorous and aggressive at the same time. He said he hadn't spent two whole evenings pouring drinks down my throat and how about we had a 'shag', as he put it, back at my place? He then lunged towards me in an attempt to kiss and grabbed my breasts.

By now I was thoroughly scared and pushed him away protecting myself as best as I could. A passer-by noticed what was happening and asked if I was alright. When Mr. Courtley saw this man, he ran off down Farringdon Road.

Although Mr. Courtley assaulted me, I do not make this statement in order for him to be prosecuted but to bring this incident to the attention of Judge Wintringham. I feel he should be informed as to how one of the barristers in the case he is trying has behaved. Thinking back, and having talked to one of the jury bailiffs in the building this morning, I realise that I shouldn't

have socialised with anyone involved in the case. I apologise to
the judge for this. However, I must add that I now feel it would
be impossible for me to concentrate properly on the trial after this
distressing experience.

Signed:

L. Sanchez.

Statement taken by Police Sergeant O.Trump. (City of London
Police stationed at the Central Criminal Court.)

My hands were shaking by now. It was a pack of lies, of course.
Nobody could possibly believe it. I would never have behaved
like that. True – I was drunk – although, in fact, I was positive
that I hadn't imbibed that much alcohol; not willingly anyway.
This girl – Debbie, as she had called herself – perhaps she had
spiked my glass?

Dazed, I ventured out of the room to find Cuffs waiting for
me.

'His Lordship is about to sit, Courtley. He'll be expecting
some sort of explanation.'

'Oh, that's simple,' I replied, 'her allegations are a
fabrication from beginning to end. I never touched her!'

Cuffs raised his eyebrows.

'I'm not sure that's really the point, you know. The actual
complaint she makes about you won't be foremost in the
judge's mind. What will be is that, on the face of it, you
suborned a member of the jury.'

'Suborned... what do you mean?'

'You picked her up effectively on the first day of the trial
and took her out for a drink on the second,' Cuffs expression
was grim. 'Do you really think that's what a defending
barrister should do with a juror involved in the same case?'

The ambience of Court One bore down on me heavily as I

rose to my feet for the judge's entry. I might not be in the dock but now I knew what it was like to be on the wrong side of the law – or, at least, on the wrong side of those unspoken conventions which applied to all barristers. The fact was that I had chatted up a member of the jury in our case not once but twice. There was a clear prima facie case against me and any defence to the charge would be a matter for a disciplinary tribunal to decide. Before Wintry even questioned me, I knew my fate had already been sealed. Whatever I said, he would be reporting me to the Benchers – the governing body of Galahad's Inn.

Luisa Sanchez was the very girl I had actually ignored on the first day of the trial. This plain little miss who wore a bobble hat (which had concealed her lustrous hair) and glasses, was the girl who had called herself 'Debbie'. I had been completely unaware of her real identity but who the hell was ever going to believe it? Certainly not Cuffs to whom I continued to protest my innocence.

'Luisa Sanchez wasn't wearing any hat on the second day of the trial, you know,' he observed. 'In fact, her hair drew everybody's attention. The only girl on the jury and such a pretty one to boot! I don't think she wore glasses either. How could you not have recognised her yesterday even if you didn't spot her the day before?'

'I... I wasn't looking.' I said lamely. Which was absolutely true, of course, although he would never believe it. It was all due to my stratagem; concentrate on the jurors that matter; *Affro, Heyman* and *Gardi* – and ignore the rest.

In due course, having heard my feeble explanations, Wintry passed judgement in the same withering tone which he used when sentencing hardened criminals.

'Mr. Courtley, your denial of any assault is neither here or there. What is crucial though is that you socialised with a juror in a case in which you appear as counsel. In my provisional judgement, you must have known that, although it will be for another tribunal to make a final decision as to the facts. This is quite a disgraceful thing for a member of the Bar to do and you will be reported to the Benchers of your Inn immediately. As far as the trial is concerned, it cannot, of course, continue. Miss Sanchez has been compromised. I shall be discharging the whole of the jury from giving a verdict and order a re-trial.'

What was already a dark day of my life was to become even blacker still. Isidore, true to his nature, happily turned the screw.

'Fuck me, man – I thought I was in trouble with the law! Not my bleedin' brief who's been chasin' pussy on the jury. Now, I lose 'em too – an' I had a good feeling I'd get off.'

In vain, I protested my innocence and to make matters worse, Worlock didn't sympathise either.

'I can't say that my firm will be impressed, Mr. Courtley. Basic rule of the court game – never go anywhere near the jury. Nor can you blame Izzy for complaining – next time, the Robbery Squad will fill all the holes you opened up and his chances will be zilch!'

A couple of hours later, I sat in front of Tufton Crump who was due to attend the House of Commons shortly. He obviously had a lot on his mind as his normal laid-back Welsh charm was absent. He raised his hand as I launched into an avalanche of excuses.

'Save your defence for the Benchers, Courtley. In the meantime, I have to consider my... the interests of the other tenants here. I see no alternative but to suspend you practising from these chambers.'

'Suspend? – but I shan't be able to earn anything then.' I spluttered.

'That's regrettable admittedly but at least on those grounds, you can ask for an expedited hearing.'

Devastated, I reeled out of chambers and decided to phone Andrea immediately after I'd had a drink. I couldn't bear the thought of visiting my usual haunts so found a pub in Carey Street instead.

Aunt Imogen answered the phone sounding breathless. Surely her bloody ankle has healed by now! I thought.

'Oh Charlie, I'm so glad it's you. I have very bad news, I'm afraid. Andrea's father died today – quite unexpectedly. She's gone home to be with her mother...'

TWENTY-SIX

As I expected, Andrea sounded very subdued on the phone.

'The doctors said that he suffered from a brain haemorrhage. Nothing to do with the operation he was recovering from – Mum's terribly upset as you can imagine. Can you look after yourself for a few days? I'll be back as soon as possible.'

'Things aren't that busy,' I replied. 'I could pop down and stay a while...'

'Oh, darling, that's so kind but it's really not necessary at the moment. I'm better off coping with Mum on my own over the next few days but I'd love you to come to the funeral.'

It was on the tip of my tongue to tell her about my problems but I thought better of it. Why cause her more upset just now?

I walked disconsolately from the phone box back to our flat dreading the dreary evening ahead of me. Gloomily, I realised that all the shops were closed by now and the fridge was empty apart from the remains of a pork pie. That, and a slug of cheap sherry would have to suffice for supper, I thought grimly.

I was about to bite into this miserable meal when the doorbell chimed.

'Charlie? Thank goodness, you're in – I came as soon as I heard what that self-serving sod, Crump, did – suspending you from chambers. He'd no right to do it and I told him so! Pity you didn't tell me about what happened first...'

'You were out of London on a case, Bill. Anyway, I felt I had to tell my head of chambers first.'

'Well, never mind that now. I've put Tufton straight. His reaction was simply to protect his own position – you know he's angling for a ministerial post in the Government, don't you? He wouldn't want anything to prejudice that as it's about his last chance of preferment. Anyway, the truth is he can't suspend you – innocent until proved guilty and all that – and Leslie agrees with me. But first, I'm taking you out to dinner pronto. We'll talk about this whole mess after a good meal!'

Soon, we were ensconced in a local Italian restaurant and only after a couple of brandies did Bill allow me to mull over my predicament.

'I haven't got much of a defence, have I?' I said gloomily. 'The fact is that I did allow myself to chat up a juror. What could be more heinous than that in the tribunal's eyes?'

'Don't be so negative Charlie – you deny, don't you, that you recognised the girl. I never took you for a damn fool and only a blithering idiot would do that deliberately.'

I began to feel more confident. 'You're right – once I've explained to the Benchers what happened, I'm sure they will believe me. Quite frankly, I want the hearing to take place as soon as possible – not least to spare Andrea any additional agony.' I told Bill of Andrea's sad news.

'I'm so sorry, old chap but you shouldn't rush the hearing, you know – you need adequate time to prepare your defence and decide who you want to represent you at the hearing.'

'He's sitting opposite me,' I replied. 'What better friend have I got at the Bar?'

'Kind of you to say so, Charlie... but I'm not a silk, and that's what you need for a hearing like this. Hub Sheckleworth's your man – he likes you doesn't he? You've told me that in the past.'

I pondered for a moment and then made up my mind.

'No, I've decided – I want to do it myself. After all, I know I'm innocent!'

Bill looked at me closely and sighed.

'Alright, Charlie. But you must ask for more time! You say the girl's lying her head off – so there's a motive somewhere. You need to instruct an enquiry agent to delve into her past.'

'That means delay and I want to clear my name as soon as possible.'

'I understand that – but surely you want to discredit her if you can.'

'Why should that be necessary? It's only her word against mine, after all – the Benchers must give me the benefit of the doubt at the very least…'

The following day, I visited the Under-Treasurer of Galahad's Inn – an amiable ex-military man called Colonel Habtree – who confirmed that His Honour Judge Wintringham had indeed lodged a complaint. As the person responsible for dealing with the administrative matters of the Inn, the former was able to indicate that a disciplinary board could be convened in a couple of weeks – just before Christmas in fact.

'I happen to know that the Lord Chief Justice will be available – of course, he will chair the tribunal. There should be no problem in finding the four other members required – three of whom will be drawn from the other Inns of Court. At least, one of them needs to be a judge as well…'

But I was too shocked to take any of this in.

'Lord Flaggett… as Chairman?' I spluttered. 'But he tore a strip off me in the Court of Appeal recently!'

'Good Lord old chap, that shouldn't matter – it's in the nature of his job, isn't it? In any event, I'm sure he won't hold it against you. Anyway, that's the convention – the most senior figure at the Inn always presides over such a hearing.'

As I walked back to chambers, I began to have real doubts about representing myself. The thought of Flaggett's good eye glaring at me malevolently throughout the hearing was just too much to bear. I would take up Bill's suggestion and contact Hub Sheckleworth's clerk.

There was an embarrassing silence as I entered the clerk's room. Dennis and our secretary bid me a hasty good morning immersing themselves in their work. Leslie, however, shot to his feet and pointed to the door.

'Let's you and I have a little chat, Sah.'

We ended up in a coffee bar in Tudor Street which was off the beaten track as far as those connected with the law were concerned.

'Mr. Tufton, with all respect to him, was plain wrong, Sah. It wasn't right to stop you working. However, you might feel a bit uncomfortable bein' in London at the moment. May I ask when the disciplinary hearing is likely to take place?'

'In about two weeks time apparently – but, in the meantime, I've got to go to my father-in-law's funeral.'

Leslie nodded sympathetically. 'My condolences, Sah. However, that works very well as it happens. What you need to keep you going is a case in the sticks. I've got just the thing – a trial down in Plymouth. Rosy, one of Mr. Brasper's regulars, has been done for robbery.'

'What sort of robbery has she committed?' I enquired.

'*She* isn't really the proper description of the client. His name is Roderick Jackson actually and it's a mugging. I'll give you the brief when we get back to chambers.'

Two days later, I was notified that the disciplinary hearing would indeed be held at the beginning of December. Dermot Cuthbertson was to be the prosecutor – which took me aback for a moment until I deduced that he was really the most obvious person in the circumstances. Meanwhile, Leslie had spoken to Hub Sheckleworth's clerk who assured him that the former would be available to represent me.

With a week to spare before going to Plymouth, I asked Bill Champney what else I should do.

'You haven't got time to instruct an enquiry agent now but write to Cuthbertson insisting that he makes full disclosure of all the material he has in his possession or is available to the police. Does she have a criminal record for instance? The copper will have done an automatic check on that. Indeed, make sure he attends court also. You'll want Hub to cross-examine him about the girl's demeanour when she first made her complaint.'

After attending to Bill's suggestions, I felt a good deal better. The truth was bound to come out – after all, miscarriages of justice couldn't possibly take place when one person was so obviously telling lies – and that person certainly wasn't myself. I cast all my legal training to the winds. This wasn't somebody else's plight on paper; it was mine!

Moreover, I wouldn't say anything to Andrea either until after Christmas (a welcome distraction) which we would be spending with her mother in Saltdean. By that time, we would no doubt be laughing about it all – I dared to hope!

TWENTY-SEVEN

'Roderick Jackson, stand up straight now and be a man! The fact is that having behaved without scruple, falsely employing your deceptive charms to confuse a prospective client, you then perpetrated an act of brigandage upon him!'

Rosy looked puzzled at this sally as well he might; the jury couldn't help sniggering and even the judge looked bemused.

The prosecutor, Pongo McGonigle was only forty but looked sixty and sounded much more antediluvian than that. He possessed a long sloping face with swept-back receding hair and a lush voice that could have come straight out of a Noel Coward play.

In contrast, Rosy – the defendant – might have been quite pretty if his long blonde tresses hadn't been so greasy and his pink, baby-doll dress clean. After all on a good day, he was a passable imitation of Marilyn Monroe; someone he had always wanted to be since the age of three. For all that, he possessed the strength of a man.

His transexuality had caused all sorts of trouble in his young life. Teasing and bullying at school led to outbreaks of violence which culminated in a variety of disposals by the criminal justice system. Finally, his probation officer had suggested a complete break from the London scene and arranged for him to take up employment in a coffee shop in Plymouth.

Rosy's love life remained complicated however. He was gay but looked so girl-like that potential partners were often confused. He also liked nice clothes; the expense of which could not be met by his meagre wages. Selling his body was one way of adding to them.

One summer night, wandering around Plymouth Hoe, he picked up a young sailor and the two of them had gone off for sex in a secluded spot. The sailor frankly admitted that he was looking for a prostitute and he had no reason to suspect that Rosy wasn't what he appeared to be. According to him, when they reached an appropriate place, Rosy punched him in the face – stunning him temporarily – and ran off after relieving him of his wallet containing his wages; some seventy-five pounds.

Rosy didn't agree with this version of events at all. True the sailor had thought him a girl at first but when he revealed his true gender, the sailor had readily agreed to play 'two way boogie' as Rosy eloquently described an act of mutual masturbation. It was after this that the punter refused to pay and a struggle ensued which culminated in Rosy taking the money from the sailor's pocket. He then made off only to be arrested after a search of the vicinity.

I had one potential weapon in my armoury. The sailor, called Joe Paridel, had waved down a police car being driven by a local policeman, PC Stubbs. After hearing the complaint, the latter had driven round with Paridel and found Rosy breathless and dishevelled by the Plymouth Bowling Green. In the event, he made no attempt to escape.

The stolid copper's note of what happened and which was duly included in his witness statement, went something like this.

Mr. Paridel asked me to stop the police car instantly as he recognised the perpetrator of the alleged robbery of his person. I duly did so and addressed the suspect in the following terms.

'Hey you – Miss! The gentleman here has complained that having made an arrangement with you for the purposes of sex, you upped and robbed him?'

'Total crap! I never – he wanked me off he did!'

By then, Mr. Paridel was standing outside the car. In the presence of the defendant, he said.

'Bleeding lies! I never touched the bastard!'

In his evidence before the court, Paridel maintained, as I had expected, that he never suspected that his prospective sexual partner was, in fact, male. This gave me a chink in the prosecution's case to explore.

'Mr. Paridel, you remember getting out of the police car when the officer apprehended my client and your allegation being put to him?'

'Yes, sir.'

'... and you recall my client telling him that you had, in effect, wanked him off?'

'Yes,'

I continued now quoting verbatim from the officer's note. 'You then said – *bleeding lies, I never touched the bastard* – because you already knew that my client wasn't a girl but a boy!'

'No, no – that's not right. What I said was, I never touched the *bitch*.'

I gave the jury a meaningful look.

'Ah, well – we'll see what PC Stubbs has to say about that in a moment. But assuming you're right, this must have come as a big shock – surely the obvious comment would have been – bleeding lies, I thought she was a girl, I never touched the bitch anyway!'

Paridel flushed. 'Maybe, I was confused at the time...'

'...or perhaps, being economical with the truth in court. Isn't that really the case?' The witness didn't answer.

For once, a policeman's normal determination to stick to the exact words of what was in his note would come to the aid of the defence. Accordingly, I kept my cross-examination of him brief.

'I take no issue with your evidence whatsoever, Officer – only one question just to confirm something Mr. Paridel said.

Looking at your notes, did he not say – *Bleeding lies, I never touched the bastard* – when confronted with the defendant?'

'He did indeed, sir.'

'Not – *I never touched the bitch* – because that's not what you wrote down, is it?'

'Quite so – I wrote down his exact words.'

The prosecution's case wasn't assisted either by Pongo's pompous cross-examination; delivered in a mocking and patronising manner and quite the wrong thing to do in the circumstances of the case. It just made poor Rosy look vulnerable, sad and bewildered. After all, it wasn't his fault that he should have been born a girl.

The judge, a laid-back QC doing his two-week stint as a recorder, summed up impartially and it took the jury only twenty minutes to acquit. Walking back to the train station and on the way home, I wallowed in that feeling of triumph which a good result always brings – until, with a shock, I was reminded of what lay in store when I let myself into our flat.

A thick, cream envelope with the Galahad's Inn crest on the back winked up at me. Tearing it open, my spirits were about to sink even lower. I discovered that the other judge selected to sit on my panel was none other than Mr. Justice Bevidere-Jones!

Remembering my embarrassing foray in the Chancery Division from which dear old Melanie had extracted me and the judge's miserable experience of criminal low-life at Inner London, I was determined to raise the matter with the Under-Treasurer the following day. It was bad enough having Flaggett preside in the first place but here was another member of the tribunal who knew me – not least by virtue of my initial display of incompetence in his court.

Colonel Habtree rubbed his chin reflectively as I poured out my concerns.

'The selection procedure is random – Benchers from other Inns are simply approached as to their availability. If Bevidere-

Jones had actually recognised your name as the accused, I'm sure he would have said.'

Accused? What a damning way to describe me! I must have looked shocked because the Under-Treasurer, who was a kindly enough fellow, looked rueful for a moment.

'Oh, my dear chap – sorry about calling you the accused. That's the term we use for soldiers when they come up for court-martial. Slip of the tongue really. You're only facing a disciplinary tribunal after all.'

'No, no, don't apologise. That is what I am in reality – a man accused of gross misconduct...'

'... but not convicted of anything as yet,' he added hastily, 'however, coming back to Bevidere-Jones, I could mention the matter to Lord Flaggett as the chairman of the tribunal and tell him you're not happy with the set-up.'

'Does it have to be Flaggett? Couldn't I raise my objection to both him and Bevidere-Jones with the Inn generally?'

'Quite impossible, I'm afraid. The Lord Chief Justice is now in charge of the case.'

Taking a deep breath, I rose to leave. I would fight them all – even with both hands tied behind my back. At least, I would now get myself represented by Hub Sheckleworth, one of the leading silks in the land.

* * *

'Chinese or Indian?'

'Er...Indian please.'

Hub waved a languid hand at his clerk. 'Pour him a cup, Rostick, there's a good fellow and go and collect the muffins.'

'Very good M'lord,' Rostick poured the tea, bowed slightly and sidled towards the door.

Flicking open a gold case, Hub selected an oval cigarette, lit it with a match and peered at me through the smoke.

'I take it you like muffins, dear boy?'

I nodded. Savoury, slightly crisped muffins were a favoured snack of barristers generally and one Inn of Court was renowned for serving them in its common room. Trust Sheckleworth to produce them in chambers, a ploy perhaps to put me at my ease.

'Whilst we wait,' Hub murmured, 'I'll just finish reading this.' He glanced at some papers on his desk.

Lord Sheckleworth's room was situated on the top story of 40 King's Bench Walk – one of the oldest edifices in the Temple. Although it was small in dimension, it had a muted splendour about it. A Stubbs hung on one wall and Spy cartoons of famous nineteenth-century barristers were interspersed between shelves of tooled law reports bound in brown calf. Rich red damask curtains edged in gold thread adorned the windows. You knew you were in a leading QC's room here.

At last, Hub turned to me. 'Interesting, interesting – quite a tale, what?'

With a start, I realised that he had been reading my own statement of events.

'Bit of a mess, though, don't you think? What worries me is you haven't any ammunition to back you up.' He sighed stubbing his cigarette out in an ashtray.

'You mean relating to the girl's background? That's true but it's her word against mine. She's lying her head off – surely, you believe me, don't you?'

Hub wrinkled his face in an incredulous frown. 'Dear boy, we all do silly things when we're young. Especially, when a pretty female is involved. Conceivably, you might not have recognised the *gel* on the first evening – but the second time – come on, you took a chance, didn't you? Hoping she wouldn't tell.'

'But I'm married…'

'…with your wife absent, as you say in your statement. The best of us are tempted to play away sometimes, you know.'

Suddenly, I remembered Hub Sheckleworth's reputation.

Hadn't he been married three times before? The last time to a Brazilian beauty queen; thirty-five years his junior.

'Put your hands up, old chap, plead guilty to the damn thing! You'll get *orf* with a reprimand – surely that's better than being disbarred.'

Now, for the first time in my professional life, I knew what it felt like to be a defendant confronted with a barrister who was leaning heavily on him to plead guilty when he hadn't committed the crime!

I stood up, knocking over my plate with a half-eaten muffin on it, which duly splodged the pale-beige carpet.

'I'm innocent – can't you see that? I'm not some old lag down at London Sessions worried about how long he's going to spend in the bloody nick, you know.'

With horror, I realised that the tension of the moment had caused me to use the vernacular – just like any other defendant. I thought this might have upset Sheckleworth but all he did was to look sorrowfully down at the mess on his carpet. What did this awful crisis in my life really mean to him?

I resolved then I would defend myself – at least, I believed in my own innocence! Muttering my excuses, I left to the sound of Hub's testy call.

'Rostick – do fetch a mop, there's a good fellow!'

TWENTY-EIGHT

The day of the hearing turned out to be a crisp and sunny day. Arriving well before the hearing was due to begin at ten o' clock, Colonel Habtree informed me of the location and explained the lay-out.

The hearing was to be conducted in a large room just off the main dining hall which was normally used as the Benchers' 'withdrawing room'- a place where the learned seniors of the Inn could quaff their port, puff their cigars and gossip well away from the ordinary barristers and students in Hall.

The five Benchers were to be seated at tables set back in the room. The windows to their rear were adorned with the coats of arms of the Treasurers of the Inn since time immemorial. Flaggett as the chairman would sit in the middle, Bevidere-Jones to his left with the other Benchers flanking them on each side. I was to sit at my own table facing them; Cuthbertson at another table to my right and the witnesses giving evidence from a stand opposite him.

At ten o' clock sharp, the tribunal's usher wearing the blue tailcoat and gold epaulettes worn by all officials of the Inn, summoned us to our places; there we awaited the entrance of the board members. The morning light blazed through the stained-glass widows adding a church-like solemnity to the proceedings and making the room stuffily hot already. By the time the board entered, my face and hands were clammy with sweat.

Dermot Cuthbertson rose to his feet.

'My Lord, Honourable Benchers, I appear before you to adduce evidence of a complaint made by His Honour Judge Wintringham who sits at the Central Criminal Court, against Charles Courtley, barrister-at-law of this Inn. The terms of the complaint are as follows.'

That the aforementioned barrister did on divers days in the month of October of this year knowingly consort, converse and keep company with one Luisa Sanchez, a serving juror in a trial in which the said barrister was engaged as counsel for the defence. (He read from a piece of paper.)

Flaggett motioned me to rise moving his arm in a chopping motion grimly reminding me of Judge Brumble.

'Charles Courtley, do you accept or deny the allegations contained in the complaint?'

'I deny them, My Lord.'

Cuthbertson rose to his feet again.

'My Lord, Honourable Benchers – accordingly, without further ado, I shall call evidence relating to the complaint which comes principally from Miss Luisa Sanchez herself. I also have available as a witness, Police Sergeant Trump whom I propose to tender for Mr. Courtley to cross-examine should he so wish.'

Luisa Sanchez was wearing different clothes to the time of the incident – a charcoal suit as opposed to a cherry-red skirt and white blouse. Her hair been cut short too in a page-boy fringe which emphasized her air of demureness and of the bobble hat, there was no sign. Spectacles were produced only to help her read the oath and then put away. She gave her evidence steadily in a low voice which seemed to bear more of a foreign accent than when we had last met. However, what she told the tribunal matched what I already knew from her statement.

Eventually, Cuthbertson completed his examination-in-chief and told 'Debbie' (as I knew her) that she might be asked further questions – as if that amounted to a real imposition!

'Miss Sanchez, do you have a nickname?' Suppressing feelings of fury, I kept my voice as level as I could.

'No, all my friends call me Luisa.'

'So the name Debbie doesn't mean anything to you then?'

'Debbie?'

'That's what you called yourself when we first met in the Magpie and Stump, isn't that so?'

She tossed me a look of scorn. 'Hardly, it is not a name that a Spanish girl would ever use.'

'But you're not really Spanish anymore, are you? You've lived in England since the age of ten – eleven years to be exact.'

'Well, nobody has ever called me Debbie – I don't know where you got that from.'

'Ah, that's obvious – I got the name from you – why should I make that up if it's not true!'

'Don't ask the witness to speculate on what may be in your mind, Mr. Courtley,' Flaggett growled, 'and confine yourself, at this stage to putting your case to the complainant.'

'I put it to you that you called yourself Debbie and told me that you were a short-hand writer at the Old Bailey who had just finished an affair with a barrister engaged in a fraud case.'

'Totally untrue – I don't know any barristers anyway.'

'Really? Well, I suggest that you were miserable because the relationship had ended that day. That's why you were in the pub – drowning your sorrows. You accept, don't you, that we both had a lot to drink.'

'Yes – and I've regretted that ever since.' There was a tremor in her voice as she turned towards the tribunal. 'Deep inside, I knew that I shouldn't be drinking with one of the barristers in the case but he said it was alright!'

'Don't distress yourself unduly, Miss Sanchez...' Flaggett spoke in a nauseatingly avuncular tone.

'Thank you, My Lord but he's also accused me of having an affair when I don't even have a boyfriend – I'm too busy at college.'

I gave her a moment to compose herself.

'Moreover, the next day it was you who accosted me as I walked past the Magpie and Stump.'

'No – you rushed up to me in the street.'

Now, the pressure began to get to me.

'You were in a state about breaking up with your manfriend, that's why we went to the Shermont Arms in Farringdon Road – I was just commiserating with you, that's all...'

Suddenly, I had an idea. 'Before you answer that, hold up your right hand, please?'

I was in luck. She was wearing the gold puzzle ring on her little finger. Noticing a reluctance to raise her arm, I raised my voice.

'You know what's coming, don't you? You took that ring off and showed it to me. Then you knocked it on the floor. It must have been at that point that you spiked my drink before I found the thing for you!'

For a moment, I thought I had caught her. She was staring at the ring and her arm began to tremble. Then she spat back.

'You leant across the table and took my hand. That's how you must have seen it – anyway, I never take it off. I bought it out of my inheritance to honour my mother and father...'

Flaggett cut in before she could continue.

'If I hear aright, Mr. Courtley, you are in terms, suggesting that Miss Sanchez maliciously added some sort of substance to your beverage presumably for the purposes of intoxication. What evidential basis do you have for making such a serious allegation?'

'Nothing specific, My Lord,' I had to admit, 'but my condition did deteriorate considerably after I returned the ring.'

'So you accept what Miss Sanchez says that you appeared very much under the influence of alcohol when you left the public house?'

'Of course – that's why I suggest she must have put something in my drink!'

'Well, did you?' Flaggett turned to the complainant once again.

'I didn't have anything to put in his drink. Anyway, why should I do such a wicked thing? He's lying again.'

'Just stop there a moment,' Flaggett scribbled noisily on his notepad. I recognised an old judicial trick – recording a piece of evidence in a manner which would emphasize its significance.

I ploughed on.

'When we finally left the pub, you were actually comforting me. I was obviously ill by this time and you said you would take care of me at your flat. You kissed me and said you wanted to make love.'

'No – you lunged at me and grabbed my breasts! I had to protect myself, that's why I pushed you away…'

'Oh yes, you said that in your statement – but it was much more than a push, wasn't it? You kicked me in the balls!'

In shock, I clapped my outstretched hand to my forehead. What a time to use the vernacular – particularly in front of that old prude Bevidere-Jones who looked suitably shocked. It didn't take Flaggett long to react.

'Please desist from using vulgar slang during this hearing, Mr. Courtley. Such language may just about be tolerable in an alehouse but it will not be condoned here!'

'I'm sorry, My Lord.' I said humbly.

'Nonetheless, I put it to you that you did indeed kick me in the groin area. I doubled up and…'

'Ran, that's what you did, you coward and I never assaulted you either. You made off because you were scared!'

'No – I was in shock. Suddenly, you changed your mind about sleeping with me and hurt me.'

'That's not what Mr. Stavely says!' Debbie added triumphantly.

'Mr. Stavely,' Flaggett interrupted, 'and whom might he be?'

'He saw everything and asked me if I was alright afterwards. I mentioned him in my statement. He gave me his phone number at the time. In fact, I spoke to him only yesterday. He's quite prepared to come to court and give evidence.'

In a trice, judicial displeasure was switched to my opponent for the first time.

'Were any attempts made by the police to trace this gentleman and have a witness statement taken from him, Mr. Cuthbertson?'

The latter shook his head. 'I regret not, My Lord – the police sergeant who took Miss Sanchez' statement did not pursue the matter…'

'Perhaps, but he could have been instructed by you to do so after the event – why wasn't that done?'

It's not often that one sees a senior prosecuting barrister put in the direct line of fire by a judge and I have to admit that I relished Cuthbertson's discomfiture. However, it didn't last long.

'My humble apologies, My Lord,' he replied smoothly, 'for overlooking it. I can only crave your indulgence as I was overwhelmed with work at the time – engaged in the prosecution of several murders and two long-firm frauds.'

'Oh quite, Mr. Cuthbertson – I know that you are always under much pressure of work. However, we need to attend to the matter as it now stands. It is only right that we hear Mr. Stavely's evidence if we can. He may or may not be in a position to confirm an important aspect of the facts.'

Talk about leading for the prosecution! I thought bitterly. But there was nothing I could do about it.

'Indeed My Lord,' Hardly surprisingly, Cuthbertson was only too ready to agree.

'Nonetheless I must bear in mind that Mr. Courtley has not

been given proper notice of this evidence. A statement should accordingly be taken from Mr. Stavely without delay and served on him. He will need time to consider this new development.'

'No – no My Lord, that won't be necessary. Let Mr Stavely say what he has to say. I've nothing to hide. Anyway, I don't want this hearing to be held up.'

Flaggett grunted in approval. Keeping on the right side of the tribunal would do me no harm but I had another motive too – I didn't want to give Stavely the chance to rehearse his evidence or, for that matter, to give the police the chance to do it for him.

Mark Luke John Stavely duly appeared in the witness box the next day. Debbie would resume her evidence later if necessary – I was given permission to continue my cross-examination of her then.

Stavely was a small, balding man wearing an ill-fitting black suit. A neat grey moustache adorned his upper lip. After giving an address in High Barnet, he was asked by Cuthbertson about his occupation.

'I own and run a shop in Fetter Lane called the *God is Just* bookshop. We specialise in religious publications – of a Christian variety, I should add.'

Flaggett glanced up approvingly. I remembered being told that our distinguished Lord Chief Justice was known to be a committed church-goer in the robust Christian mould. This didn't augur well.

'Tell us, Mr. Stavely about a particular night in October – the date is not in dispute – when, I believe, you witnessed an altercation.'

'I did indeed – as a result, I gave a telephone number to a Miss Sanchez. The whole thing was quite disgusting!'

'Please confine yourself to what you actually saw, Mr. Stavely. The interpretations of the events is a matter for the tribunal alone.'

'Well, I saw a man reeling out of the Shermont Arms in a drunken condition. He was prevented falling by a girl. Suddenly, he lunged at her – groping obscenely at her body.'

'Thank you,' Cuffs resumed his seat.

'Mr. Stavely, it was quite late in the evening by then, was it not, about ten o' clock? Presumably, your shop shuts at the normal closing time – about five-thirty – why were you still in the area?' I asked.

'Having my own business requires me more often than not to work overtime in the shop. Stock taking, accounts – that kind of thing. I live alone also and so do not keep to prescribed times.'

'But I imagine your actual route home to High Barnet doesn't vary. You walk up Farringdon Road to the station, get on the Circle Line and then change for the Northern at King's Cross?'

'That is so,'

I decided to take a gamble – asking a question to which I didn't know the answer; an advocate's nightmare.

'You don't like pubs much do you, Mr. Stavely? Beery noisy places – and that's because you're a teetotaller, isn't that correct?'

Please God, he would agree!

'I don't drink that's true but…'

'So seeing a drunk outside the Shermont Arms – something you witness only too often, I imagine – is a source of considerable irritation, I dare say. You're bound to think the worst of anybody behaving like that!'

'Well…'

'You see, I accept that to you I may have looked drunk, Mr. Stavely. I was certainly staggering about outside the pub – you may even have seen us coming together in some sort of clinch – but I never touched her sexually, that's something I suggest you're mistaken about. Indeed, she actually kicked me in the groin area.'

'No – there was no kick and you groped her. That is the plain unvarnished truth which I have sworn to on God's holy book!'

'Might you not be mistaken?' I was wheedling by now.

'Never!'

I sat down – any further questions would simply deepen the hole in which I was rapidly sinking.

There was a pause. Then Flaggett asked me.

'Mr. Stavely's evidence having concluded, do you wish Miss Sanchez to be recalled?'

I shook my head. 'No My Lord. I think that the dispute between myself and Miss Sanchez is clear enough.'

Flaggett glanced at his colleagues on both sides. 'It is – at least, as far as I am concerned, Mr. Courtley.'

The others nodded in turn, not looking at me. Things aren't looking good – I thought grimly.

Sergeant Trump was called to give evidence next. I was anxious to establish what sort of state Debbie was in when he first saw her.

'Calm enough sir – but then she had spoken to a jury bailiff already before I was contacted. After being informed generally of her complaint, I gave her directions to the police office on the first floor of the old building opposite the main staircase. I had some other matters to discuss with the jury bailiff which were not connected to this matter.'

'You didn't feel any need to actually accompany her in person then?' I enquired.

'No, she was composed at that stage...'

'So what was her demeanour like when you eventually went upstairs?'

Trump scratched his nose and pondered for a moment.

'No different, sir – but, perhaps, there's one thing you should know. Not a factor I thought as significant at the time but I did see her before getting to the police office – actually leaving Court Number Fifteen.'

I felt a prickle of excitement. Could this cast any light on her motive for lying?

'Did you ask her why she had gone into that court?'

'No, she simply came out, saw me and we walked up to the police office together. I had told her that I might be twenty minutes or so and suggested that she have a coffee first.'

'Except that's not what she did, is it? Instead, she went into a court where she had no business to be...'

'That's a rather harsh comment Mr. Courtley,' Flaggett put his oar in. 'Once inside the building, jurors, unless actually serving, are quite entitled to sit in the back of courtrooms and observe other cases.'

'Quite so My Lord – but we didn't hear anything about this from Debbie – I mean Miss Sanchez. I do now wish her to be recalled.'

'Very well,' Flaggett had to agree.

'Miss Sanchez, why did you go into Court Fifteen?'

For the first time, she looked flustered.

'Court Fifteen? I don't know where that is...'

'Oh, I think you do. After Sergeant Trump spoke to you in the jury waiting area downstairs – you didn't go straight to his office, did you? Instead you went into Court Fifteen downstairs. Later, you ran into each other as you were leaving – he's told us that. Why go into that court at all?'

'I don't know... I suppose I must have done if he says I did. Perhaps I realised that I hadn't been in any of the other courts apart from the one where we'd been sitting. So I was just taking a peek – Court Fifteen is different from Court One, isn't it? One of the new ones I believe.'

'Come on – you were supposed to have suffered an ordeal the night before and the police were about to take a statement. Hardly the moment to satisfy your curiosity, now was it?'

She gulped. 'Well...'

Then Flaggett destroyed my advantage at a stroke.

'You're quite right Miss Sanchez,' he said breezily, 'Court

Number Fifteen is one of the newer ones built some sixty years after the original four, as it happens.'

'Oh yes, My Lord. The jury bailiffs told us on arrival that we would be much more comfortable if assigned to one of these…'

'But as it turned out you were sent to Court One. Unfortunately, justice and comfort do not always go together…'

There was a titter of amusement at Flaggett's little joke which I didn't find remotely funny. Debbie had regained her composure and the moment was lost.

After I gave my account in evidence, I expected Cuthbertson to grill me in cross-examination as I had seen him do many times to defendants in the dock but he was far too subtle for that.

'Pretty girl, Miss Sanchez – stood out on that jury, didn't she? There was a bit of banter about it in the Bar Mess on the second day of the trial, don't you remember? I happened to mention the fact whilst we were having our mid-morning coffee – I believe you were present?'

I did remember Cuffs joining a group of us at a table but I hadn't really been listening to any conversation.

'I may have been there but I was reading my brief at the time. Anyway, I only noticed the girl when the jury were sworn in on the first day. On the second, I was concentrating on…'

I stopped mid-sentence. The reasons were, of course, tactical. I had focussed exclusively on my favourite jurors by then – *Affro*, *Heyman* and *Gardi* – but I could never disclose this. Flaggett would be bound to think that singling out jurors as individuals as opposed to addressing them collectively amounted to sly trickery; pompous old prig that he was. It was better to be uncandid.

'Er… nothing specific as such – I just didn't notice her, that's all.' I answered unconvincingly.

I was to make my closing address to the tribunal after

lunch. Despondently, I ate my sandwich on a bench in Temple Gardens without much appetite. What could I say? Before Stavely, it had been her word against mine but now this 'independent' witness had scuppered me completely. Then I felt a flash of inspiration – perhaps *Turnbull* would save the day!

Turnbull was a leading case decided by the Court of Appeal only a few weeks beforehand. It involved the difficulties and problems which occurred when defendants were wrongly identified. Judges were now required to issue warnings about how careful juries had to be before relying on such evidence and a particular specific direction sprang to mind.

A judge should always warn a jury that an honest witness, absolutely sure he or she is telling the truth, can sound very convincing, but for all that, still be mistaken.

Why shouldn't the same principle apply in my case? Stavely was obviously sure of what he saw – but he might still be wrong!

Despite my waxing eloquently on this point, the tribunal remained stony-faced during my peroration and I sat down to dead silence. I had seen enough of judicial body-language by then to realise that this was an ominous sign indeed...

TWENTY-NINE

'The stock's kept in our warehouse – underneath High Street Kensington,' Mr. Sorbury told me.

'But that's miles away!' I protested. 'How do we collect it?'

'You use the underground tunnel from the store and load up one of the hand-trolleys.'

I glanced at my shelves. There were plenty of packets of rice stacked up on it but of what variety, I had no idea.

Sensing what I was thinking, Sorbury wagged a finger. 'You'll find the customers asking for any number of brands – best to keep a good selection in your outlet area.'

Just before Christmas, I had found a job working as a 'merchandiser' (actually a shelf-filler) at one of London's department stores, Harple's of Knightsbridge. At least this way, I would earn some ready cash – enough to buy Andrea a decent Christmas present. The overdraft was right up to its limit (taking into account the recent payment of chambers rent, VAT and clerks' fees) and Tinby had expressly forbidden any extension. Also, I needed to escape from the law…

Just days before, I had been disbarred and with Flaggett's condemnatory remarks ringing in my ears, went straight home in a daze. Unable to settle to anything, I had gone up to Oxford Street and applied for a job through a temporary employment agency.

As it turned out, Harple's were looking for shop assistants

in their food halls to cover the Christmas rush. Stack shelving might be boring (I was assigned to those devoted to rice) but I never suspected that it would turn out to be stressful.

However, I hadn't reckoned on Mr. Sorbury; the Chief Merchandiser- a small man with a Napoleonic complex – who was my boss and relished his position as our 'generalissimo'.

As merchandisers, we all wore green knee-length coats with the Harpie's symbol emblazoned upon it, over a white shirt and plain black tie. Mr. Sorbury wore the same coat, but his buttoned up the front and sported a tunic collar, which bore gold facings. That was his badge of authority and he certainly made the most of it.

At quarter to eight, on my first morning after we had been kitted out in the staff cloakroom, he gathered us together.

'Merchandisers! Your shelves must never be ever less than half-full – so make sure you pay regular visits to the warehouse during the day. Bear in mind too that customers may very well ask for something which isn't on the shelves – so be prompt and see if it's in stock. Never, never – tell the customer we don't keep it. Remember Harple's motto *"Harple's have even if other stores haven't'*

With that he gave a curt nod of dismissal reminiscent of the famous Emperor of the French and it wasn't long before his lecture was put to the test.

'Excuse me! You work for the store, don't you?' A snappily dressed executive-type woman addressed me. '*Arborio* – there's none on the shelves – I'm sure I bought it here last time.'

'If you give me a few minutes, Madam – I'll see if we have any in stock.'

Beginning my first long trek to the warehouse gave me time to brood once again…

Charles Courtley, we find you guilty of professional misconduct. Had you admitted your wrong-doing at the outset, we might have been able to exercise a degree of clemency in the penalty we impose, but that you did not do. Instead, you brazenly denied your guilt despite the compelling evidence of Miss Sanchez backed up by the corroborative testimony of Mr. Stavely. There can be no place in this Honourable Society for a discredited individual such as yourself. You are disbarred forthwith...

Disbarred forthwith! Never would I forget those words uttered in Flaggett's sepulchral tones – but now it was incumbent upon me to concentrate on rice!

There were about twenty packets of *Arborio* left, so I stocked up my trolley with them and loaded two other varieties as well – *Basmati* (which I had actually heard of) and *Della*.

I returned to the store to find Mr. Sorbury waiting with another customer. 'Ah, there you are Charles, this lady here is asking for *Manoomi* – there isn't any on your shelves.'

'What happened to the woman who requested *Arborio*?' I enquired.

'Obviously gone – customers don't like to be kept waiting, you know. How long is it since you left the store?'

'Twenty minutes – time to get to the warehouse, load up and come back...'

'Much too long – anyway, *Modom* here,' he bowed unctuously towards a tall butch-looking woman puffing a cigarette through a holder, 'is from the United States and wants *Manoomi* for a special birthday meal.'

'You got some out there, buddy? My partner's half-Indian and I'm cookin' her a special meal with wild rice from Apache country...'

Dutifully, I trotted off and fetched a consignment of *Manoomi* and loaded several packets of *Jasmine* as well for good measure.

After the American woman left, I felt I could relax – after all I now had a good selection of rice on my shelves, didn't I? Then a diminutive Japanese woman approached me; pretty as a picture on one her country's exquisite vases.

'*Gohan* rice, plees – no having on shelf!'

I groaned inwardly. 'Just give me fifteen minutes, Madam – we may have some in stock elsewhere.'

227

Once again, I trudged back to the warehouse where I identified several packets of *Gohan* rice. Better still, there seemed to be two varieties – *Asa* and *Hiru*, so she could take her choice.

The customer carefully examined a sample of each type for a couple of minutes. Then she turned to me, frowning.

'No, no -no good. Wanting *Ban – Ban* rice, plees? '

'*Ban?*' I queried. 'But you asked for *Gohan?*'

'*Gohan*, yes plees but *Ban Gohan* wanting – for deener…

Asa – morning rice, *Hiru*- afternoon rice, *Ban*- evening rice!'

So I trudged back to the warehouse and eyed the masses of packets once again. I'd only noticed the two varieties of *Gohan* before but somewhere there might be some *Ban*. After an extensive search, I did find one packet and hurried back without loading a trolley. The whole journey took more than a half-hour this time.

Still, I had satisfied another customer. By this time, it was twenty past five and feeling footsore, I sank down on a bench (really for the use of the customers) in a corner of the shop.

'No time for sitting down, Charles! We have a complaint that your shelves are under -stocked once again. The good lady here is very cross indeed!' The wretched Sorbury was at my side once again.

The woman with him was a scrawny harridan with metallic hair and piggy eyes to match.

'I wish to purchase a packet of *Uncle Chang's Paddyfield Rice*. I'm astounded you don't keep it on your shelves.'

'Harple's extends it most sincere apologies, *Modom* but I'm sure there's plenty in the warehouse. Charles? Just run along and get some, will you?'

Totally ignorant of rice varieties, I might have been before taking this job, but even I had heard of *Uncle Chang's Paddyfield Rice* – the most widely advertised brand in the land. Why couldn't this bloody woman buy it somewhere else? I might no longer be a barrister but suddenly I couldn't accept Sorbury's peremptory treatment any longer.

'Madam,' I said in my best professional voice, 'it will take fifteen minutes for me to fetch a packet of *Uncle Chang's Paddyfield's Rice*. This store is supposed to close in five minutes. Across the road, there's an ordinary supermarket which stays open until seven. Why not buy it there? – It's a lot cheaper anyway.'

'How dare you be so impertinent. As an account customer, I always buy my rice from Harple's!'

'Charles, go and fetch the rice this instant!' Sorbury added for good measure.

'No, I won't, you little twerp – go and fetch it yourself. In fact, thinking about it, sod your rice and bugger your merchandise!'

I left the store an hour later, having been summarily dismissed without pay but I felt so much better having let off steam. One thing I had proved to myself and the world – I was no salesman and not cut out to work in a shop. Penniless and unemployed I might be but I still had Andrea – it was time to travel down to Saltdean and tell her the whole story.

The journey home turned out be a nightmare – signal problems at London Bridge meant long delays – and I was developing a hacking cough. I bought a bottle of brandy to blot out my problems and decided not to travel again until the following day but a welcome surprise lay in store. When I got back to the flat, Andrea was waiting for me.

'Darling, where have you been? I rang chambers and Leslie said he hadn't seen you since the result. What result is he talking about? He wouldn't tell me and just clammed up. What is going on – please tell me?'

I collapsed into a chair weakly.

'God, it is so good to see you – give me a moment and a slug of that brandy first. Then, I'll tell you everything – but what about your mother?'

'Gone over to Aunt Imogen's for Christmas. Vera's there too – she actually offered to take mum off my hands as I was so good to Imogen when she broke her ankle. Despite what we've said about her in the past, she's been a real brick. Anyway, I thought we'd spend Christmas at home – just the two of us and the cats – you can see they're delighted to be back.'

Katie and Winston were indeed roaming the flat enthusiastically sniffing every corner and mewing lustily. Suddenly, I burst into tears.

'Darling – what on earth is the matter?'

So I told her the whole story taking gulps of brandy until the bottle was half-empty. I was beginning to feel woozy and it wasn't just the effect of the alcohol. Then I began to cough – and couldn't stop.

Andrea moved to my side and removed the bottle.

'You're sweating, sweet creature and beginning to shiver. Let's get you to bed – you must have picked up a bad cold.' My breathing had become constricted and I could hardly stand as Andrea helped me to undress.

'Oh God,' I croaked, 'what a failure I've been – I wouldn't blame you if you left me!'

'Don't be so silly, of course I shan't leave you…' She paused and stared into my face. 'Except I want to know one thing. Would you have slept with Debbie if you'd had the chance?'

I decided to be absolutely truthful. 'Certainly not on the first night – I was just flirting that's all – and on the second, I didn't want to meet her at all. Only when she told me her sob-story did I take her for a drink. Then – well, she did spike my glass! I suppose if I had made it back to her flat I might have tried but I really can't be sure what would have happened.'

Andrea moved away from the bed – a look of determination on her face.

'You can't be held responsible if the bitch put something in your drink when you weren't looking. Now, before I tuck you up – tell me where you have put all the case papers.'

I gestured feebly towards my briefcase in a corner of the room. All I remembered then was the sweating and shivering getting progressively worse before the final relief of oblivion…

EPILOGUE

The memorial service for His Honour Judge Champney was well attended as Bill had been a popular judge, sitting at the Central Criminal Court for many years, until his untimely death of cancer at sixty.

Attendees included Rex Huggins – now a Lord Justice of Appeal, Dermot Cuthbertson – recently appointed a High Court Judge himself and many of Bill's erstwhile colleagues both from the Bench and the Bar. Regrettably both Dan Rydehope and Tufton Crump had died some years before of heart attacks, and entirely in character – Dan, in Tom Tug's, whilst knocking out his pipe one evening, and Tufton, in the arms of a 'lady of the night' on a House of Commons fact-finding trip to the island of Tobago.

After the service in the Temple church was finished, I caught a taxi to Victoria declining an invitation to join a group heading for Tom Tug's. The hour-long train journey to Brighton would be partly spent in reading my brief for the following day but I had something else to ponder too...

Revealing to my chambers that I was about to quit.

As the train trundled through Clapham Junction, I opened my briefcase and glanced at the large manila envelope which I hadn't yet opened. I knew that it contained details of my already confirmed judicial appointment so instead I removed a scuffed plastic folder taking out several sheets of paper covered in Andrea's neat hand. The folder travelled with me everywhere as a good luck charm and this seemed an appropriate moment to read its contents once again...

Darling boy,

So much has happened since you fell ill that I'm going to describe everything in full in this letter, ready for you to read when you're up to it. I've just rung the hospital and they told me that your condition is improving all the time – although the doctor said you're not capable as yet of following a conversation. Hence this letter which will put everything in sequence.

After I put you to bed, you slept for a bit (that was probably the brandy), but woke up coughing again and choking as well, so I rushed to use a neighbour's phone and called an ambulance to take you to Lambeth General. I stayed the night there worrying like hell as you remained unconscious, but by the morning, the doctor said your condition was quite stable which, at least, gave me the opportunity to read Debbie's statement and the notes you made at the hearing.

That afternoon, the consultant told me that you had contracted viral pneumonia and there wasn't much they could do. Your body just needed time to fight the disease. As you were young and fit, that shouldn't, according to him, be a problem although the over-indulgence in brandy hadn't helped initially! Still, who could blame you after what you'd been through in the last few days.

One thing kept niggling at me – something I had read in your notes of evidence – about Debbie going into Court Fifteen. Then I remembered...

There was a story in that new woman's magazine I've been taking written a few weeks back, by a journalist called April Greenspan. She writes about the problems which women encounter in modern society and this article concerned a rape trial at the Old Bailey which involved a young student from a Polytechnic in north London. You know how I tend to hoard things and sure enough I found the back copy at home.

The article, written from the victim's point of view, was called 'Ordeal in Court Fifteen' and did describe, I feel a complete travesty of justice but, I know darling, you always say that there are two sides to every case and unless you hear the evidence for yourself in full you can't really judge. Whatever, the girl was interviewed by Ms Greenspan after the verdict which turned out to be 'not guilty'. Apparently, this traumatised her completely as she had been accused of leading the man on and positively inviting sex. But the complaint she made wasn't just about that – it was over the way the young defence barrister had cross-examined her. He had been gratuitously cruel and the judge actually upbraided him for it on several occasions. Even when being asked about neutral matters, his manner had remained sneeringly supercilious.

The girl wasn't identified by name – the heading of the piece simply read 'Ordeal in Court Fifteen – SL's story.' I began to wonder – what if SL bore a deep grudge against the defence barrister because of the way he had treated her and decided to get her own back on somebody in the same profession? Then comes the perfect opportunity for revenge when she's called up to do jury service, sees the young barrister in her present case drinking on his own and that very same barrister starts to chat her up!

Suddenly, it all clicked. 'SL' must be Luisa Sanchez – her initials had simply been reversed.

You silly creature, if only you had done some research on Debbie's background, as Bill Champney advised, you might have uncovered her motive and this disaster could have been avoided.

Well, I decided to put that right if I could by confronting Miss Sanchez myself! I checked the statement and nearly despaired when I saw that her address didn't appear on it but fortunately it was mentioned in Sergeant Trump's.

You know the funny thing was that I couldn't help feeling sorry for Debbie even then, knowing what she had done to us.

She was obviously devastated by her treatment in court and it sounded as if she lived a lonely life without family or friends.

So it came as no surprise when she answered the door to her flat herself when I went round there in the evening. Instinctively, I just knew that no-one else would be present.

I was quite calm and collected, you see, intending to introduce myself quietly and suggest we have a chat. Then I was going to beseech her on your behalf to stop telling lies and admit the truth – woman to woman. But when I actually saw her, perfectly composed as if answering the door to the postman, I just froze. After telling her who I was, I was certain that she would slam the door in my face – that's what I would have done in the same circumstances.

Then came a flash of inspiration.

'Court Fifteen – going in there must have been hell after what you'd been through. But it was the only way that you could possibly psyche yourself up enough to tell lies about Charles Courtley, wasn't it? Don't deny it, I'm his wife!'

Well, she actually staggered back as if going to faint. I took her arm to prevent her falling and, at the same time, entered her flat. You have often said that women on juries seem to instinctively detect when a female witness is telling lies – and it applied here, the other way round really – I just knew that she wouldn't lie to me!

So it all came out – her lonely existence after her father died, that awful rape which has put her off sex for life and then being humiliated by a member of your profession at the Old Bailey. She wanted to get back at a barrister and you were in the wrong place at the wrong time. Spiking your drink was easy too; she'd been prescribed valium after her father's death and it was easy to crush the tablets into powder.

At the end of her tale, we were sobbing in each other's arms – please forgive me for that but I couldn't help feeling deep compassion for her even though she had ruined your career.

Anyway, the end result was that she rang Sergeant Trump's

private number – she had been given it so she could ring him at any time. He came round immediately and took another statement – Luisa insisting that I remain present so that the full story could be explained. In fact, he took a statement from me too.

Trump handled it all very sensitively but told me privately she could face allegations for wasting police time. However, much would depend on whether you Charlie, would wish to press charges and I took the liberty of telling him I thought that unlikely.

Oh Charlie – it will be all over soon! I phoned Bill Champney from her flat who said he would speak to Dermot Cuthbertson straightaway. Later, a message came back from him that he had now seen Luisa's statement (Trump had delivered it to his house personally) and that the Lord Chief Justice would be invited to quash the finding against you without another hearing – an automatic process, he reassured Bill as the case against you was now totally discredited...

My eyes misty with tears, I couldn't read any more; remembering once again the way Andrea had all but saved my life.

As the train pulled into Brighton Station, I resolved to purchase some flowers and a bottle of champagne to take home. Of course, my beloved Andrea wouldn't be surprised about the appointment – I had discussed applying for it with her months before. Now, a new chapter was about to open in our lives – we would no longer have to suffer the stresses and strains of being self-employed. Instead, I would henceforward be earning a salary and become entitled to a pension.

But would the work of a judge advocate (military judge) ever prove to be so exciting?